Fatal INTENTIONS

SINS OF A SIREN II

A NOVEL

ALSO BY CURTIS L. ALCUTT
Sins of a Siren

Fatal
INTENTIONS

SINS OF A SIREN II

A NOVEL

Curtis L. Alcutt

SBI

STREBOR BOOKS

NEW YORK LONDON TORONTO SYDNEY

Strebor Books
P.O. Box 6505
Largo, MD 20792
http://www.streborbooks.com

ISBN 978-1-59309-377-8
ISBN 978-1-4516-2877-7 (ebook)
LCCN 2011938445

First Strebor Books trade paperback edition August 2012

Cover design: www.mariondesigns.com
Cover photograph: © Keith Saunders/Marion Designs

10 9 8 7 6 5 4 3 2 1

Manufactured in the United States of America

For information regarding special discounts for bulk purchases, please contact Simon & Schuster Special Sales at 1-866-506-1949 or business@simonandschuster.com

The Simon & Schuster Speakers Bureau can bring authors to your live event. For more information or to book an event, contact the Simon & Schuster Speakers Bureau at 1-866-248-3049 or visit our website at www.simonspeakers.com.

I DEDICATE THIS BOOK TO MY DAUGHTER, CuSANDRA ALCUTT; throw your shoulders back, hold your chin up and show life who's the boss... I love you, Baby Girl...

ACKNOWLEDGMENTS

As always, I have to thank the Almighty for *everything*; good, bad and otherwise. Through You, I have learned that every day is a lesson and a blessin'. I'd also like to give a gigantic hug to EVERY reader out there. Without you, we writers are as useful as a wet match...

*Repay no one evil for evil, but give thought to do what is honorable
in the sight of all. If possible, so far as it depends on you,
live peaceably with all. Beloved, never avenge yourselves,
but leave it to the wrath of God, for it is written,
"Vengeance is mine, I will repay, says the Lord."
To the contrary, "if your enemy is hungry, feed him;
if he is thirsty, give him something to drink; for by so doing
you will heap burning coals on his head."
Do not be overcome by evil, but overcome evil with good.*

—ROMANS 12:17-21

One

"I want that green-eyed bitch *dead!*" the late Officer Darius Kain's widow, Beverly Kain, yelled as she picked up the heavy crystal candy dish off of her coffee table. She then threw it into the flat-screen TV mounted on her living room wall. The image of the woman whom she had placed most of the blame for the death of her husband on, blinked out after the explosion of glass and sparks. In her mind, the Baltimore PD also shared some of the responsibility.

On this, the second anniversary of her husband's death, the ache in her heart ran to her head as she collapsed on her sofa. Tears of sorrow and anger leaked out of her brown eyes. They ran down her face and neck, and onto the collar of her pink robe. Every day since the grisly discovery of her late husband's body, she'd watched the videotaped newscast that featured a short conversation with Trenda Fuqua.

Trenda Fuqua.

The same woman alleged to have had an affair with the late Baltimore police officer, Darius Kain. Nightmares of his acid-eaten, mutilated body launched her into chronic insomnia. "She ruined our lives!"

The belief that Trenda had corrupted her husband and helped the Baltimore PD murder him was undeniable. News that Trenda was due for an early release from prison further pissed her off. As tears smeared her mascara, she recalled the smug look on Trenda's face as she was stuffed into the patrol car after her interview.

Once her crying fit stopped, she reached into the pocket of her robe. A maniacal smile formed on her face after pulling a piece of paper out of the pocket of her robe. She then picked up the phone, blocked her number and dialed the number written on the back of her late husband's funeral program. She *thought* she had blocked her number but in her stressful state of mind, she put in the wrong number blocking code. The number she called was for Lionel, a friend of Darius's. He'd given her his number at Darius's funeral. He promised he'd look after her.

His gruff voice answered. "Wassup?"

As she had done many times before, she hung up without answering. Upstairs, the muffled cries of her two-year-old son, Darius "DJ" Kain, Jr. got her attention. She hurried up the stairs, walked over to the Birchwood baby bed, picked up the blue pacifier next to the baby's head, and put it in his mouth. *You look so much like Darius...because of that red-headed tramp, he didn't even get to see you.* She stroked the child's curly, dark hair. Finding out that she was pregnant a month after Darius's death had filled her with bitterness.

Two

"That's a lotta money," Trenda said as she examined the contract on the table. A verse she often read while incarcerated came to mind. It alluded to a majority of her past troubles.

For the love of money is the root of all kinds of evil. Some people, eager for money, have wandered from the faith and pierced themselves with many griefs. — TIMOTHY 6:10

She rubbed the green rosary beads in her hands and looked across the table at the tall, blond woman. "But I can't take it. Sorry."

Alexis Cannon, top reporter for StarShine Entertainment, folded her arms on the table and focused her ice blue eyes on Trenda. The smell of new paint still lingered in the air of the recently painted conference room. The three-year-old Cockeysville Correctional Center—or "The Cock" as some inmates dubbed it—was the most modern prison in Maryland. "Ms. Fuqua, this is one hell of an opportunity for you." She tapped the contract. "You can leave out of this hell-hole a very wealthy woman."

The seven-figure deal to tell her story was awfully hard for Trenda to resist. But in order to make a real change in her life, sacrifices had to be made. Two years ago, after the bodies of the two crooked cops that had extorted and abused her for years turned up, her story had been in high demand. Along with the fact that the officers were in the middle of one of Baltimore's most high-profile corruption cases, their gruesome murders had grabbed national headlines.

Tempting as it was, Trenda realized that going on TV would garner her a lot of unwanted attention. After spending the last 24 months behind bars—and in her Bible—she had come to enjoy her anonymity. Also, she didn't want to make too many waves. Word around The Cock was they were going to release a few low-risk inmates due to overcrowding. After finding out from the D.A. that she was almost on the list, Trenda went out of her way to stay out of trouble. It worked. The D.A. told her she was going to be paroled early because of her good behavior combined with the overcrowding.

Besides self-change, self-preservation was an issue also. Even though the Island Boys had withdrawn their contract for her life, she had a new set of enemies to deal with. A few days ago, she found an unsigned envelope containing a letter, a copy of her mother's funeral program, and pictures of her elderly father and brothers and their families in her mail delivery. The letter warned her to keep her mouth shut about Darius and Tyrone's "street business" if she and her family valued their good health.

Although the guard who delivered the letter to her denied knowing where the envelope came from, Trenda knew she was lying. *Need to get out of here though…Daddy needs my help, especially since Momma died.* Images of her frail father played in her mind. She shook her red, shoulder-length French braids and stood up. "I gotta go."

Alexis puffed out her cheeks, exhaled, put the contract back in her alligator briefcase, and closed it up. She then pulled one of her business cards out of her purse and slid it across the table to Trenda. "I *will* be talking to you again."

Trenda watched the well-dressed woman exit the room. "I'm

sure you will." The prison guard motioned for her to follow. She stood, adjusted her baggy orange jumpsuit, picked up the card, and stuffed it into her pocket. *Two more weeks*, she thought as she was led back to her cell. *Two more weeks and I'm outta here. Hallelujah.*

ଛଠଔ

Twelve days later, at one in the morning, Trenda was rudely awakened by a Cockeysville Correctional Center Correctional Officer. "Wake up, Red! Time to get your ass outta here," the bulky, six-foot-tall female officer said. She banged on the bars of her cell door with her billy club. She then tossed a letter from the court and two empty pillowcases into her cell. "Get up and get packed *now!*"

What the fuck? Trenda thought as she blinked her eyes. The bright light of the C.O.'s flashlight blinded and angered her. "Can't you turn off that goddamned light?"

The guard, Monique, "Big Mo'" for short, grinned. "I thought you church folks didn't cuss?"

Trenda swung her legs out of her bunk. They were well-toned and fit after the two hours a day of running in place. Her washboard abs flashed as she pulled down her t-shirt. Having been in solitary confinement for two years, she spent a majority of her time doing push-ups, running in place and a host of other isometric exercises. She grimaced at the big dyke. "I ain't never claimed to be perfect...I just read the good book every now and then." She pulled her orange jumpsuit on in a hurry. She hated the way the guard's eyes fixed on her cotton-panty covered pussy. "Why you wakin' me up, anyway? This a random search or somethin'?"

The husky guard signaled to have the cell door open. "No, sexy. Time for you to get out. Go home."

Trenda froze midway through zipping up her jumpsuit. "Wha...? I ain't supposed to leave for a couple more days...you sure you know what you doin'?"

Big Mo' tapped her club against her thick thigh. "It's ya lucky day. The warden doesn't want to get caught up in a big media circus because of you."

Perplexed, Trenda shook her head. "Wait, wait, wait. What the heck are you talkin' about? What media circus?"

"Well, when word got out that you were on the early release plan, folks started talking about your case again. Everybody still wants to know what you know about those murders. When word got back to the warden that the tabloids were gonna be camping out to catch a picture of, or get an interview with you, he decided to 'be nice' and let you go a lil early. So guess what? You're leaving right now." She pointed at the cell floor. "Your parole information is in that letter."

In a daze, Trenda picked up the letter and pillowcases and started packing up her stuff. She kissed her rosary beads, said a silent prayer, and packed them into one of the pillowcases. Dazed or not, her time spent in the streets taught her to get out first, and ask questions later. She briefly recalled the parade of reporters and other celebrity stalkers when she was first flown into BWI from Oakland. "Shi—, I mean *shoot*, them folks already out there?"

"Not yet, but they'll be here soon. We're gonna sneak you out the delivery dock inside an unmarked van. From there, we can drop you off anywhere within fifty miles of here, as long as it's in the city limits. You wanna go to your parents' house?"

"*Hell*, I mean, *heck no!*" The thought had never occurred to her where she was going to go when she was released. She'd toyed with the idea of going to see her father, but facing him after almost two decades of absence was difficult. Especially for the reasons she'd stayed away.

Thirty minutes later, Trenda was handed an old friend of hers; her "Travelin' Bag." The empty, six-year-old, black and white Reebok bag was a welcome sight. She looked into the bifocals of the property clerk. "Where's the rest of my stuff?"

The heavy-set, elderly black officer looked at her with a shade of contempt. "Calm your ass down…I'm gettin' it now."

Big Mo' stood behind her and chuckled. "Ol' Sarge don't play that shit. You better calm down, Shorty. You don't wanna upset that man. He's the only one that knows his filing system. You don't want your shit to come up 'lost.'"

Trenda took a step back from the drab, gray and white counter. The faint sound of blues music drifted out of the otherwise silent room. Minutes later, Sarge came back with a plastic bag full of the clothes she'd had in her bag at the time of her arrest. He placed the bag on the counter, pulled out the pile of clothes, and put them on the counter. His hand rested on her sheer, pink thong. "You can wear some of this as ya change out; I guess it's still clean. I'll be right back with the rest of your stuff."

Nasty muthafucka, rubbin' his hand all over my drawers…sho ain't gonna put those on! She stuffed her clothes into her bag. A thousand memories returned to her as she packed her beat-up bag. The loss of her butterfly knife she affectionately called "Baby" hit her like a stake to the heart. She and it had been through a lot. Most of it not so good. *Sure hope I can find enough peace in the Bible to change all that.*

With all of her items returned, along with a check for the balance of her commissary account, she changed into her pink velour sweatsuit and waited for her ride into town. As she was escorted out of the prison, she looked up into the star-filled night. Any second now she expected to hear a whistle, bell or guard yelling for her to stop. She paused and took a deep breath before taking the final step out of the prison and onto the blacktop where the tan, unmarked van waited for her.

"Go on and get outta here," Big Mo' said, twirling her club. "Or you can stay; I'll see your sweet-ass back here in 'The Cock' soon enough."

"Don't count on it, bitch," Trenda said as she flipped Big Mo' the middle finger and strode to the van. "I ain't *ever* comin' back. Believe that."

Big Mo' chuckled behind her. "That's what they all say...I'll be here waitin' for you."

Trenda ignored Big Mo's mockery, looked past the white officer standing next to the open sliding side door, and tossed her bag inside. She looked back at the dismal, dark prison. It reminded her of the entrance to Hell. A Bible verse jumped out at her:

The Lord knows how to rescue the godly from trials, and to keep the unrighteous under punishment until the Day of Judgment.

—2 PETER 2:9

Amen, Peter. She hopped into the back of the van. The guard slammed the door closed and locked it.

They pulled out of the loading dock onto the road. The driver, a Puerto Rican guard, asked, "Where you goin'?"

She thought about the letter in her bag, which contained information on how to contact her parole officer, the $400 check, and $10 in cash. A strict budget was definitely in order. With no real destination in mind, she said, "Take me to the Greyhound station. You can let me out there."

The guard shook his head. "You do know your parole restricts you to the state of Maryland for the next eighteen months, don't you?"

Damn, forgot about that... "Yeah, let me out there anyway...I'll just chill there for a minute."

"Good, and don't forget to check in with your parole officer on Monday morning."

☜☞

At half past one in the morning, they pulled up to the curb at the O'Donnell Street Greyhound station. Even at that hour, a smattering of people still roamed the streets. "All right, last stop on the prison express," the jovial middle-aged black guard said. "Get your shit and git."

Trenda grabbed her bag as she waited for him to get out and open the sliding side door. When she hopped out, a mild breeze brushed against her. She hitched her bag up and looked at the guard. "Well, I'm out."

The look he gave her as she turned to walk away was a little more caring than she expected. "I don't ever wanna see your ass again, you hear me?"

Without looking back, she said, "Take a *real* good look; this is the last time you're *ever* gonna see my backside."

Three

A chilly spring breeze proved to Trenda that her velour sweatsuit was not a good clothing choice. She stood and watched the prison van disappear down the road. The light signal suspended above her swayed in the constant wind gusts.

Damn, it's cold as shit out here! She looked up and down the street. Most of the streetlights were either burned or shot out. Not much was open or inviting at that time of the morning. The only possible havens were the Greyhound station and the Wash World laundromat a few doors down, across the street.

An old, sky blue pickup truck slowed as it approached. The freckled, salt and peppered-haired, burly black man driving the truck grinned at her. His smile looked like a picket fence with a few boards kicked out of it. "You workin', baby?"

Trenda glared at him. "Excuse me?"

He licked his lips. "You wanna take a ride wit' me? I got a few dollars..."

When it dawned on her what he was trying to say, anger swelled in her like an angry, red-hot tidal wave. "*What?* You think I'm out here lookin' for *tricks*?"

He shifted into park, pulled a half-pint of gin from between his legs, and took a swallow. "What the hell else a fine-ass honey like you doin' out here this time of night? If you ain't ho'in, then you damn sure need to be...you finer than all the other bitches out here tonight. You could make *all* the money, sweet meat!"

A siren wailed in the distance. It sounded like the stream of obscenities she wanted to unleash. But, her newfound spirituality held her back. She took a step back. "Look, I ain't the one. Go on 'bout ya business. I ain't no hoe. Not even close."

A few other cars drove by. Some of the male drivers gave her more unwanted attention. The scent of burning motor oil found her nostrils. A symphony of noises came from the truck's tired engine. He leaned over the seat, bottle in hand. "Come have a drink wit' me. Ain't no harm in that."

Trenda longed for her old friend, "Baby." Experience told her men like him were trouble. "No thanks. I don't drink."

His tone became stronger. "Why you trippin'?" He shook the bottle again. "I'm just tryin' to be ya friend."

Time to go. The laundromat looked like a safe haven. She began walking toward it. "No...I don't need any new friends right now...thanks anyway."

Twenty feet from the truck, she heard him shift into drive. Seconds later, he pulled alongside her. The engine coughed, then died. "Shit!" he yelled as he tried to restart the engine. After several cranks, it turned over.

Please let there be some people in here, she thought as she neared the laundromat. The light inside Wash World spilled out onto the dark sidewalk. On that unlighted street, it looked like a luminescent, white rug.

"Hey! Slow down, girl! I just wanna talk."

Ignoring him, she hitched up her bag and kept moving. The sound of his tire scraping against the curb made her look. He seemed to be oblivious to the fact that he was ruining the sidewall of his tire. Trenda increased her pace. The entrance to the Wash World was thirty yards ahead. A loud *bang* almost made her jump across the street. "What the heck?"

She looked back just in time to see the man wrestling with the steering wheel. He'd struck the corner of a metal gutter in the sidewalk. The collision had ripped a hole into the side of his front tire. "Fuck! *Son-of-a-bitch!*"

Just before stepping into the Wash World, the large man pried his large frame out of the truck and slammed the door. She watched him adjust his dirty yellow sweatpants. The outline of his stiff dick nauseated her. *Nasty ol' freak!* She hurried inside.

The *clop-clop* of a pair of tennis shoes bouncing around inside a nearby dryer competed with the drone of an infomercial. A dusty TV, mounted to one of the support pillars, featured some Spanish man pitching the merits of his teeth-whitening gel. The buzzing of a fluorescent light above her sounded like a swarm of bees. It blinked off and on like baby lightning flashes. A down-and-out looking Caucasian couple sat in the hard, white plastic seats, smoking and watching the boring show. *Smells like straight piss in here*, Trenda thought as she walked in the opposite direction of the couple.

In the far corner, Trenda took a seat next to the detergent vending machine. She sat her traveling bag in the seat next to her, leaned back, and closed her eyes. *Ain't been out a good hour and already the devil's fuckin' wit' me!*

The desire to have the comfort of her butterfly knife within reach ate at her. But if she did have another "Baby," she'd use it. Oh hell yeah, she'd use it. Even in that hard, uncomfortable seat she found herself dozing off. A swirl of her dead mother's face and Bible pages clouded her mind. The fact that she didn't get to see her mother before she died fueled her guilt. She could have gotten a pass to attend her funeral, but she was too chicken-shit to go. She'd allowed her petty grudge against her family to ruin that once-in-a-lifetime moment.

The sound of the shoes in the dryer and the off-and-on coughing fits by the couple across the room helped lulled Trenda to sleep. Although the rock-hard chair was a tad less comfortable than the bed in her prison cell, she used her refined power of adaption to help her sleep.

હⓈ◯◖

So deep was her sleep that she didn't hear the doors open and close. The smoking couple got up, grabbed their basket of clothes, and left as the huge, lumbering figure looked around. He then fixed his sights on the cute woman sleeping on the far side of the laundromat. *Little bitch*, he thought as he pulled his bottle of gin out his pocket, took a long swallow, put it back in his pocket, and walked toward Trenda. *Made me flat my damn tire!*

હⓈ◯◖

Put on the full armor of God so that you can take your stand against the devil's schemes.
—EPHESIANS 6:11

Between her broken sleep and the stress of her situation, nightmares filled her head. Her father sat at their old kitchen table having dinner with a skeleton. The skeleton was dressed in her mother's favorite church outfit.

"Momma, no! You can't be there!" In her mind she screamed those words, but only a low whimper escaped her sleeping body. The apparition of her mother looked up from the table. The skeletal head had a pair of accusing, bright green eyes. The same shade as hers.

The dream version of her father continued eating. He acted as though he was eating alone. The frailness of his thin body was all too real in Trenda's tortured mind. She could feel the heat of her spectral mother's glare. Her father dropped his fork and grabbed at his throat. He was choking. Her mother continued to glare at her. "What you gonna do? Let him die, too?"

The fear of going anywhere near the ghostly, mother-like thing kept her from assisting her choking father. "What are you gonna do?" the apparition bellowed. "If you weren't such an evil child, you'd help your father! Heathen! You demon child!"

In her dream, she placed her hands to her ears, frozen with fear. Her father's face contorted into a mask of pure horror. He held out one shaky hand to Trenda before falling face first into his plate of food. His thin body hitched one last time in his baggy pajamas and then lay still.

The green-eyed accuser pointed a bony finger at Trenda. "You did this! You! You! You!"

Trenda couldn't pry her eyes off of her dead father. The mother-thing rose out of its chair and slowly walked toward Trenda, finger wagging—the same way her real mother had done when Trenda was a child. "I curse you to Hell! Lucifer is waiting for you, you evil, evil child! I'm going to take you there by my own hand!"

Unable to move, she started screaming in her dream. She could feel her mother's hand on her shoulder.

Her eyes flew open. In front of her was another nightmare. A large, calloused hand shook her shoulder.

"Hey! What you makin' all that noise fo' in ya sleep?"

Disoriented, Trenda was shocked to see this huge, gin-breathed man shaking her shoulder. The rest of Wash World was deserted. Even in her fugue, she saw his erect penis outlined in his grimy yellow sweatpants. Instinctively she tried to shake out of his grip and couldn't. "Let me go, man!"

His grip tightened. He flashed his drunken, unbecoming smile. "Not 'til you say you gonna have a drank wit' me. You owe me after makin' me bust my tire."

A wave of anger replaced her fear. She almost slipped up and said the MF-word for the first time in almost a year. "*Mutha—!*" She angled her foot between his legs and kicked as hard as she could.

"*Ooooaf!*" escaped his throat as he back peddled and collapsed to the stained, gray tile floor like a folding chair. The bottle of booze in his front pocket shattered in his pocket, lacerating his large thigh.

Trenda grabbed her bag, and hurdled the moaning, fallen ogre as he winced and held his genitals. She ran to the door, then skidded to a stop. Red, blue and amber flashing lights bounced off of the surrounding buildings. "Dang it!" she looked out the window and saw a Baltimore PD patrol car and a red and white, *All-City* tow truck. They were parked in front of the drunken man's disabled truck. The tail end was at least five feet from the curb, sticking out into the middle of the lane. "I can't catch a dang break!"

Cursing and the sound of a fist slamming a washing machine made her snap her neck around. The drunk had managed to get to his feet. A blooming bloodstain the size of a bagel grew on his left thigh. He pulled shards of the broken bottle out of his pocket and slammed them to the floor. His red, mad eyes found Trenda. "*Hoe!* You gonna die tonight!"

A sickening sense of déjà vu swept her, then was gone. As he headed toward her, she calmly exited Wash World. Without looking in the direction of the cops and tow truck, she walked as fast as she could in the opposite direction. *How the fuck can I be havin' this much bad luck?*

Four

"'m sorry, Mr. Langford, but as I told you before, Ms. Fuqua was released early because of good behavior."

"How can that be, Detective? Since when did the state of Maryland become a safe haven for criminals?"

Detective Marv Brice rubbed his temples with one hand and held the phone with the other. *Goddamn Trenda Fuqua. I swear everything associated with her is cursed! And gettin' my ass chewed out by this dickhead friend of the Mayor is out of my pay scale.* "I'm sorry, Mr. Langford, but—"

"Damn right, you're *sorry*...you and the rest of you incompetents! If you can't do your job, I'll have to see about getting someone in there who can!"

Marv pulled the phone from his ear after Thurston Langford, father of murdered Piper Langford, rudely hung up on him. Her case, although still open, remained unsolved. He slouched down into his creaky old desk chair and drummed his thick, brown fingers on the scarred and nicked wooden desktop. *What the hell is this bitter bastard doing calling me this late? Better yet, why am I still here at two in the morning?*

He knew the answer to that question before he even asked. Because of his impressive record of solving cold-cases, he was assigned to the Langford case. Because of the nature of the unsolved case, Trenda Fuqua was in the crosshairs of his investigation. A two-year-old pile of folders about the Langford case sat in the center of his old desk. Just as he was about to pack them away for the night, an instant message from his cousin, Jules, popped up on his computer screen. He was a Correctional Officer at The Cock. "Messy Marv! Guess who got released from here an hour ago?"

The nickname "Messy Marv" was given to him by his old commander. He earned that moniker after chasing a homicide suspect seventeen years ago. The suspect unfortunately tried to run across Interstate 95. After being struck by a pair of speeding tractor-trailers and a few cars, there wasn't much left of him. After witnessing the aftermath, Commander Richmond dubbed then rookie detective Marvin Brice "Messy Marv."

Marv answered the instant message. "Who?"

"Ya girl, Trenda Fuqua. She's gone. She got checked outta here 'bout an hour ago."

He jumped to his feet. "What the hell?" It took a minute for the information to register with him. He stroked his bare chin as he stared at the message on his computer screen. *She's out already?* Ignoring the message, he ripped through his stack of folders until he found one labeled "D-Day." Inside, he found all the information relating to Trenda's case. Every move she made was documented—including her proposed early release date. That date was two days away. Jules's message awaited a reply. He leaned over, his slight beer-belly touching the desk, and typed, "Thanks for the info. I'll get back to you in a few." Without waiting for a reply, Marv shut down his computer, grabbed his jacket and cell phone, and hurried out of the office. On the way down the elevator, he placed a call to a friend of his at The Cock.

"Property Clerk; Sarge speakin'."

"Sarge, it's me, Marv. Do you recall checking out a prisoner named Trenda Fuqua?"

"Yeah...checked her out a lil while ago. Is sumthin' wrong?"

Marv opened the door of his gold, unmarked patrol car and got in. "No, I'm just surprised she got out this early. I was hoping somebody woulda told me."

"Well, I heard they had to rush her out because of all the damn media snoopin' around. I heard she got dropped off at the Greyhound station. Good thing they let her go when they did; the goddamn press is already linin' up down the road for a chance to talk to her. They gon' be mad as a wet cat when they find out she's already been let out."

Marv started the car, backed out of his stall, and exited the parking garage. The Cock was a forty-five-minute drive away. "Yeah, but it still irks me that the powers-that-be didn't feel it wasn't important enough to let *me* in on it. I'm *only* the detective that's been following her fuckin' case since she got locked up." He slowed down as he approached the front of the police station. "Hey, Sarge, thanks for the info. I'll check with you later."

"Okay, Messy, lata."

Amazed at the scene in front of him, he pulled over to the curb and stopped. *This is nuts!* Half a dozen news vans, satellite trucks, and an assortment of print media vehicles lined the streets. Yawning, coffee drinking technicians milled around, some smoking cigarettes, some talking with newscasters under the increasingly cloudy, star-filled, chilly night. *You would have thought that Charles Manson was being released.*

A bright light almost blinded him. "What the hell?"

The spotlight from a shoulder-mounted TV camera illuminated the interior of his car. A middle-aged white man—a news anchor he'd seen before—tapped on the passenger window of his car. "Excuse me! Is Trenda Fuqua inside? May we have a word with you?"

Other newshounds soon ran toward the unmarked car. *Oh hell no!* His brown eyes glared into the bright light. "Back up! Back away from the car, *now!*" Before the swarm could reach him, Marv mashed the gas pedal and raced down East Eager Street. He burned rubber around Greenmount Avenue, losing the media vultures.

As he drove toward the Greyhound station, he hoped that he could at least find out where Trenda was heading. Hopefully, if she'd boarded a bus, one of the clerks could provide him with the destination of her bus. Although he had no legal reason to detain her, he was professionally dedicated to keeping a tab on her as long as he was still working on the Darius Kain cold case.

℘℃℞

Too high and angry to notice his truck about to be towed away, the huge drunk yelled, "Hey, bitch...Bring yo' ass back here! Gonna beat yo' ass...kicked me in my balls and shit!" He then staggered and placed his hand on the wall to hold himself up. "Gonna fuck...you up...hoe!"

"Hey, Archie! Quit all that yelling!"

The drunk clumsily turned around to see who'd called his name. "What?"

The skinny, red-headed cop, twenty yards away, shined his flashlight beam in Archie's face. "I said, stop making all that noise. You're already in trouble for parking your goddamned truck in the middle of the street."

Archie squinted as he fought to see whom the voice belonged to. "Aww shit...Is that you, Nick?"

The cop walked toward Archie. "Yeah, it's me. How much have you had to drink tonight?"

Officer Nick Leland had worked for the Baltimore Police Department for over twenty years, most of it patrolling the mean streets of West Baltimore. He was known as one of the most crooked and meanest cops in the streets—second only to his former coworker and rival, the late Darius Kain. Although he was slight of build, he was known as a bad ass that didn't mind brawling with, or shooting, ruffians. His disposition earned him the moniker "Nick the Dick" in the streets.

Archie tried to appear sober, but his alcohol-saturated body betrayed him. As he tried to walk over to his truck, his feet got tangled and he fell, face first, to the sidewalk. The black, over-weight tow truck driver laughed out loud at the drunk before securing the safety chains to Archie's truck.

Nick walked over, shook his head, and helped Archie to a sitting position. A trickle of blood ran out of one of his nostrils. A quarter-sized scrape on his cheek bled a little bit. "Archie, I thought you told me you were givin' up the juice?"

Archie leaned back against the wall. "I ain't drunk...I tripped ova my shoelace."

Nick kicked Archie's left foot. "Hey, ass; you have on slip-on deck shoes. No laces, fucker."

Archie snored in response.

Irritated, Nick kicked him in his bloodstained thigh. "Wake up!"

"Hey, man!" Archie yelled. "Why you messin' wit'...me?"

"Who were you screaming at earlier?"

Archie broke out in a drunk, lusty grin and looked down the street. "I was callin' my girlfriend...that fine green-eyed hoe." He pointed in the direction Trenda had walked. "There she goes...no good bitch..."

Nick looked down the street and spotted a figure half a block away, about to turn the corner. He looked back at Archie. "Did she have anything to do with your leg injury?"

Again, Archie snored in response. Instead of waking him, Nick let him sleep. Horniness and boredom got the better of him. He stood and waved at the tow truck driver. The driver tapped his horn in response and hauled away the truck. Archie snored loudly behind him. Nick kicked the bottom of Archie's feet. "Wake up, drunky."

Archie's eyes fluttered awake. "Hey, man." He wiped drool off the corner of his mouth. "Where'd that bitch go?"

Nick stuck the nightstick back in the ring on his belt. "Get up here, turn around, and put your hands behind your back."

The drunken behemoth swayed like a leaf in a breeze after getting to his feet. The wound on his thigh didn't seem to bother him. He wiped his mouth and frowned. "Why? You takin' me in?"

Nick removed his cuffs, twirled Archie around, and cuffed his thick wrists. "I told you last time you were walkin' around drunk in public, I was gonna haul your ass in."

"Awww c'mon, Nick! Gimme a…break…I just needed a sip." He looked over his shoulder at the officer. "Man, I just been goin' through some shit…wit' my wife. Can't you lemme go this one…time?"

Nick winced from Archie's toxic breath. "*Jeeez!* You been eatin' shit sandwiches? Holy cripes, your breath *stinks!*"

As Archie slurred a rebuttal, Nick marched him to his patrol car, opened the rear passenger door, and stuffed Archie inside. Before closing the door, he looked Archie in his bloodshot eyes. "If you throw up in my car, I'll take you somewhere quiet and shoot your ass. You hear me?"

Archie nodded as he fought dozing off. He shut the door as

Archie mumbled something. Nick took off his cap and hung it up on the wire-mesh screen that separated him from his passengers. He ran his hand through his thick crimson mane, started the car and drove off.

Two blocks ahead, he made a right turn. A moment later, Archie yelled, "Hey! Hey! There she goes!"

"What the hell are you yelling about? Sit your ass back and be quiet!"

"That's her! That's that bitch who made me get hurt!"

Nick pulled over to the curb and look in the direction Archie nodded his head. A fit and trim, sexy, pink velour-covered ass swished and swayed halfway down the street. Even on that poorly lit street, he could see that wasn't your everyday piece of ass. *Oh my!* He pulled away from the curb. *Now that's a body that brings tears to your eyes!*

"Half-slick hoe! Got yo' ass now," Archie said, drifting in and out of sleep.

"Shut up and sit back!" Twenty yards behind the shapely woman, Nick turned on his flashing red and blue beacons and pulled up alongside her.

Five

re you serious? Trenda wondered as the walls of the abandoned bakery she stood in front of and the few surrounding cars were bathed in red and blue light. Lights she was more than familiar with.

She let her bag slide down her arm to the sidewalk. All the talk she'd heard about convicts returning to jail at an outrageous rate jumped into her head. For a second, she considered running. She was familiar enough with the area to give the cop a run for his money. But the aspect of returning to The Cock killed that noise.

As soon as the officer got out of the car, her blood frosted over; she recognized Nick right away. *God, why are you treatin' me so bad?*

He adjusted his utility belt and walked over to her. His smirk let her know he recognized her, too. "Excuse me, *ma'am*." Sarcasm coated his words. "I need to ask you a few questions."

Trenda folded her arms over her breasts. "Did I do somethin' wrong?"

His eyes traveled every curve on her firm frame. "I have a guy in the back of my car that says you assaulted him. I just wanna hear your side of the story."

She broke eye contact with Nick and gazed into the back of the squad car. Archie flicked his tongue at her like a drunken snake. *Nasty bastard!* She returned her attention to Nick. "I don't know that man. He tried to holla at me outside the laundromat and I turned him down...then he got all crazy and tried to attack me."

Nick didn't seem to pay attention to anything she said. He was much too busy letting his eyes rove her body. The 6 to 8 hours a day she'd spent exercising in her cell had put her in the best shape of her life. Her butt was like a beach ball. Her muscular thighs were still sexy and feminine. A tiny waistline separated her awesome ass from her firm, perky tits. "Well, Trenda, I have a citizen that says different. He claims you tried to pickpocket him."

Since he'd dropped the façade of not knowing who she was, Trenda followed suit. For years, Nick had had a crush of lust on her. Darius was the only buffer she'd had from his advances. He'd made it clear to every "dirty" cop on the force that she was off limits. For the first time in her life, she wished Darius was still alive. The swelling she saw in his crotch disgusted her. "C'mon now, Nick. You know as well as I do, homeboy is drunk and lyin'. All I'm tryin' to do is get home. I'm on parole so you know I ain't botherin' nobody."

"When did you get out The Cock?"

"A lil while ago."

"Knowing you, that's plenty of time for you to return to your old tricks and bullshit."

She glared at him. "Man, you trippin'. How you think you just gonna strong arm me out here? You must be on one!"

A patch of clouds drifted by and obscured the moonlight. The only light besides the red and blue beacons came from a streetlight half a block away. Nick advanced on Trenda and grabbed her by her right arm. "Step behind the car and place your hands on the trunk."

Trenda shook her head and took a step back. "What you doin'? How you gonna try and take me in for some bull crap?"

Nick flashed his small, weird-looking teeth, snatched her, and made her look him in the eye. "Look here, bitch; don't play your fucking games with me. *I'm* the big dog, now that your boyfriend took an acid bath. I suggest you get used to following *my* orders."

Lord, why do You forsake me so? flashed through her mind as Nick breathed in her face. The urge to dig her fingernails into his eyes fought her good sense. "I dunno what you talkin' about, but I'm not into drama."

Without a word, he glared at her, yanked her behind the squad car and sandwiched her between the trunk and his pelvis. His voice whispered in her ear from behind. "I'm gonna have to search you real good, convict...*real* good."

As happened to her at times of stress, a Bible passage emerged from her subconscious:

Perseverance must finish its work so that you may be mature and complete, not lacking anything.

—JAMES 1:4

The feel of his stiffness against her ass sickened her. He'd placed her in the perfect spot behind the car; Archie couldn't see what was going on. There were no witnesses to his harassment of her.

"*Man!* Get ya hands off me! What you doin'?" She felt him grinding on her ass. His pecker was right above her covered asshole.

His chin rubbed against her ear as he wrapped his arms around her waist and ground on her butt. "Quiet down before I put you in a three-way with me and my nightstick."

His hands groped her hard nipples. She cursed herself for not being able to stop her tits from responding to his touch. But having been untouched by a man for over two years made it a difficult task. His breathing became more labored as he rubbed her tits and rode her ass. A wave of hot anger crashed into her as she felt him trying to pull down her sweatpants. *Gotta get this muthafucka off of me!*

"Quit fightin' me, goddammit!" he said as she bobbed and weaved her hips. "All you're doing is pissing me off! You might as well get used to it, bitch. From now on, I'm your *new* Darius. You don't make a freakin' move in this city unless I know about it."

Just as Trenda prepared to slam her head backwards in the hopes of breaking his nose, a second patrol car approached them. Since they were traveling on the opposite side of the street, they couldn't see what Nick was doing. "Shit!" he yelled as he spotted the patrol car. "You say anything out of line, and I'll make what happened to Darius seem like a church picnic—with you as the main course."

Nick eased his skinny body off of her ass and pretended to pat her down to her ankles. He nodded to the officers in the other patrol car as they double-parked. A pair of African American cops got out, walked over, peeked at the passenger in the backseat of Nick's car, then looked at Nick and Trenda. The taller of the two grizzly bear-sized cops took his eyes off of Trenda and looked at Nick. "Everything okay?"

"Yeah, everything's fine. Had a case of mistaken identity." He looked at Trenda. "You can go, ma'am, but remember what I told you about being in this area this time of night. Bad things sometimes happen. "

The message in his eyes was clear; keep your mouth shut or else.

Fuck you too, cop. She dropped her glare, picked up her bag, and stormed off before the two black officers could get a good look at her.

Six

After the two patrol cars pulled off, Trenda managed to calm down a little. Boarded up, dilapidated and vacated homes and businesses occupied the last six blocks she walked. Stray dogs, cats, and the occasional vermin accompanied her. She stopped and sat down on a bus stop bench, which sat in front of a boarded up hardware store. The decay of the surrounding buildings matched her mood; her newfound morality was slowly eroding. She collapsed back on the bench. *Fuckin' cops ain't shit.*

Loud rap music played in the distance. The bass thump and high-hat symbol snaps told her "The Hood" was wide awake. She scanned the area. *Can't stay around here long.* About a block away, she spotted a group of individuals walking toward her. The sound of the music increased as they neared. Her street instincts kicked in like Spiderman's senses. *Might be some members of them Dip Set Purple City gang members I heard about at The Cock. Ain't tryin' to let them fools run up on me and I ain't strapped.*

The group of people and the music were half a block closer. She saw one of them riding a three-wheeled bike with a car stereo and speakers cleverly mounted to it. She stood up and looked around. Behind her, a narrow alleyway ran between the old hardware store and the burned-out remains of Wing Wong Chinese Cafe. After pulling her bag up on her shoulder, she hurried down the litter-strewn alley.

The stench of piss, garbage and despair permeated the air. The music became louder. She looked around desperately for a place to hide. An unusual number of beer bottles, empty cigarette and cigar packages covered the ground. In the minute about of streetlight that trickled down the alley, Trenda saw unfamiliar graffiti on the walls of the alley.

The temporary cyclone fencing around the burned down cafe was useless. It had holes in it big enough to drive a bus through. After a quick evaluation, Trenda determined the back of the café, with its easy access to its burned out interior, was where most of the action went down. She scanned the back of the hardware store. At first look, it appeared to be boarded and sealed shut. *Fuck! Ain't shit to hide behind back here!*

A mixture of loud voices and loud music filled the alley. *Fuck! Fuck! Fuck!* rang out in her mind. Desperate for a weapon, she picked up a broken beer bottle by the neck. It made her long for her old butterfly knife, "Baby." Just as she prepared to drop her bag, ready for confrontation, a gust of wind rattled the plywood covering the back door of the hardware store.

Lord please! The sound of glass breaking, laughter and somebody getting cussed out echoed down the alley. Trenda ran over and tried the plywood. It pulled away enough for her to see the back door had been broken down. She tossed her bag and the broken piece of bottle inside and tried to squeeze through the narrow opening. *C'mon, dammit!* Her sexy, eye-pleasing sweet ass was a few inches too luscious to fit through the opening.

The sound of somebody snorting and spitting was too close. *Muthafuckas gonna see me!* Panic worked a miracle. A three-inch tear opened up on the side of her favorite sweatpants as she forced her way inside the opening. She prayed the sound of the rap song blaring from the bike masked the sound of the plywood slamming back in place.

Trenda lay on the filthy floor, panting and listening. Voices outside the door froze her. They were so close, she could hear them over the music.

"I'm tellin' you; I saw somebody run back here."

"You just high, fool! Ain't shit back here but us and maybe a crackhead or rat. You need to quit fuckin' wit' that kush if you can't hang."

A fist pounded on the wall next to the door. "Fuck you, punk! I know what I saw. They're back here somewhere."

Trenda hopped to her feet as quick as a cat. *They come in here and my ass is done.* As her eyes adjusted to the darkness, she saw she had been lying on a bed of used hypodermic needles, empty matchbooks, a few condom wrappers and a thick layer of dust. *Shit!*

A female voice joined in the conversation outside as the volume of the music was lowered. "Both y'all need to quit actin' like bitches and pass me that bottle of Henny; I'm ready to get my drank on!"

Trenda tuned out the conversation and assessed her situation. She appeared to be in the shipping and receiving area of the decades-old, abandoned business. The dim glow from the only working streetlight in the alley managed to filter between a few of the boarded up windows. Walls lined with empty shelves surrounded her. A few scattered boxes of different sizes adorned the room. Every now and then the wind rattled the massive steel roll-up door, which led to the loading dock. The broken rollers lining one side of the door assured it would never open again. She spotted her bag and crept over and picked it up.

Trenda paused to listen to what her company was up to. The aroma of high-grade marijuana smoke made it to her nostrils. "Nuh-uh! Get yo hands off my ass, fool! I told y'all already, ain't no touchin' or fuckin' goin' on 'til I get ready. I ain't even high yet!"

Yeah, freak-bitch, keep them fools busy so I can work on gettin' the hell outta here. As if walking on eggshells, Trenda cautiously and quietly worked her way toward the door leading out of the storage room and toward the front of the store. The litter strewn about and the darkness made navigating the room difficult. "Ouch! What the...?" she whispered as she banged her knees into the partially lifted blades of an ancient forklift.

It took five good minutes for the pain to subside enough for her to continue walking. Meanwhile, the party outside was raging. A second woman's voice joined in the conversations. The sound of the music was replaced by laughter, swearing and sexual innuendo. Trenda successfully navigated the darkness and maze of trash and tried the door. *Shit! Locked...* The steel-lined fire door's knob failed to turn. In the darkness, she couldn't see where many had tried, unsuccessfully, to pry open the door.

"Dip Set Purple City, fool!" one of the thugs yelled. "DSPC runnin' shit!"

Trenda cringed. *Just like I thought; they are some of those wannabe blood gang members.* Just like she knew of the gang's name, she also knew of their reputation of being robbers and remorseless murderers. One of them leaned back against her plywood entrance, making the wood creak.

Looking around, she saw no suitable hiding place. On the wall next to what looked like the shipping and receiving office, she saw a metal ladder bolted to the wall. As she studied the ladder, a new sound got her attention; the sound of rain pelting the roof.

"Awwww, shit! Rain gonna fuck up the blunt!" Trenda then heard wood creaking. "Yo, Mondo, help me pull this wood off so we can go inside and smoke."

Panic rode Trenda like a cowboy. She hoisted her bag up on her shoulder and hurried up the steel ladder. *God, please don't let this old-ass roof collapse!*

Her solid 140 pounds made the roof of the shipping and receiving office groan and moan, but it held. Seconds after she scrambled up the ladder, the plywood covering the door gave way from the squealing, protesting nails that once held it. As she lay flat on the inches of grime atop the office, the gang entered her hideout.

A mere five feet below her, walked men that would certainly rape her and possibly do a lot worse. As the gangsters partied to the sound of a Lil Wayne song, Trenda remained sprawled out, making herself as flat as possible. She closed her eyes.

Be strong and courageous. Do not be afraid or terrified because of them, for the LORD your God goes with you; he will never leave you nor forsake you.

—DEUTERONOMY 31:6

That verse had gotten Trenda through many rough spots in prison, but in her current position, she would much rather have had an assault rifle. She took a chance and lifted her head. Stacks of boxes, an old filing cabinet, a small desk and other office furniture came into view. She noted that the top of the office was also used as storage space. *Wait a minute; what's that?*

Even in the poor light, Trenda spotted an eight-inch-long screwdriver lying about three feet away from her. She reached for it and came up several inches short. Meanwhile, weed smoke wafted up to her, threatening to give her a contact high. She eased a few inches to her left and tried for the screwdriver again. This time she managed to grip the blade just above the rubber-covered handle. Having a potential weapon gave her a small bit of relief. *It ain't Baby, but it'll work fa now.* Confident the group wasn't aware of her, Trenda scooted up to the edge of the roof and cautiously peered down. Three guys and two girls danced, drank, smoked and rapped to the music as the rain poured down outside.

Ain't this a bitch? Fresh out the pen and already caught up in a gang of shit. She eased back from the edge, folded her arms under her head and pondered her existence. *God, why'd You let me get out— early at that—just to have me fall into the same ol' bullshit I was in before I got locked up? Did I piss You off that much?*

Her conversation with the Lord was interrupted by the sound of the radio crackling, then going silent, and loud, angry shouting. Trenda scooted back to the edge and looked down. *Oh shit!*

Seven

"Hey…Why you stop, baby?" Kelvin, Beverly's boyfriend, asked as she climbed off his inflated dick. "I thought you said you was ready to do this?"

Beverly laid her nude, high-yellow body next to his, on top of her thick, multicolored comforter. The fourth attempt at sex with her new boyfriend, Kelvin, had turned into another failure. She'd gone without sex for nearly as long as her foe, Trenda. Five months ago, she'd met Kelvin at a bookstore in Galveston and they'd hit it off right away.

He was the first man she'd dated since moving to Houston, Texas, a day after her husband was killed. Once she came home from visiting her sister in Washington, D.C., found her home ransacked and a death threat spelled out on her living room wall in her late husband's blood, she immediately hopped a plane out of Baltimore.

After months of dating, she'd finally given in and agreed to have sex with him. "I'm sorry, baby…I…I guess I'm not as ready as I thought."

He grabbed one of her fluffy pillows, covered his chocolate face for a moment, then pushed the pillow off of him. "How you gonna get me this hard, then just roll off me? That's some foul shit."

Beverly gripped the comforter, pulled it over her body and closed her eyes. "I'm trying, Kel, but it's a lot harder than I thought…"

"Shit! So is *this*." He sighed, grabbed her hand, and put it on his stiffness. "Just when I thought you were ready for us to get to the next level..."

His words barely registered as her thoughts returned to vengeance. *That fucking cunt is still fucking with my fucking life.* Inspired to defy Trenda's influence on her world, Beverly wiped her twisted, shoulder-length hair out of her face, then stroked his dick. Her hand glided up and down the vein-lined shaft of his tool.

Residue of her pussy juice coated his staff. Even though the pleasurable feel of him inside her as she rode him for five minutes was wonderful, she couldn't get fully into the act. Anything associated with sex reminded her of all the rumors she'd heard about her late husband's debauchery.

With the image of Trenda sucking Darius's penis in mind, as she did on the video that was leaked to her of Trenda actually sucking off the late officer, she released Kelvin's dong, wiped her hand on the comforter, turned her back on him, and balled up into the fetal position. *Lord, please help me...*

"What the fuck *now*?" Kelvin rolled over and lay behind her. "Is this some kinda game? I told you I was feelin' you, but if this is how you respond, maybe I ought to bounce out ya' life."

In the few seconds of silence before her response, the tick-tock of the brass alarm clock on her nightstand matched the beat of her stress-filled heart. As she stared at the clock, a whisper escaped her. "Please leave..."

She felt Kelvin stiffen up next to her. *"What?* It's damn near three in the mornin' and you puttin' me out?"

Another whisper. "Kelvin, please just go...I'll explain later..."

He grabbed her by the shoulder. The angrier he got, the thicker his Southern accent got. "What's wit' all the whisperin'? I'm right here. Turn over so we can talk this shit out...fuck all this bullshit, turn over and tell me what's really goin' on."

Her heartbeat accelerated way past the speed of the ticking alarm clock. This time the whisper was a little stronger. "Please don't grab me like that...it hurts..."

"I will as soon as you turn over so we can talk this shit out."

"Kelvin, *stop it!*" She eased over to the nightstand and pulled the drawer open a few inches. Her whispers were replaced by an ominous, normal vocal level. "I told you I don't feel like talking right now...please don't make me ask you to leave again."

Incensed by the thought of driving fifty miles home with blue balls, Kelvin shook her by the shoulder. "What part of the game is this? You some kinda tease?" He then flopped back on the bed. "You know what? You ain't givin' me the bum rush like that...I'll leave when I leave."

In silence, Beverly eased her hand into the open drawer. Inside, her fingers wrapped around the grip of her compact, Beretta PX4 Storm pistol. She'd purchased it shortly after her husband's murder. The weekly trips she'd taken to the local shooting range made her very comfortable and extremely accurate with her weapon. Her temples throbbed with anger. "I'm not going to ask you again, Kelvin; please leave."

He folded his hands behind his head and closed his eyes. "Fuck that and fuck you. Ain't lettin' no female punk me like that...hell naw..."

Ferocious anger filled her every cell. Beverly rolled out of the bed, stood, and fired a round into one of the beams in her vaulted ceiling.

Bang!

Bang!

Another round went into the floor, the third into the middle of her bed, less than a foot away from the cowering Kelvin. "Whoa! Whoa! Whoa!" He held his hands up, afraid to move.

She deeply inhaled the aroma of gunpowder as she pointed the pistol at Kelvin. Her nipples, fully erect, pointed at him like accusing fingers. A bead of pussy juice leaked out of her twat. The act of using her pistol always made her as steamy as McDonald's coffee. Something about the power of the steel in her hand made her almost climax at times. Her eyes locked on him like a vise. "Get your fucking keys and leave..." She pointed the gun at his crotch. *"Now!"*

"Girl...you *trippin'*!" He eased one leg out of the bed and onto the floor. "Careful wit' that thing...fuck around and go off."

Fortunately, Beverly had dropped her son off at her new best friend, Paula's, house for the weekend, sparing him the mayhem going on in her bedroom. A spray of spittle flew out of her mouth like machine gun fire. "If you don't get your wannabe thug-ass out of here, I'll put the next round in your skinny black ass!"

"Bev, quit trippin'!" Kelvin cautiously took his eyes off of her long enough to spot his clothes on the cedar chest at the foot of her bed. "This is some deal-breaker shit you pullin', girl."

"Fuck you, asshole!" She fired another shot into her bed, inches away from him. "Get your goddamned clothes and get out of my house!"

As he gathered up his clothes, his shaky hands dropped his shoes twice. "Hold up! Let me get my clothes on; shit."

Bang!

A bullet pierced the toe of one of his eel-skinned shoes. Her laughter filled the room as she watched him run out of her room, down the stairs and out the front door as naked as the day he was born.

The powerful smell of gunpowder filled her nostrils. The gun dangled at her side as she stood at the top of her staircase. *Fucker left my door wide open.* As she descended the stairs, she wiped a lock of hair out of her face with the hand she held the pistol in. *Guess I'm back to being single.*

She was so hyped-up on adrenaline, she wasn't aware that she stood in her doorway just as naked as Kelvin was. After making sure he had driven off, she closed the door, looked at the keypad to the right of the door, and set the alarm system.

Too wired up to sleep, she went into the kitchen, opened the freezer, and took out a half gallon of rocky road ice cream. She flipped the safety on her gun, put it and the ice cream carton on the marble top of her kitchen island, opened the dishwasher, and removed a clean tablespoon.

Moonlight coming through the bay window over her double stainless steel sinks washed over her. As she stared at the Man in the Moon, her adrenaline high came crashing down. Images of her shooting up her bedroom flashed in her head. She leaned over and vomited into the sink. She cried as she used a dishtowel to wipe her mouth. *Oh my God! What have I become?*

Eight

These are some straight freaks! Trenda thought as she peered over the edge of the office roof. Below, one of the thug-ettes was on her knees, busy sucking the dick of the tallest of the thugs. A few feet away, the other woman sucked on a blunt. The other two men pointed and yelled at each other while looking at the three-wheeled bike.

"Fuck you, trick-ass nigga! I ain't spilled shit in ya fuckin' radio!" the husky thug said to his slim friend.

"You a muthafuckin' lie!" Slim said as he placed his hand inside his jacket. "You was so busy rubbin' on this bitch, with ya high-ass, you let half of ya drink spill on my radio!"

"Bitch? Who you callin' a bitch, punk? My name is Letty Paul. Don't you eva forget that!" the loud mouthed woman yelled, hands on her wide hips. Her large tits spilled out of her un-buttoned blouse. The fat blunt dangled from her full lips.

This ain't lookin' good. Trenda watched the two thugs square off. Each man had a hand under their coats. The tall thug completely dismissed them as he focused on his oral treat.

"What? Am I supposed to be scared of you reachin' in ya coat? I got some shit under my coat, too, muthafucka," the husky thug said, his hand inside his black *Baltimore Ravens* starter jacket.

"Both you fools need to chill the fuck out," the tall thug said as his drunken head-giver let his dick pop out of her mouth. "A nigga can't even bust a nut wit' y'all arguin' like a pair of lil girls."

"Fuck that shit, Mondo." The slim thug pulled a black pistol out of his jacket. "This nigga been talkin' way too much shit lately. I ain't havin' it no mo'."

The husky thug pulled out his chrome pistol. "Fuck *you*, punk!" He cocked his pistol. "What you gonna do?"

The tall thug, Mondo, shook his head and pushed the chick off of his dick. "Put them goddamn guns up! You niggas too drunk to be slangin' them gats. This ain't no request muthafuckas; it's an *order*!"

Mondo's stature as a senior member of the gang held suitable weight for the two combatants. The husky thug un-cocked his pistol and put it back under his coat. "You lucky Mondo here."

The slim thug kept his pistol pointed at Husky. "He ain't gonna be here every time, bitch-ass nigga!"

"I ain't gonna tell you again to put that fuckin' gun up," Mondo said as he pulled a chrome .44 caliber pistol from beneath his jacket and let it dangle at his side. "And you know I don't point my shit at you unless I'm 'bout to pull the trigger. Put ya shit away before I put holes in you."

After a couple seconds of defiance, Slim drunkenly swung his pistol away from Husky. Unfortunately, his trigger finger twitched and a slug flew from his pistol and buried itself into the left breast of the female blunt-smoker.

"*Oh fuck!*" Slim yelled.

Trenda froze as she watched the gang clog up the entrance, trying to escape. Taking up the rear, the slim thug pushed his bike to the doorway, forced it through, and sped off.

"Stupid muthafuckas!" She grabbed her bag and quickly descended the ladder. The wounded woman lay on her back, quiet and still. Having seen death numerous times, Trenda didn't need a second opinion to conclude the woman was very dead.

After stepping over the corpse, she made the sign of the cross and bolted out the building.

෨෬

Gotta go back and check on that bitch, Slim thought as he made a U-turn. A firm believer in the saying, "Dead men tell no tales," he sped back to the alley, ready to put another bullet into the body just in case she had a pulse. The two felonies he already had on his record dictated his actions.

"I ain't tryin' to do no lifetime bid." He turned into the alley and almost ran head-on into a cute, dirty, wet woman as she ran out of the building. Their eyes met for what seemed like forever. He turned to the right and blocked her path. "What the fuck you doin' comin' outta there?"

"What you doin'? I just stopped here to take a piss…I'm leavin'."

Slim felt time running short. He also didn't trust the look in her eyes. "Naw, bitch…you seen too much. Can't let you go nowhere."

෨෬

Awwww, shit! Trenda thought as she calculated her next move. When she saw him getting off of his bike, she realized she still held the screwdriver. Knowing he was high and drunk, she figured she had at least one good shot at escape.

Before he could dismount the three-wheeled bike, she closed the small gap between them and plunged the screwdriver twice in his belly and once in his right bicep. The bicep of his shootin' arm. The shanking skills she'd learned in The Cock came in handy.

"Owwwww! Hey! What the…fuck? Bitch, you *crazy*?" he yelled as Trenda pushed the bike aside, tossed the bloody screwdriver against the wall of the defunct hardware store, and ran away. "Gonna kill yo muthafuckin' ass!"

Bullets whizzed past her as the angry thug fired a few rounds at her before collapsing to the ground in pain. Light rain basted her as she ran down the alley, out to the street. The falling rain turned the dust and dirt on her clothes into a muddy mess. Still she ran. Dirty puddles of water splashed under foot as she ran. *Stalked by a drunk, assaulted by a cop, witness to a murder and shot at. All this just hours after gettin' out of prison. God, You got jokes!*

Three blocks away, she turned a corner and literally ran into some of the other gang members. Winded, she intermittently jogged and walked. Too late to turn around, she picked up her pace and ran past them. One of them yelled something at her. *Fuck you crazy bastards.*

With several blocks between her and the thugs, she slowed to a fast walk. Rain water ran between the rows in her braids, down her neck and back. *Gotta get out this rain.* As she approached a residential part of town, she spotted an old church.

A sneeze escaped her. She wiped her nose with her soggy, dirty sleeve. *Sure don't need to be gettin' sick now.* The rain came down harder. A second sneeze shook her. Using her bag as an umbrella, she walked over to the St. Peter's Church of God in Christ. Peeling white paint covered the diminutive church. Rainwater saturated the low-cut lawn that ran along both sides of the cracked and pitted concrete walkway. A three-foot-tall bronze cross was mounted over the archway.

She hurried up the five creaking wooden steps, thankful for the shelter from the downpour. She leaned over the rickety wooden railing, and looked into the drapeless window. Darkness looked back at her. After three sneezes, she dropped her bag on the porch and hugged herself. "Fuck, it's cold!"

One of her mother's favorite quotes rang in her ears: A good church will never forsake you. Her eyes went to the brass door-knob. *Lemme see how true that shit is...*

She tried the doorknob and gasped as the door swung open. "Oh shit!" A quick glance around told her she was alone. Grabbing her bag, she walked inside and closed the door. When she tried to lock the door, she realized it had no lock. "I guess Momma was right."

The interior of the church was only slightly warmer than it was outside. Directly in front of her was a double row of wooden pews. At the end of the red-carpeted aisle stood a white altar. A huge wooden cross was mounted to the wall behind it. To the right of the altar sat a piano that looked older than the bottom of the hills. Three large arched windows ran down each side of the church. The high ceilings did little to contain heat. Remarkably modern track lights dangled from the ceiling. *Wonder how many poor folks helped pay for that...*

The sound of dripping water caught her attention as she walked toward the altar. To her left, a steady stream of rain water fell from the leaky roof. *All that water is gonna fuck up these hardwood floors.*

She sneezed and the sound echoed through the empty church like a barrel-bomb. As she wiped her nose with her damp sleeve, she saw a small puddle of water forming around her. Itching to get out of her soggy clothing, she looked around and saw a door at the rear of the church, to the far right of the altar. Numerous depictions of Jesus Christ filled the walls of the church. That included the stained glass tops of the arched windows. A melancholy chill shook her. *Shit reminds me of havin' to go to church damn near every day when I was a kid.*

A dirty thought soared into her mind. She recalled the summer day she'd committed a major sin in church. As a seventeen-year-old, she'd had the body of a grown woman. And that bought her the attention of many grown men. On that particular summer day, her mother decided to punish her for going to bed without washing the dishes. She made Trenda spend the day polishing the wooden pews of her father's church.

Pissed off, she waited for her mother to leave, then pulled a joint of Indo weed out of her bra, went out the back door of the church, and fired it up. She loved getting high on hot days. The eighty-degree, humid, midmorning weather suited her just fine. After five good puffs, the sound of an approaching vehicle startled her. Fearing it was her mother, she ground out the fire on the wall and tried to stuff the remains of the joint into the pockets of her too-tight, cut-off jean shorts.

Once she saw the familiar white Toyota pickup truck belonging to Earl, the handyman her parents often used, she relaxed. The thirty-something handyman smiled as he got out of his truck. Something about his skin tone made her young twat hot. His gray uniform fit his average-sized build well.

"Hey, Trenda! What you doin' out here?"

She stretched and gave him a nice glance at her white, Minnie Mouse T-shirt-covered boobs. It was tied in a knot, showing off her sexy midriff. "Slavin'. My momma got me out here polishin' the pews. Way too damn hot for that shit."

Earl held his hand up. "Hey, that's no way for a young lady to talk." She watched him pull his eyes off of her sweet body. "Don't make me tell your folks you out here cussin'."

"Whatever." She pulled the pink Bic lighter out of the folded cuff of her shorts. "You can tell 'em I'm gettin' high, too."

A bead of sweat rolled off his bald head and down his jaw as she put the joint in her mouth and fired it up. "Girl, what the heck you doin'?"

She took two deep pulls, exhaled, and held it out to him. "Wanna hit it?"

He hesitated, then reached for the spliff. "Hell, why not? It'll make preppin' this building for paint a lot easier."

The potent marijuana disarmed her inhibitions. She openly gazed at his crotch area. A year ago, while hiding her weed stash in the garage, she'd secretly caught him taking a piss in their backyard. She'd never forgotten the black beast he'd tucked back into his zipper before going back to working on the fence. Her nipples rose as that memory faded.

She handed him the joint, then rubbed her long reddish-brown ponytail. "You got a girlfriend?"

He took a few long drags. "Yup, sure do. Why?"

Trenda smirked and let her hand fall to her vaginal region. "'Cause I might have to steal you from her."

His half-closed eyes opened wide. "Girl, please."

She chuckled as he put his hands in his pockets, trying to hide his hard-on. "I ain't no girl; I'm all woman." She rubbed the thin trail of fuzzy light-brown hairs that ran beneath her navel and disappeared under the top of her shorts. "C'mon up in here and see for ya self."

Shock stalled him for a moment. He must have thought about the consequences of statutory rape in the state of Maryland. He backed away and almost tripped over the bumper of his truck. "I, uhhh…I gots work to do."

Trenda laughed as she dropped the last of the joint, ground it under her sandaled foot, and kicked the remains into the parking lot storm drain. "Whatever, Mr. Earl; you know where I'll be."

She gazed at the aroused, blushing handyman, licked her full lips, and switched her well-developed ass back up the wooden steps and into the church. Her pussy leaked with desire. She walked over and turned on the huge stainless steel fans that sat on both

sides of the rear of the church. The breeze did little to cool her
heat. Her mother, being the spendthrift she was, kept the A/C
thermostat locked. And at the moment, it was turned off.

Instead of picking up her rag and bottle of furniture polish, she
walked to the back of the church and looked out of the window.
Earl was busy untying the ladder mounted to the rack on his
truck. Her clit twitched with thoughts of him digging her pussy
out. Her hand found the hot spot between her legs. She moaned
as she rubbed her pussy through her shorts.

When he pulled off his shirt and she got a glimpse of him in
his wife-beater T-shirt, her knees buckled. She unbuttoned the
top button of her shorts and slid her hand down to her tingling
clit. All she could do was imagine his onyx-like skin rubbing on
hers. After placing the ladder against the building, he wiped sweat
off of his forehead. He then looked up and nearly caught her
rubbing herself in the huge window.

Let me get this polishin' done before I have to hear Momma's mouth.
Just as she pulled her hand out of her shorts, she heard someone
coming up the back steps.

Earl entered the calescent church, wiping sweat off of his
forehead. "Hey, which way is the bathroom?"

She and her erect nipples pointed to the right. "Down there.
You'll see a sign tellin' you which way to go."

"Thanks." He grinned and pointed at the rag and bottle of
furniture polish on the pew next to him. "Get to work."

Without moving her eyes from his zipper area, she said,
"Whatever," and watched as he walked past the gold-plated, holy
water basin behind the altar, toward the bathrooms down the
hall. After hearing him close the bathroom door, temptation
forced her hand. She slowly crept down the hall and placed her
ear against the bathroom door. Just the thought of his penis

hanging out of his pants increased the pulse rate of her spasm chasm. She found her hand back inside her shorts, massaging her mound. It felt so good, she closed her eyes and imagined Earl's dick punishing her cunt.

In the midst of her self-love, the bathroom door swung open. His eyes flew wide open. "What the...?" He swallowed hard. "Oh *shit!*"

Realizing she was busted, Trenda kept her hand in her pants and grinned. "You gonna tell my momma about this, too?"

"About what?"

Trenda giggled as he tried to pretend he didn't know he'd caught her playing in her pussy. Shyness was one thing she lacked in a big way, especially when she had a good buzz working. She pulled her pussy juice-soaked finger out of her shorts and sucked it dry. "You need to quit it; you know what I was doin'."

He licked his lips and focused on her nice tits and pink lips. "You too nasty for ya own good."

She rubbed her tits and gave him a wicked smirk. "What you sayin', Mr. Handyman?"

Buzzing and no longer able to stand the teasing, he walked over, grabbed her ass in both his big hands and pulled her to him. "You still too young to fuck, but you can jack this dick off."

Breathing hard with anticipation, her supple breasts rose and fell. She sucked in a deep breath as he unzipped and unleashed his pole. His chocolate, vein-covered dick was fully erect. She wrapped her hand around his thick stick. "*Damn!*"

He looked around, then placed his hand on her head. "Mmmmm, stroke it...rub it faster..."

Having given many hand jobs, she needed no instructions. Many of her high school jocks could attest to that. She fell to her knees and stroked his rod. *His dick big as hell!*

"Faster...jack me faster!" Earl groaned, ten minutes into his stroke-fest.

Hot and wet, Trenda man-handled his manhood. Soon, she felt his pre-cum dribble out. She had never tasted cum, but the desire to have a sample overcame her.

When she wrapped her soft, pink lips around his throbbing dick, he moaned loudly, gripped the back of her head, and fucked her in her hot throat. Trenda, both frightened and turned on, went with his motion. His large tool bounced off the roof of her mouth and inside her jaws.

Minutes later, his body stiffened and trembled. "Ohhhhhh goddamnnnn! Don't move! Don't...you...moveeeee!"

A gusher of warm, creamy cum shot down her throat and filled her mouth. The taste instantly addicted her. He seemed to cum forever. After swallowing all she could, she still had a mouthful. The familiar creaking sound of her mother's vintage Buick Electra 225 pulling into the church parking lot chilled her.

Oh no! Momma's here!

She ripped her mouth off of Earl's dick and stood wide-eyed, trying to find a place to spit his jizz. She knew if she swallowed one more drop, she would heave.

Earl, dazed and grinning, gazed at her. "You aight?"

Trenda, still looking around, pointed frantically to the back door. Earl walked over, looked out the back window, and froze. "Oh goddamn!" He ran across the church and out of the front door like a wide receiver seeking the goal line.

Don't you spit on the floor! Momma will see this shit all in that brown carpet!

The car door opened and closed. On the verge of tears, she had only one choice as her mother's foot falls sounded on the steps. She leaned over the holy water basin and spat out the sperm.

The church seemed to creak with anger. Deep in her soul, she *knew* she had committed an unforgivable sin. Panicking, she sloshed the water around with her hand, ran to the pew she was polishing, grabbed the towel and polish, and pretended to be hard at work.

After taking a scolding from her mother for working slow, Trenda grinned, tickled at her deviousness. Her journey down the dark path had begun. A week later she would run away and make the streets her home.

Nine

"Sorry, Detective, but I've been here since my shift started at eight and I don't recall anybody like this lady buying a ticket," the crew-cut, freckle-faced clerk said to Detective Messy Marv.

Marv shook his head as the clerk slide the mug shot of Trenda back to him. "No problem." He tucked the picture back into the inside pocket of his dark blue suit jacket. Inside the same pocket, he pulled out one of his business cards and slid it under the slot in the bulletproof glass barrier between them. "Give me a call if you happen to see her."

He rubbed his growling belly as he headed for the exit. *Knew I should have taken my ass home and had some dinner.* A spring rain shower drenched his normally ultra clean undercover car. Using his hand to brim his forehead, he strolled to his car, got in and started the engine. He yawned, turned on the wipers and defroster, then pulled away from the curb. *Forget it; I'll get a fresh start Monday.*

A quarter mile away from the Greyhound station, chatter on his police scanner got his attention. Reports of a gang member named Percy Wells—aka—Slip, whom he was very familiar with, was found in the middle of a street not too far from him, bleeding from multiple wounds. "That boy stays in trouble."

After a moment's thought, he listened to his "cop intuition," busted a U-turn in the middle of O'Donnell Street, and headed for the location of the bleeding thug. Minutes later, he arrived at his destination. He pulled up between a fire truck and a PD patrol car. *Son-of-a-bitch! Fuckin' Nick's here*, he thought as he got out of his car. He and Nick were *not* the best of friends. Not by a long shot.

Nick and one of the firemen stood next to a three-wheeled bicycle, seemingly discussing the custom-made contraption. The rain eased up a bit as Marv walked over to where two firemen kneeled next to a drenched, slim young man who lay grimacing on the asphalt. Another fireman stood talking on his cell phone. The wail of an approaching siren filled the air. After showing his badge to the firemen, he leaned over and shook his head at the fallen thug. "What's new, Slip?"

ഇറ

Slip grimaced and rolled his eyes at Messy Marv. They'd met on numerous, unfortunate occasions. He instead focused on the cop and fireman standing directly over the sewer grate. He'd tossed his pistol and a thick, sealed envelope he had tucked in his waistband into it after his wounds forced him off of his bike. *Sho' hope all that rainwater washes my prints off that gun. If they find it, my ass is through…I'm gonna have to avoid Red long enough to make up for that cash I just tossed in that gutter. Can't afford to get busted with twenty grand of dope money on me…*

ഇറ

Marv leaned over further and the mug shot of Trenda fell out of his pocket, landing inches away from Slip's nose.

"Awww, shit!" he said, reaching for the photo.

Marv stopped and watched Slip do a double take as he looked at the photograph. His gaze went from the mug shot, to Marv, and back to the mug shot.

Marv studied Slip's nervous look. "You okay? That somebody you know?"

Slip avoided all eye contact with Marv. He shook his head, closed his eyes and clutched his stomach. *He's lyin' like a Persian rug.* "C'mon, Slip; what you know 'bout her?"

"Ambulance is here, Messy," a familiar, grumpy voice said behind his back. "They need to get him to the hospital."

Marv exhaled, slowly turned his head, and looked at Nick. "I'm completely aware of that, officer."

He picked up the picture of Trenda and noticed Nick, just like Slip, paid a lot of attention to the mug shot. He shook the water off of the photo and held it in front of Nick's face. You know who this is?"

"Can't say I do." He removed his plastic-covered patrol cap and shook water off of it. "What? She run off from you?"

Marv read the lie in Nick's face as he tucked the picture back in his pocket. "Nope, just a person of interest."

They parted as the paramedics pushed a gurney over, lowered it, and worked on the injured gang member.

Nick spat out a disgusting wad of phlegm onto the wet ground. "Well, if you need help findin' her, give me a holler."

Recognizing that as one of Nick's "You-been-behind-a-desk-too-long-to-do-real-work" jabs, he adjusted the collar of his jacket and looked Nick in his pale face. "I seriously doubt I'll ever need *your* help with anything, but thanks anyway."

Nick glared at him, grunted, turned and left. *Good; take your simple-ass down the street somewhere.* Marv turned and caught Slip staring at him as a Hispanic male paramedic placed an oxygen mask on his face. "I'll talk to you later, Slip."

The injured man turned away from Marv's gaze as the paramedics slid him into the back of their waiting ambulance.

Ten

The recollection of her first time sucking down cum left a bad taste in her mouth. *Was way outta control with my young, dumb ass*, Trenda thought as she shook off the embarrassing memory. She hitched her bag up on her shoulder, walked over, and tried the door behind the altar.

"Oh cool!" The door opened up to a short hallway with three other doors. Two were restrooms; the third had a plaque on it stating "Office."

She entered the women's restroom and flipped the light switch. A grimy stranger stared at her. "Dang! I look like straight *doo-doo*!" The mirror mounted over the small sink reflected the filth of her journey. Streaks of dirt covered her face like camouflage paint. Her once cute, pink sweatsuit was beyond the skills of any cleaners. The mixture of blood, dirt and funk assured her of that. Her fingernails were caked with dirt.

I'd give blood for a hot bath, she thought as she stripped. Dirty water drained off her pile of waterlogged clothes, onto the old, linoleum floor. After taking a "bird bath" in the sink, she stuffed a massive amount of used paper towels into the tall, white plastic garbage can that sat next to the door. Her conscience awakened. She grabbed the garbage can, carried it out to where the roof was leaking and placed it under the dripping water. She went back, got her damp shirt, and dried up as much of the water on the floor as she could.

Back in the restroom, she went through her bag and found her last outfit; a pair of red, French-cut panties, a pair of black jeans and a black Baltimore Ravens sweatshirt. She dug deeper in her bag. "Cool." She found her pair of black Timberland boots.

Twenty minutes later, she emerged out of the bathroom carrying her wet clothes and her bag on her shoulder. *Can't leave these bloody clothes in here…hell-to-the-naw!* She took her bag off of her shoulder and set it on the floor. *Wonder if they have a dumpster?*

Walking down the hallway, she looked to her right and saw a door with an illuminated EXIT sign over it. After checking to see if it was alarmed, she was relieved to see it wasn't. Outside, the rain had let up. The clouds gave way to the starry skies. She walked outside and spotted a small green dumpster. As she got closer, she sighed. A large padlock on the lid killed her plan. *What am I gonna do now?*

She walked to the edge of the church and looked out onto the street. In front of the vacant lot next to the church, she spotted a mound of illegally dumped garbage. The low-income neighborhood still looked fast asleep. *Fuck it.* She hurried over to the pile of rubbish and stuffed her clothes underneath the mangled and filthy cushions of a green, crushed-velvet loveseat.

A few drops of rain fell. She yawned, wiped her hands on her pants, and walked back to the rear of the church. Back inside, she went to her bag, picked it up, and tried the office door. Not surprisingly, it opened up. The small office contained a small desk, a four-drawer black file cabinet, a bookshelf full of Holy books, an aging black leather office chair and a large picture of an elderly black couple, dressed in their Sunday best, holding hands. "Must be the preacher and his wife."

Trenda yawned again. She walked around to the office chair and smiled when she pulled it from under the desk. *Thank the*

Lord! Underneath the desk was a fairly new portable heater. It looked like the only thing in the whole church worth stealing. She sat her bag on the desk, grabbed the heater, and looked for a plug.

Directly behind her, she found an extension cord plugged into an outlet behind the chair. "Oh, baby!" she exclaimed as the heating element glowed red and heat found her. After turning the heat up as high as it could go, she stood and rotated around the heater like a chicken on an automated roasting spit.

During her thawing out process, her mind raced. The possibility of the church having an early morning service bothered her. If they did and it started at seven in the morning, no telling how early they would show up to get ready. She scratched her dirty, itchy braids. *Need a bath, bad.*

She could think of only one place she could go on short notice. She rubbed her red eyes. *Gotta do what I gotta do...*

ଈଔ

Can't stand that prick, Nick thought as he watched Marv get into his car and drive off. What really bothered him was the fact that he was carrying around a mug shot of Trenda Fuqua. It was no secret in the police department that he was still investigating her, but still, something about him with her photo in his jacket pocket, on this night, bothered him. *Has that bastard been tailing me?*

He stared out of his windshield after getting behind the wheel of his patrol car. Now that he had the chance to make Trenda *his* "hustle-hoe," like the late Darius Kain did, he wasn't eager to see Messy Marv fuck it up for him. Nick was well aware of how proficient Marv was at tracking his prey.

He recalled how he and Marv had almost come to blows during

Darius Kain's funeral. After making a few insensitive jokes within earshot of the fallen officer's widow, Marv lost his cool and took a swing at Nick. Fortunately, Nick managed to lean back from the punch. It took half a dozen officers to separate the two.

"Fuckin' pussy," Nick said as he shook Marv out of his system and focused on finding one of his street walking friends. He needed sexual release after having "browsed" Trenda's body.

Gonna have to keep tabs on that green-eyed tramp... He cruised the streets of west Baltimore until he spotted three hookers. One of them was his favorite prostitute, Cherry. She had the biggest ass and darkest skin in West Baltimore. He flashed his high beams on Cherry, letting her know he was ready for action. When he pulled over to the curb, Cherry's two female friends scattered.

He got out and pointed his billy club at her. "Time to pay your taxes, Cherry."

Eleven

Wish somebody would turn that music down...too early for that shit...never heard them guards playin' gospel music before... It took a few moments before Trenda realized she wasn't in her jail cell. Her eyes flew open and she looked around cautiously. *What the hell?* She felt the weight of a blanket around her shoulders. The heater still glowed next to her as she sat in the chair behind the desk.

The melodious sound of the church's organ drifted in between the cracked office door. Pale sunlight glowed behind the yellowing window shade behind her. She sat up and saw someone had wrapped the prettiest quilt she'd ever seen around her shoulders. A woman's hound's-tooth jacket and man's trench coat hung from the wooden coat rack that stood next to the door.

Oh shit! Somebody's been in here while I was asleep!

She had no idea what time it was, but from her years of growing up attending both morning and afternoon services in her father's church, it sounded like the current service was about to end. A deep, booming voice preached to the audience. As soon as Trenda stood up, the door to the office opened up. A very grandmotherly looking, white-haired black woman in a conservative light blue skirt and jacket adjusted her round eyeglasses and gave her a smile.

"Well, hello, honey! How you sleep?"

Shocked, all Trenda could do was stand still. She finally found her voice. "I...I'm sorry. I was cold an—"

Before Trenda could finish her explanation, the old lady held her hand up and shook her head. "Child, you ain't gotta explain. Ain't nobody need to be stuck outside on a cold, rainy night." She then graced Trenda with a sweet smile. "Besides, it's the least we could do after you put that garbage can under that leak in the roof. Would have ruined our whole floor if you hadn't come inside our church. Praise the lord!"

Trenda gently sat the quilt on the chair. "Uhhh, okay." She bent over and turned off the heater. "I'll go 'head and get outta here. You got the time?"

The chubby matriarch checked her watch. "It's a little after ten." She walked over and placed her hand between Trenda's shoulder blades. "You ain't gotta leave, honey. Besides, we still have a little food left from breakfast. I bet you could use a lil something to put in that belly."

Goddamn! I slept that long? Only meant to take a short nap and cut outta here. Trenda looked around for her traveling bag. "No... that's okay. I'll get somethin' later."

The old lady studied Trenda's face. "I'm Emma Brookfield... What's yo' name, child? You look familiar." She picked up the quilt, folded it and placed it on the desk. "You got eyes like somebody else I know."

Trenda's stomach howled for food. Emma had just thrown her a curveball. She wasn't sure if she should use her real name or one of her aliases. Her instincts told her to go with the latter. "Gina."

Emma's eyes seemed to bore through Trenda. "You related to the Fuquas?"

Trenda almost tripped over the chair. "No...never heard that name."

"You sure? You look just like Father Fuqua. He runs the St.

Philips Church over in Randallstown." The organ music stopped, followed by clapping and murmuring voices. The first service of the day was over. Emma took a deep breath and sighed. "Where do you live? You have family out here?"

Time to bounce. Trenda looked on the side of the desk, saw her bag, picked it up, and cleared her throat. "I'm just passin' through; I ain't got no family out here."

Just then, the door swung open. A tall, slim, light-skinned man entered the office. It was the man in the photograph with Emma, on the wall. "Well, good morning, angel!"

His smile was as bright as a full moon on a summer night. Trenda ran her hand over her fuzzy braids. "Thank you, sir."

Emma walked over and stood next to her husband. "Drake, don't she look just like Father Fuqua?"

The early signs of cataracts showed in his brown eyes. He squinted at Trenda. "She sure does...got them same deep green eyes."

With both of them blocking the door, it was hard for Trenda to make her escape. Her stomach growled again, giving her an idea. "Excuse me, Mrs. Brookfield, did you say you had some food?"

They both nodded and smiled. Emma held the door open and motioned for her to follow. "Come this way, child. We've got some coffee, doughnuts, and maybe some bacon and eggs left."

Trenda couldn't remember the last time she'd had "real" food. She was almost tempted to actually stay and eat, but that wasn't in her game plan. She showed them a faux smile. "Sounds good!"

She left the office and followed Emma and Drake out to the altar area. Several people still lingered in the church—too many for Trenda's taste. Drake tapped her on the shoulder. "Right this way. Follow Emma."

Straight ahead was a door Trenda didn't see last night. It led to what looked like a small kitchen. Emma stood there holding the door open. Meanwhile, Drake walked down the aisle, shaking hands and seeing people out. Just a few feet shy of Emma, Trenda stopped. "You mind if I go to the bathroom first? I'll be right back."

Emma pointed back down toward the office. "You know where it is? In the same hall as the office?"

"Yes, ma'am. Thank you."

Emma smiled. "Good, I'll go make you a plate and have it ready for you when you come back. You want coffee or orange juice?"

Ohhhh, coffee sounds so good right now... "I'm not sure yet. I'll see when I get back." She could feel Emma's eyes on her as she walked away. Guilt rode her like a saddle on a horse. She looked back over her shoulder. "Thanks for everything, Mrs. Brookfield."

Emma's smile faded a tad. "You say that like you ain't comin' back."

Trenda felt like shit. Her lifetime of lying was still a part of her. And it was annoying the hell out of her. "I'll be back...just need to wash up a lil bit."

Emma nodded as her eyes fell from Trenda's to the floor. She turned her back to Trenda. "Take care of yourself, baby." She walked into the kitchen and let the door swing closed behind her.

For a moment, Trenda had the urge to run into that kitchen, eat, and enjoy the kind woman's company. But, circumstances dictated that she do the opposite; break camp. Gripping her bag, she walked into the hallway, past the restrooms, and out the back door.

The pleasing warmth of the springtime sun fell on her. Instead of basking in it as she very much wanted to, she picked up her pace and hurried away from the church. Several cars containing members leaving the first service passed her as she strolled down the street. She kept looking back, expecting to see Drake and Emma following her. *Hated lyin' to 'em, but can't take no chance on them tellin' folks who and where I am.*

Three blocks away from the church, a patrol car cruised past her. The pair of African-American officers gazed at her but kept moving. She thought about the gang member she'd shanked the previous night. *Hope they ain't tied him to me.*

Nervous and hungry, Trenda stepped inside the Old Soul Coffee Shop. The quaint, neighborhood caffineatorium was exactly what she needed. A fistful of early risers were there, sipping coffee and working on their laptops. Trenda found a table in the far corner that sat next to the large picture window. She put her bag on the table and opened it up.

Almost forgot about this. She attempted to power-up her three-year-old cell phone. She found the power cord in her bag, plugged it into the outlet next to her chair and hooked up her phone. It looked like an antique compared to the sleek new smartphones most of the other patrons had. No surprise to her, the service was shut off; account canceled.

Ahhh, at least I still got my phone numbers. She browsed the contact information. Her eyes lit up when she got to the F-section. "Ol' Fox... just the person I need to see."

A pierced-lipped, skinny waitress stopped at Trenda's table. "Good morning! Can I get you anything? Coffee? Latte? Bagel?"

Trenda looked past the cocoa-colored woman and into the glass display case filled with edibles. "You got cinnamon raisin bagels?"

"Sure do." She scratched her order on her pad. "Anything to drink?"

Trenda squinted, trying to read the coffee menu. "What y'all got?" After running down the list of various flavors of coffees and teas, Trenda's head swam. *Where the fuck did they come up with all them crazy flavors?* "I'll have a large hot chocolate."

While waiting for her food, she went through the contents of her bag. Besides the phone, charger and wallet, the only things left were her well-worn New York Yankees cap and letter explaining who and where her parole officer was located. Memories of the places she'd been and shit she'd been involved with swarmed her thoughts. Before being swept away in nostalgia, she slapped it on her head, over her itchy braids. *Gonna have to let that old life go...*

Inside her wallet, she found she had no identification. *What the hell?* Besides an old prepaid Visa card, the $400 check and her ten-dollar bill, all of her fake IDs were gone. She closed her eyes, then lowered and shook her head. The police had confiscated them. Now she had no way of cashing her check. Her patience with God was wearing thin. All of the Bible studying she'd done in prison was starting to lose hold of her. To center herself, she reflected on the verse, James 1:12:

Blessed is the man who perseveres under trial, because when he has stood the test, he will receive the crown of life that God has promised to those who love him.

It did little good. Reality was kicking her ass. "Here you go, ma'am," the barista said as she put a plate with the bagel and the cup of hot chocolate on the table. "Will there be anything else?"

Trenda opened her eyes as the hot chocolate aroma pleased her nostrils. "No...I'm good."

The waitress put the bill face down on the table. "Have a good day."

The sun crawled across the sky as she wolfed down her food and read the contents of her parole letter. *Gotta report to my P.O. Monday mornin' at nine. Better stay close to downtown.* After paying for her meal, the three dollars and change left from her last ten bucks troubled her. She was about seventeen dollars short of the cost for a new ID in the state of Maryland.

Outside, the exhaust from a passing MTA bus almost made her gag. While fanning the front of her face, she spotted a bank of payphones across the street. After trying two of the three phones, the third one gave her a dial tone. She then opened her bag, took out her phone and looked up the phone number for her former attorney and lover, Dennis "The Fox" Wilcox. On the fourth ring, as she was about to hang up, his familiar, extra proper sounding voice entered her ear. "Hello?"

"Wassup, Fox?"

"Who's calling?"

"Oh, you forgot my voice already? It's only been a couple years."

After a long silence, he said, "*Trenda*? Trenda Fuqua?"

"The one and only. Surprised?"

"Wow! I'm uhhh...quite surprised. When did you get out?"

Another bus approached. Before she sucked down any more fumes, she turned her back to the traffic. "Yesterday."

"Really? Where are you now? What are you going to do with yourself?"

She looked into the large picture window of Drew's Dry Cleaners, which was right behind the bank of payphones, and grimaced at her slovenly reflection. "I dunno yet. That's part of the reason why I called you."

She heard what sounded like a muffled woman's voice in the background. "Hmmm, and just what is it that you're looking for?"

Several cars loaded with folks dressed in their Sunday best passed her. She surmised that they were headed to St. Peters for the late service. Turning away from the window, she focused on Dennis. "I've got a situation here that I need ya help with."

Again she heard the muffled female voice. "I'm not sure...I can be of much help right now. I'm kind of...busy."

Sounds like you over there fuckin', Trenda thought. "It's just a small favor, Fox..."

"I...I don't know..."

"C'mon, Fox. All I need is a small loan so I can get me a new ID card. The cops took mine after I got booked. Now I ain't got no way to cash my check and I'm broke as hell. I'll make it up to you, you know that."

"I don't know...I'm a little tied up..."

A recorded voice broke in and told her she needed to deposit two more quarters. But she could tell he was thinking about the great blowjobs she'd blessed him with. "Fox, baby, you know I wouldn't be askin' if I didn't need it...come meet me real quick." The voice demanded more change. She was out of coins and had to lasso Fox in before she got cut off. "Look, do me this lil favor and I'll make you feel real right."

She could almost hear the wheels turning in the Fox's freaky dome. After a minor pause, he said, "Where exactly are you?"

Thank you, Lord! The phone shut off just as she finished spitting out the address of the cleaners.

Twelve

"That's the last one, thank God," Beverly said as she filled the bullet hole in the beam above her bed with wood patch. She climbed down the ladder and wiped her forehead. "I have got to do a better job of controlling my emotions."

After checking the time on her nightstand clock, she folded up her aluminum ladder and prepared to haul it back to the garage. The splotches of yellow paint on it reminded her of the time she and Darius had painted the kitchen together early on in their marriage, years before it began unraveling. Even though she'd caught him cheating on her a few times, she still loved him.

After all, he was a great provider. Although she knew his police salary wasn't enough to explain their upscale lifestyle, she'd never questioned it. But a part of her knew something in the milk wasn't clean. Oh hell no, it wasn't.

She managed to get the ladder back down the stairs without banging it against the mahogany railings of staircase. *Almost time for me to pick up DJ*, she thought after checking her watch. Ten minutes to noon. For a moment, she stared at the vanilla-colored car cover covering her late husband's beloved Corvette. It hadn't been moved or uncovered since she'd had it shipped to her new house in Houston from her former home in Baltimore.

A mist of despair fell on her soul. The seething hatred of Trenda re-emerged. She found herself grinding her teeth. It had gotten so bad, she'd contracted Bruxism. Her dentist had instructed her to wear acrylic night guards on her teeth.

Besides the anger, she was still horny. Very horny. But the fact that she hadn't been able to climax since Darius was killed added to her frustration. Too proud to see a psychiatrist, she instead sought other means of dealing with her issues—visiting the gun range and smoking copious amounts of weed were two of her release valves.

Need a fat joint right now. Walking between her baby blue Escalade and the covered Corvette, she searched her mind to see if she had any bud left in her stash. Between the life insurance policy she held on her and her late husband and the cash settlement she'd accepted from the Baltimore PD, she was financially set.

Upon reentering the house, she heard her cell phone ring. *Hope that's not Kel's ass.* By the time she got upstairs to her bedroom and checked her phone, she'd missed the call. She called her voicemail and her knees buckled. She sat down hard on her bullet-riddled bed.

A voice she both wanted to hear and feared spoke to her on a recorded message: *What's the deal, friend? I see you called me but didn't leave a message. You okay? Need help with something? You know I got you; told you at the funeral that I'd take care of you. Darius was one of my best friends; it's the least I could do. Gimme a call back. One love.*

His deep, gruff voice watered her twat. *Good thing he's a couple thousand miles away*, she thought as she stood and ran her fingers over the bullet holes in her mattress. *Thank God these thick mattresses slowed the bullets down enough to not have gone through the floor.*

Her trying to "Jedi-mind trick" her brain failed. Thoughts of Lionel's' thick, full Teddy Pendergrass-style beard, thick lips and muscular frame caused her to lie back on her bed. Her hand soon found her steaming hot vagina. After several blissful minutes of finger-fucking herself, the alarm on her cell phone went off. "Shit."

Her clit tingled with desire as she sighed and eased herself off of the bed. "Let me go get this boy."

As she turned off the alarm on her phone, she stared at the missed call from Lionel. The temptation to return his call almost won out. She quickly put the phone down. A part of her brain told her that once she made that phone call, she would set into motion things that could easily get out of hand.

ಬಿಎಲ್

Minutes crawled by like hours as Trenda waited for Dennis to show up. Not only was her hunger irritating, so was her griminess. There were times she'd felt more morally dirty, but never had she felt so physically filthy.

She sat down on the bus stop in front of the cleaners, sat her bag next to her, and leaned back. The feel of the late morning sun helped relax her. An elderly man, resembling her frail father, walked toward her. He tipped his aged, Baltimore Orioles cap at her as he stood next to the bus stop sign. "Mornin', young lady."

"Mornin'," Trenda mumbled as she closed her eyes and pulled the brim of her cap down to her eyebrows. She had no intentions of engaging in conversation. *Wonder what Pops is up to?*

The guilt of having dodged and shamed her family pushed that thought away. Even though she had only closed her eyes for a minute, she was already drifting off to sleep. A replay of almost getting shot dominated her thoughts until the sound of a beeping car horn snapped her awake. *'Bout time.*

The sly smile of Dennis "The Fox" Wilcox shined on her from behind the windshield of a gunmetal gray, wide-bodied Porsche. She stood up as he pulled to the curb. *Damn, when they start makin' four-door Porsches?*

He lowered the passenger window. "Well, how goes it, Ms. Fuqua? Can I offer you a lift?"

The aroma of high-grade marijuana wafted out of the window. She bent over and looked inside the car. "Yeah...I could use one of those."

He squirted Visine into his bloodshot eyes as she sat down on the dark gray, leather seats. He tucked the small bottle into his shirt pocket and grinned. "Wow! Looks like you've seen better days."

She wasn't feeling his candid personality. He was an even bigger asshole after he smoked a little ganja. "Ya think?"

He chuckled as he checked his mirror and pulled into the traffic. "Never thought I would see the fabulous Trenda looking like a pauper."

The beginnings of a tension headache loomed in her temples. "Dang, you love pickin' at folks, don't you?"

A red traffic light stopped them. "You know I have your best interest at heart," he said as pulled off at the green light. "Speaking of that; I heard you turned down a lucrative deal from StarShine. Is that true?"

Trenda turned away from his gaze and looked out the window. "Somethin' like that."

He pulled over to the curb. "Looks to me like you could use that kind of deal right now. Why didn't you take it?"

She massaged her temples. "All money ain't good money."

"Touché." His hand landed on her thigh. "Now, what is it I can do for you?"

His hand moved up and down her thigh. She recognized, from experience, that was a sign the Fox wanted her—badly. "Well, I just got out the pen, as you know, and I need to get my shi—I mean, *myself* together. All I have is a check and no ID to use to cash it. I need you to let me hold a few dollars so that I can get one and cash this check. After I do that, I can break you off what I owe you."

A tall, slim Puerto Rican man admired Fox's car as his leashed, black and white pit bull pissed on streetlight pole. "How much is the check?"

Trenda ignored his groping hand and looked out of the window at the dog. "Four hundred bucks."

His hand paused for a moment. He then playfully slapped the brim of her cap. "I have an idea. How about I take you back to my place so you can clean up? Then we can further discuss your financial plight."

She glanced into his lap and saw the outline of his bulging penis under his tan slacks. *Same ol' freaky Fox.* The speed at which her old life was overtaking her new life astounded her. Circumstances made her commitment to becoming a better person a hell of a lot harder than she thought it would be. "You gonna bring me back here when we get done?"

He chuckled as he looked out of his window at the decaying neighborhood. "Yes, if that's what you really want to do."

"It's what I really want to do *right now*." She recalled her status. "Hey, I'm on parole. I ain't supposed to leave the state of Maryland. You live in D.C., don't you?"

After one last squeeze of her leg, he grinned and pulled away from the curb. "Don't worry about that; you have a good attorney."

As Fox navigated to the freeway entrance, Trenda contemplated her next moves. For some reason, staying in Baltimore seemed like a bad idea. The adventures she'd been on over the past twelve hours proved that. *Where do I go if I leave here?*

She even considered going back to California. Maybe look up her old friend, Lollie, and take another crack at starting over out there. Her parolee status put that plan on an eighteen-month hiatus.

Fox cursed as his precious car bounced in and out of a rainwater-filled pothole on the entrance to Interstate 695. He turned down the volume of the classical music he was listening to in order to answer his ringing cell phone. The German side of his half-German, half-West Indian composition was showing itself today.

Trenda closed her eyes and tuned out his phone conversation and corny music. Four hundred dollars would not get her far. And finding a job with her record and infamous status would truly be a challenge. She frowned in her semi-sleep at the aspect of giving in to StarShine and selling them her story. The thought of putting her family in danger put the kibosh on that plan. *Ain't gonna let nobody hurt my folks over some money...fuck that...*

An hour later, they pulled off the highway and into the affluent city of Georgetown. A sense of déjà vu swept over her. She had spent many weekends at Fox's impressive estate. As they drove alongside the Potomac River, they passed up several high-end stores and eateries. He turned onto Wisconsin Avenue and pulled into the parking lot of Urban Chic.

Trenda turned to him. "What are we doin' here?"

He flashed his famous Fox grin. "You'll see."

Thirteen

*C*an't believe this trifling little hoochie turned down all that money from StarShine! Dennis thought as he grinned at the grimy but hot woman sitting in his passenger seat. *I wish I could talk her into selling her story and retaining me as her legal counsel. I'd make enough money off her to afford that second home in Los Angeles I've been dreaming of.* He dropped his hand to her thigh, caressed it and sighed. *It sucks for me that she is so true to the "no snitching" code.*

His bloodthirsty drive for riches was legendary. His ability to defend anyone with enough cash sickened most law enforcement personnel. Many believed he was a stooge for the Mob, but Fox could not care less. His outstanding record for getting social "undesirables" out of jail terms was his calling card. After parking his car, Dennis walked around to open Trenda's door for her, but found she had already gotten out. *So much for chivalry.*

She looked him in his brown eyes. "Wassup, Fox? Why'd you bring me here?"

"Just thought you'd like to get out of those rags and put on something more fitting for a hottie like yourself."

She studied all the new clothing styles behind the huge storefront windows. He was well aware of her addiction to fashion. "I can't afford the shi—I mean, *stuff* in this store. I gotta strict budget."

He chuckled. "I see you've been trying not to curse...is that something new?"

A pair of well-dressed African-American women gave Trenda dirty looks and a wide birth as they exited the store. She returned their glare, then looked back at Dennis. "You could say that. Tryin' to break a lot of bad habits."

Hope that doesn't include your freaky side, he thought, watching Trenda use the passenger mirror of his car, and attempt to brush down some of her fuzzy hair with her hand. "C'mon; let me treat you to a new outfit to celebrate your liberation."

℘℃℞

This fool's up to somethin'. Never seen him do a damn thing without wantin' somethin' back, Trenda thought as she looked into the mirror, into her troubled eyes. She slapped her cap back on her head and followed him into the store.

The store was stocked with the hottest, hippest, wildest fashions Trenda could imagine. Racks of skirts, blouses, dresses, and pants beckoned her. Instead of rushing over to the clothes, she used restraint. Dennis walked over, stood behind and put his hands on her shoulders. "Go ahead and put together a couple of outfits—my treat."

She looked over her shoulder at him. "And you say this is on you, right?"

"Yes, my friend. Look at it as a welcome home gift." He waved a hand at the waiting clothes. "Go get yourself something nice."

With no further goading needed, Trenda made her way to the pants section. *Aight, Fox, I'm gonna play ya game.*

An hour later, Trenda and Dennis left the store with four outfits in three bags. While he put the bags in the trunk, Trenda got inside and waited.

"Nice selections," Dennis said after getting in and starting the Porsche. "Can't wait to see you model them for me."

"Ah ha! I *knew* you had some kinda twist involved."

He grinned and backed out of his parking stall. "Not at all! I was just kidding, friend."

"Yeah, right," Trenda said as she folded her arms across her tits. "I'm gonna hold you to that."

A few minutes later, they arrived at his fully renovated, three-story, five-bedroom, four-bathroom, brick house. The million-dollar home was over one hundred years old. Instead of pulling into the five-car garage, he drove onto the brick, circular driveway and parked behind a yellow convertible Mustang. "I hope you have time to stay for dinner, or at least a late lunch."

"Lunch maybe...I still gotta get to where I'm goin'." She un-buckled her seatbelt and opened the door. "You still gonna be able to cash this check for me?"

He unbuckled and took his keys out of the ignition. "Don't worry about that right now. Let's go inside and have a bite."

It had been quite a while since the last time Trenda had entered the palatial mini-mansion. It was almost too nice to live in. It looked more like an exhibit in excess than a dwelling. The rainforest-brown, Italian marble tile that lined the floor of the foyer cost as much as a *nice* used car. Soulful female vocals over a smooth jazz track leaked out of the speakers hidden throughout the house.

"Who is that singin'?" Trenda asked as Dennis closed the front door and carried her bags inside.

"Ahhh...that's one of my favorite vocalists, Samantha James. Have you heard of her?"

Trenda followed the tile into an immaculate sitting room. The unmistakable smell of high-octane marijuana hung in the air. She sat down on a cognac-colored leather loveseat and yawned. "Nah, can't say I have. She new?"

He sat the bags down on the floor next to Trenda. "No, she's been around for a while. Sounds good for a white girl, huh?"

Disbelief filled her face. "Say what? She *white*?"

"White as new snow." He took off his chocolate-brown sport coat and hung it over his arm. "Just proves that soul is colorblind."

"I guess..." She removed her cap and scratched between her braids. "Awww, shi—ah, *shoot*! I forgot to get a comb and shampoo. I need to take my hair down and wash it."

He removed his brown and yellow tie and unbuttoned the top three buttons on his white shirt. "No worries. My friend, Carly, may be able to help you with that."

Trenda narrowed her eyes and studied Fox. "Who the hell is Carly?"

His chuckle echoed off the sand-colored walls of the sitting room. "My friend. Hold on a second and I'll introduce you to her."

"I ain't interested."

"Sure you are."

Without another word, he turned and walked away. Trenda shook her head, picked up one of the bags, and sorted through the stuff inside. She pulled out and examined the three, sexy panty and bra sets. After looking at the silky materials, she put them back in the bag. *Think I'm gonna rock the black set after I wash my ass.*

Dennis's creepy laugh, along with a woman's laughter drifted to her from down the hall. Moments later, she heard the *click-clack* of shoes on hardwood floor approaching. Dennis entered the sitting room accompanied by a gorgeous brunette with ice-blue eyes. "Trenda, I'd like to introduce you to Carly."

As hot as Trenda *knew* she was, even she had to do a double take at the curvy, Caucasoid beauty. She reminded Trenda of

Lynda Carter of *Wonder Woman* fame. After looking her up and down, she mumbled, "Wassup?"

She handed the small wooden weed pipe she held to Dennis, then offered Trenda her hand. "Hello, Trenda! Dennis speaks very highly of you." She took her hand back and caressed Trenda with her gaze. "You are *much* prettier than he described."

Trenda smirked. "Thanks."

Dennis pulled a lighter out of his pocket, sparked up the bowl of weed, and took a deep hit. He then stepped behind Carly, handed her the pipe, and placed his hands on her shoulders. "Carly here is a visiting attorney friend of mine from Omaha. She's on vacation and working her way to D.C. to check out the Smithsonian."

Trenda noticed that the nipples on Carly's enhanced boobs were erect beneath her white, Georgetown Hoyas T-shirt. Somehow, it worked well with her blue jeans and high heels. To Trenda, they looked like a pair of jackals stalking prey. "That's all good." She scratched the back of her head. "Y'all goin' together?"

Carly took a hit of weed, looked over her shoulder at Dennis, smiled, looked back at Trenda, and offered her the pipe. "You want a toke?"

Trenda wanted to hit that good grass bad as hell, but knew a dirty drug test would put her right back in The Cock. Fuck that. "No...I'm good."

Carly took another pull off the pipe. "Actually, we were hoping you'd show me around. Dennis told me you know the area better than almost anyone."

Hmmmm, this slick bastard...no wonder he was so eager to take me shoppin'. Same ol' snake. She looked him in his red eyes. "Sounds like fun, but I got a lot of stuff to handle and not a lot of time to handle it."

Dennis held his grin, dropped his hands, and stepped beside Carly. "Don't be too hasty, friend. I know you just got back 'in town,' but I'm sure we can arrange for you to get where you need to go." He placed his hands on Trenda's shoulders and massaged them. "How about we go have dinner and continue this conversation later?"

Having people put their hands on her without being invited to do so was a major pet peeve of hers. That simple act had led to bad things happening to the offenders. Trying to hold back her temper and continue on her path to a new and better Trenda was becoming one hell of a challenge. She eased his hands off of her. "Thanks for the offer, but I *really* need to do somethin' with this head, you-know-what-I'm-sayin'?"

He snapped his fingers and looked at the very mellow Carly. "Oh that's right. Babe, do you have a comb, and perhaps some shampoo, my friend here can use?"

Carly sucked her lips in, deep in thought. Her eyes lit up. "Yes! As a matter of fact, I just bought a bottle of shampoo and a few other things especially for this trip."

Dennis looked at Trenda. "Will that work for you?"

Trenda took her eyes off of the white girl's surprisingly nice hips. "Yeah…that'll work."

Carly showed Trenda her bright smile. "Cool! I'll be right back."

As Carly dashed off, Trenda grabbed Dennis by the arm. "Aight, Fox. I know your butt is up to somethin'; go head and let me in on it."

He laughed. "So suspicious. You just can't accept that I'm doing this out of the kindness of my heart, can you?"

She smirked. "Hel—err, *heck* naw! I know how you get down."

He grinned and shrugged. "Okay, okay…maybe I would like for you to help me entertain my cute country friend."

Trenda knew damn well his definition of "entertain" was a tad bit different from the definition the rest of the world used. Most times his meaning of the word included high levels of debauchery. "Well, before you go any further, I gotta let you know a couple things. First, I'm serious about gettin' away from some of my old bad habits, includin' premarital sex. Two, I really need to get this check cashed. And I'd like to handle that ASAP. I have to go get started on my new life."

He studied her in silence for a moment. "Okay, friend of mine, let's handle one hurdle at a time." He reached into his back pocket, pulled out an ostrich-skin wallet and flipped it open. He pulled out a cluster of hundred-dollar bills. "Where's your check?"

Trenda went to her traveling bag, opened it up, and pulled out the wrinkled check. "You got a pen so I can sign it over?"

He gave a cursory look around the room. "Crap...I thought I had one lying around here somewhere..." He counted out four, hundred-dollar bills and handed them to Trenda. "That's for you. We can worry about that check signing business later." He counted off six more bills and flashed that devious "Fox" grin at her. "And you can have these, if you do me a favor."

Fourteen

"I appreciate you coming all the way out here, Ms. Cannon, but I haven't heard a word from my daughter in years. I had no idea she'd been released from prison already." He ran a finger under the tab collar of his black, friar tuck shirt. "Every time I hear my daughter's name in the media, I just turn it off… most times it's just filthy talk."

Alexis Cannon, top reporter for StarShine Entertainment, stood on the porch of Trenda's father's house, with a well-practiced look of empathy. "I'm awful sorry to hear that, Father. But I promise you, I have only the best intentions and utmost respect for you and your family."

"Thank you, Ms. Cannon. Lord knows we've had enough unwanted attention over the past couple years." He shook his head and stared down at his feet. "Those buzzards even managed to contact my son who's stationed over in Afghanistan. That's a doggone shame."

She shielded her eyes from the late afternoon sunshine. "Again, Father Fuqua, I'm sorry for bothering you. I was concerned because she hasn't answered any of my letters or phone calls. I have a great opportunity for her that would greatly help her reintroduction into society."

Father Fuqua held the white, wrought iron bannister in one hand and leaned on his cane with the other. "I'm sure there's a good reason you ain't heard from her." He removed his fedora, and then wiped sweat off his forehead with his sleeve. "But if I do hear from her, by the grace of God, I'll be sure to have her get in contact with you. And oh, thank your company for the generous donation to my church. It really saved our financial hide."

Alexis removed her dark sunglasses from her expensive gold clutch and placed them over her hazel eyes. She then offered her hand to him. "You're more than welcome, Father. Thank you for your time. Feel free to call me anytime; night or day."

"I'll remember that. You take care, young lady."

After releasing his hand, she hurried over to the black Lincoln Town Car parked in front of Father Fuqua's nice home. Her Liberian driver, Titus, opened the rear door of the luxury sedan. "Where to now, Ms. Cannon?"

She eased herself into the car. "West Baltimore."

Titus lifted his eyebrows. "*West Baltimore*? That's a pretty rugged part of town. You sure that's where you want to go?"

"Rugged, my ass." She grinned at the dark chocolate man. "This South Philly girl can handle it. We'll start over near the ESPN Zone."

Before closing her door, he said, "Didn't that place shut down a while back?"

"Yes, but I'm not looking to go inside; just check out the surroundings."

Titus closed the door, took his seat and started the car. As he pulled off, she rolled up the privacy glass, sat back and let her mind go to work. Now that the rest of the world knew the tight-lipped Trenda Fuqua was out of prison, the race to get her story was on again. She had already heard that everybody from *The National Enquirer* to Oprah Winfrey were on the hunt.

But that didn't intimidate StarShine Entertainment's seven-time Reporter of the Year. Her tenacity, connections, and cunning were well known in the industry. With the number two person under her boss having passed away a couple of months ago, she had a golden opportunity to move up. The spot was still open. Landing the Trenda Fuqua story would surely shoehorn her into that position.

She reached into her clutch and pulled out the list of Trenda's friends she was able to compile. The vast majority of them lived, or did business, in the Baltimore/D.C. areas. Of the short list of names on that sheet of paper, one name held more promise than the rest; Constance Brimmer. Alexis was able to find out that she and Trenda were good friends. Alexis believed that if anybody would know Trenda's whereabouts, it would be Constance.

₧₨

The extra hundred-dollar bills Dennis dangled in front of her nearly made Trenda salivate. But she managed to keep her cool. "What kinda twist are you tryin' to get me into?"

They both turned around to the sound of Carly coming down the stairs. Dennis put the cash in his wallet and stuffed it into his back pocket. "I'll tell you shortly. First, you can go ahead and freshen up. I'm sure you know where everything is."

Before she could answer, Carly walked up and handed her a large-toothed comb, a bottle of lilac-scented shampoo and an unopened bar of Tone soap. "Here you go; enjoy!"

"Thanks." Trenda put the items into the bag that contained her new underwear and began grabbing the other shopping bags. "I'll be back in a few."

Dennis picked up a couple of the bags. "Hey, Carly. How about putting together some lunch for us while our friend freshens up?"

Carly walked over and kissed him on the cheek. "Sure thing, sweetie."

Trenda watched Dennis pat Carly on the ass, as she walked toward the kitchen. *Well, guess I ain't gotta wonder no more; they are definitely fuckin'.* She followed Dennis to the ground floor guest bathroom—the one she used most of the time during past visits to his home.

He placed the bags on the floor, next to the black marble sink. He looked into the mirrored wall behind the sink and into Trenda's eyes. "I sure have missed your company." He moved behind her and hugged her from the back. "We have a lot to catch up on."

At his height, his hard dick poked her in the lower back. That sensation sent an uncontrollable tingle to her attention-starved clit. Trenda eased out of his embrace. "Cute…" She put her traveling bag on the floor. "Seems like you have all the company you can handle already."

He smirked. "You mean Carly?"

"Yeah, and I'm sure she's not the only one that's been here in the 'Foxes Den.'"

He examined his fingernails. "Even if that were true, you know none of them measures up to you."

She took off her cap and sat it next to the sink. "C'mon…miss me wit' all that, Fox; I *know* how you get down."

Down the hall, his telephone rang. "We'll talk more about this later."

Trenda closed and locked the door behind him. *His touchy feely, half-breed ass is startin' to get on my nerves. He really starts trippin' after he smokes some weed.* Even with that, Trenda knew better than to rock the boat right now. She needed exactly what Dennis could provide; a temporary safe haven and financial support—for a price of course.

She pulled off her sweatshirt, dropped it to the floor, and unsnapped her bra. As it fell, she gazed at the lightning bolt-shaped scar on her right shoulder. A brief and painful flashback of the horrific night when she'd received that scar reemerged. She leaned close to the mirror and studied the small scar on her right cheek. Fortunately, it wasn't as deep or long as the one on her shoulder. One would only notice it if they were up in her face. And *very* few got that privilege.

Her eyes went from the scar to her perky, full breasts. Her brown nipples stood up. She slipped out of the rest of her clothes and admired her chiseled body in the full-body mirror mounted behind the bathroom door.

She held her arms up and posed like a body builder. She smirked. "Body ain't ever been in this good of shape," she said as she rubbed her well-defined six-pack belly. "Be damned if I wanna go to jail just to get in shape, tho'…nah, heck no."

Wish I had a razor. Her pussy was much hairier than she liked. Her thighs never looked tighter. She turned around and looked at her backside over her shoulder. *Damn! Where all that ass come from?* After admiring her cakes, she picked up the comb and started taking down her braids. Fifteen minutes later, she had a big, dirty, reddish-brown Afro.

Next, she opened up the bar of soap, slid open the glass shower doors, and turned on the water. After turning on the ceiling fan, she stepped into the steamy oasis that was the shower. Never had hot water felt so good. She let the cascading water drown her grimy hair.

Mmmm, shit…her twat twitched the entire time she washed it. *Been way too long without some action.* Tired of teasing her slit with her fingers, she shut off the water and stepped out. She grabbed two of the burgundy and gold towels, tied one around her head and dried the rest of her with the other. Once done, she wrapped the biggest towel around herself.

Need to flat iron this mess, she thought as she looked at her head full of nappy curls. Her hair reminded her of the girl she had seen get shot to death last night; she wore her hair in a similar style. As she stared at herself in the mirror, she couldn't help but wonder how in the world she'd became such a trouble magnet. Not even the ominous passage, *Luke 12:21,* could deflect her attraction to temptation:

"This is how it will be with anyone who stores up things for himself but is not rich toward God."

It seemed like no matter how hard she tried, temptation always won out in the end. What's worse was she oftentimes didn't try and fight it off. The lure of action, danger, hot sex, and fast money was her kryptonite. A knock at the bathroom door snapped her back into reality. "Who is it?"

"Hey, it's Carly. Just wanted to let you know that lunch is ready whenever you are."

Trenda opened the bag containing her black underwear and pulled it out. "Aight, I'll be out in a minute."

After fifteen minutes of trying to do something with her hair, she gave up. She then looked in the bag that contained her new toiletries items and recalled she had forgotten to buy some toothpaste. "Crap. Lemme go see if Carly or Dennis has some I can use."

Outside the bathroom, as she approached one of the downstairs bedrooms, she heard a familiar sound; the moans of sexual pleasure. "Oh heck no."

The mahogany door was halfway open. She stopped and peeked inside. Two pale, naked bodies were intertwined on the king-sized bed. Dennis had his face planted between Carly's thighs, grazing on her pussy. The aroma of sex overtook the smell of food in Trenda's nose. *Nasty bastards.* The sight of Carly's stiff pink nipples moistened Trenda's mouth. *Nice tit job!*

Before she knew it, Trenda had pushed the door open and was staring at her host and hostess. Carly turned her head and grinned before closing her eyes and resuming her enjoyment.

Dennis finally noticed her. He lifted his head, wiped his wet chin, and smiled. "Hey, Ms. Fuqua! Just in time for lunch!"

Trenda folded her arms over her perky tits, hiding her stiffening nipples. "I knew your ass was up to somethin'…just *knew* it!"

Carly sat up and wiped her long hair out of her flushed face. "I hope you're not offended. I told Dennis to close the door but he said you wouldn't mind."

Trenda stood her ground, assessing the situation. The sight of Dennis's hard, light-brown dick made her involuntarily lick her lips. *Ain't sucked that thang in a long time.* She adjusted her towel, composed herself, and looked from one of them to the other. "Well, y'all do what y'all was doin'; I'm gonna go on and get me somethin' to eat."

Dennis eased out of the bed and walked over to Trenda. She fought to keep her eyes off of his member. She almost won. Once he got within a couple of feet, her eyes fell to his chunk. He placed his hands on her shoulders. "Remember that side job I offered you earlier?"

She turned her head as he circled around and placed his hands on her shoulders. "What?"

He leaned his head in and spoke in her ear. "Remember that extra cash I offered you? Well, I'll give it to you if you teach Carly the '*special*' treat you give me."

Trenda furrowed her eyebrows. "*Special treat*?" She thought for a moment, then recalled how much he loved having his ass fingered as she sucked his dick. She watched Carly finger fuck herself. "You serious?"

His hands found her soft breasts. "Very much so."

Again, temptation was working overtime on her. She brushed

his hands off of her. "I'm tryin' to get my shi—*stuff* together. Why you wanna try and trip me up?"

He held his cock as he spoke. "Now you know I'd never do anything to hurt you. Just thought it would be a nice exchange; we both get something we desire." He walked over and rubbed her bare shoulders. "How long has it been since you had some dick?"

The cyclone of events she'd endured since being released from jail pressed on her conscience. She fought it off the best she could. "None of ya business." She lifted her eyebrows. "If I was to take that deal, I want cash up front. No negotiating that."

He let his hands fall to her tits. "Deal."

She wiped his hands off of her, adjusting her towel. "And I'm *not* joinin' in. All I'm gonna do is instruct her."

Dennis grinned and stroked his meat. "Okay, okay…wait right here and I'll be back with your fees."

Trenda took her eyes off of the masturbating Carly. "Hey, don't forget the finger condoms."

He snapped his finger and smirked. "Right."

Once Dennis left, Trenda walked over and watched Carly play in her pussy. Carly opened her eyes, held out one of her wet fingers, and grinned at Trenda. "Wanna taste?"

Trenda shook her head. "Nah. I'll pass for now."

Pink was the theme of the room. The walls were painted light pink; the bedspread maroon and pink. There was even a large, pink throw rug on top of the maroon shag carpet. She recalled years ago telling Dennis that this was his "Pussy Room."

Her eyes were repeatedly drawn to Carly's beautiful vagina. The lips were bright; hot pink. The clit stuck out like a small, pink penis. The landing stripe of black hair on her cunt accented it well. The hand resting on her vagina featured fingernails painted pussy pink.

Carly rubbed her tits. "God, you're hot!" She reached for Trenda and missed. "Come here so I can see what's under that towel."

Trenda took a step back. "I'm afraid that's not part of the deal."

Carly rubbed her nipples with the palms of her hands. "What *deal*?"

At that moment, Dennis entered the room, walked over and stood next to Trenda. He looked from one girl to the other. "Getting started without me, ladies?"

Carly smirked at Dennis. "What's this 'deal' Trenda mentioned to me?"

He turned his head to Trenda. "You told her about my surprise?"

Trenda folded her arms. "Nope…just had a conversation and she asked me a question."

He shrugged. "Oh well…" He held out the handful of cash and the condom to Trenda. "As we agreed."

Trenda counted the six hundred dollars as Carly gawked at her and Dennis. Her mouth finally began working again. "What the hell?"

Dennis smiled, sat down on the bed next to Carly, and stroked her hair. "Our friend, Trenda, here is going to show you how to do a 'magic trick.'"

Carly's eyes widened. "You mean the 'trick' you were telling me about a few months ago?"

He put his arm around Trenda's shoulders. "That's the one, and this young lady is going to show you how it's done."

Trenda corrected him. "No, not *show* her how it's done; *teach* her how it's done."

Trenda never could understand how sticking her finger in Dennis's ass, while sucking his dick, caused him to have multiple orgasms. It was both erotic and repulsive to her. But the fact that he paid well for that treat and her discreetness made it worth her while. Plus the fact she loved the taste of his cum was another bonus.

After putting the money on top of the dresser, she walked over to the bed and looked down at the naked duo. She took her eyes off of Carly's pretty pussy lips and looked into her blue eyes. "All you gotta do is do what I tell you and it'll be all good."

She sat up on the bed. "I'm ready."

Trenda looked at Dennis and tapped the finger condom in her hand. "Lay on your back."

He was as happy as a kid at Christmas. "Anything you say, Professor."

Trenda adjusted the towel wrapped around her body. "Carly, bite his nipples."

Her jaw dropped. "You want me to do *what?*"

Trenda lifted her eyebrows. "I said, bite his nipples."

Dennis's light-brown face blushed heavily. His breathing increased substantially. Carly bent over and suckled his left nipple. She then looked at Trenda. "Like this?"

Trenda shook her head. "No...I said *bite* it."

Carly gently put her teeth on his nipple and pulled it. Dennis sucked in a deep breath of pleasure. "Yes...like that...mmmmmm..."

Trenda watched as Carly moved to his right nipple and chewed on it. *Straight freaks.* The harder she bit his nipples, the more turned on he got. After ten minutes of that, she said, "Okay, Carly, lick your way down to his balls."

Fully with the program, Carly used her long, pink tongue as a washcloth and tongue-bathed his abdomen. His dick was stiff as a plank and his nipples were cherry red. The sight of his staff tossed some kindling on Trenda's freak furnace. *Naw, can't afford to get caught up.* Just as Carly closed in on his genitals, Trenda stopped her. "No, don't touch his dick; just the balls."

Carly licked and sucked his testicles like a woman possessed. She juggled each one individually in her wet mouth. Trenda tapped her on the shoulder. "Hold up." She placed her hand on Dennis's shoulder and pushed him over on his side. "Assume the position, Fox."

He grinned with half-closed eyes full of pleasure. "Anything you say, Professor."

Trenda ignored him as she ripped open the condom wrapper and tossed the package on the floor. "Kiss him, Carly...tongue the heck out of him."

Being a good student, Carly slid up in front of Dennis—her tits rubbing his chest—lightly licked his lips, then shared her tongue with him. Trenda caught herself breathing heavily as she watched them tongue wrestle. She moved over, took Carly's hand, and placed it on his ass. Carly broke her lip lock. "You want me to rub his ass?"

"No, I want you to grab it hard, grip it—all over."

Dennis shuddered with desire as Carly squeezed and gripped his butt. When Trenda noticed Dennis was panting, she took the condom and slipped it over Carly's right index finger, then put her lips on Carly's ear and whispered, "Stick it in his ass slowly."

Sensing her unease, Trenda spread his ass cheeks for her. Dennis whimpered with delight as Carly eased her finger into his opening.

"Ahhhh...that's it," he moaned.

Carly continued kissing him as she fingered his ass. Trenda could tell by the stiffness of Dennis's blood-engorged rod that he was close to climax. The desire to taste a dick kicked her willpower in the face. She let her towel fall to the floor.

What the hell am I doin'? What happened to livin' by the good book? Before she could answer her conscience, she found her hand wrapped around Dennis's chunk. *Fuck it; one blowjob can't be that bad after all this time.*

Carly, in the meantime, found a nice rhythm; fingering Dennis as she bit his nipples. Dennis moaned and groaned with extreme pleasure. Carly looked up once she felt Trenda get on the bed. She wiped her long black hair out of her face and grinned. "You joining in?"

Trenda slowly stroked Dennis's throbbing cock. "Just for a minute," she said as she crawled between the sideways lying couple so that his dick was in her face and Carly's pussy was on the back of her bushy, red Afro. She held the thick, hot, half-foot of dick and rubbed it on her face. *Sooo fuckin' good!*

Carly continued her finger work and nipple biting as Dennis pushed back on her finger. She moved up so Dennis could suck her tits. The scents, sounds and feel of the three bodies sent Trenda into a freak tizzy. But just as she was about to wrap her soft lips around his waiting dick, a powerful verse popped up in her head:

"Thy own wickedness shall correct thee. Thy backsliding shall reprove thee. Know therefore and see that it is an evil thing and bitter that thou hast forsaken the Lord thy God, and that my fear is not in thee, saith the Lord God of Hosts." —JEREMIAH 11:19.

Her eyes flew open as she pushed his dick away from her face and sat up on the bed. Carly stopped fingering Dennis and gazed at her. "Why'd you stop? That looked *so* hot!"

Trenda grabbed the back of Carly's hair. "It's all about you, baby." She pulled Carly's head down to the dick. "Suck it while you finger him. He's dang near ready to nut."

Suddenly, she wanted another shower. *The devil is busy as a muthafucka!* she thought as Carly swallowed Dennis's average-sized penis. The sight of Dennis enjoying Carly fingering and sucking him was hard to watch.

The fact that she had gotten so close to giving into temptation frightened her. *Bad enough I'm takin' his money In exchange for a sin, but to actually join in the fornication...that's doin' too much.*

She stood up and watched as Carly sucked and licked his dick like a champ. The sex smells, slurping sounds, and moans were hard to ignore. Trenda's pussy leaked for release. Leaked so bad Trenda had to pick up the towel and rub the excess pussy juice off of her swollen slit-lips.

Dennis howled with delight as he shot hot sperm down Carly's throat. Trenda grabbed the back of Carly's head and forced her to keep sucking. "Don't stop! Keep goin'; he's got more cum for you. Work ya finger faster!"

Carly followed instructions and was soon rewarded with another gusher of cum as Dennis shuddered and whimpered. A stream of jizz leaked out of the side of Carly's mouth as Dennis ejaculated again. The urge to lick the run-off, off of Carly's chin almost drove Trenda insane.

Carly's finger and mouth work—along with Trenda's coaching—drew a third nut out of the sweating, panting flushed attorney. After his last release, both Carly and Dennis collapsed on the bed, on their backs. Dennis cracked his eyes, gave Trenda a weak smile and a thumbs-up. *"Awesome!"*

Trenda smirked, dropped the towel, grabbed her cash and went back to the bathroom. She could barely look at her reflection. *You weak!*

She ignored the voice of guilt and stepped into her new skinny jeans. They gripped her hips and ass appreciatively. After pulling her pink and white tunic tee over her wild hair, she looked more like the Trenda of old; hot as a lava flow. She really liked her new Steve Madden, black, knee-high boots. They were the same style she wore when she ran the streets hard back in the day. They were a good hiding place for her old, stainless steel butterfly knife she affectionately used to call "Baby."

Miss my Baby...instead of even trying to run Carly's comb through her coarse hair, she shaped it with her fingers. *Got the Jill Scott hairdo goin'*, she thought as she looked in the mirror. After one last check of herself, she packed up her stuff and left the bathroom. She looked into the "Pussy Room" and saw Carly and Dennis enjoying a sex-induced nap. *Lucky asses.* Back at the sitting room, she dropped off her bags. Her stomach rumbled. *Never did make it to lunch. Lemme go see what's in the kitchen to eat.*

Inside the modern kitchen, the faint aroma of pizza lingered in the air. She walked over to the wall-mounted, stainless steel, double oven and peeked inside the top unit.

A fully loaded supreme pizza stared back at her. Three fat slices later, she was as full as a tick. The digital clock mounted on the stove showed a quarter to six. She drummed her fingers on the wooden tabletop. *I'm ready to go.*

She walked back down the hall and looked in on Dennis and Carly. Both were still knocked out. *Oh well, time to break this up.* She walked over and bumped her knee against the bed. "Wake up, folks."

Dennis wiped a thread of slobber off of his jaw. "What's up?"

Trenda lifted her eyebrows. "I gotta get back to Baltimore."

He yawned and rubbed the sleeping Carly's right nipple. "When do you have to be back?"

"As soon as I can. I don't like the idea of bein' outta state while I'm on parole."

He rubbed his hands over his neat, wavy haircut. "Okay. Give me a minute to throw something on."

Fifteen

"A re you sure this is the right location, Ms. Cannon?" Titus asked as he guided the Lincoln around West Baltimore.

Alexis surveyed the ghetto surroundings behind the tinted glass. "Yes...I'm pretty sure the person I need to see is around here somewhere..." She nibbled on her left thumbnail as she studied the street dwellers. Through her many connections she was able to get information on practically everyone Trenda associated with on the east coast. A block away from the Harbor, she spotted a trio of hookers smoking next to a mailbox. She reached over the seat and tapped the driver on his shoulder. "Pull over there next to those girls."

He slowed the car. "You mean those prostitutes over there?"

She checked the contents of her purse. Her .38 pistol and wallet were in easy reach. "Yes, I need to talk to the tall one in the red wig. Park across the street from them." As soon as the car stopped, she opened the door without waiting for Titus. "Stay here. I'll be right back."

His reply was muffled as she hopped out and closed the door. She tossed her hair back as she waited for the traffic to clear so she could cross the street. The eyes of the hookers fell on her instantly as she walked toward them. The lone black girl turned her head and said something to the white girl in the red wig. The third hooker, a short, chubby white girl, wearing a much-too-tight pink spandex outfit, mean-mugged Alexis. Twenty feet from the trio, Alexis slowed her pace and smiled. She adjusted her glasses and looked the tall hooker in her brown eyes. "Is your name Constance?"

The tall hooker exhaled a plume of cigarette smoke. "Depends… It can be for the right price."

The black hooker flicked the butt of her cigarette in Alexis's direction. "Who the fuck are you, comin' over here askin' stupid-ass questions, bitch?" She tugged at the hem of her red shorts but failed to alleviate her camel toe. "And I hope like hell you don't think you about to sell no pussy over here."

Alexis smirked as she watched the black girl struggle with keeping her enormous tits from popping out of her tiny tank top. "Honey, you *definitely* don't have to worry about me wanting to do anything out here." She turned her gaze back on the woman in the red wig. "Now, as I was saying, are you Constance Brimmer?"

The red wigged hooker narrowed her eyes. "Why you wanna know?"

Well versed in the ways of the streets, Alexis opened her purse and pulled out her wallet. "I'll give you a hundred bucks for fifteen minutes of your time, if you're the Constance I'm looking for."

After she pulled out the c-note, she had all of their attention. The tall hooker took one last drag off her smoke and tossed it in the street. "You a cop?"

"No, not even."

The tall hooker lifted one eyebrow and pointed at Alexis's purse. "Then why do you have that gun in your purse?"

Alexis chuckled and shook her head. "You saw that, huh? Well, let's be real. You think a scrawny white girl like me is going to be comfortable walking around *this* neighborhood without some kind of protection?" She went back into her wallet and pulled out one of her business cards and handed it to the hooker. "As you can see, I'm with StarShine Entertainment. And I'm also licensed to carry a concealed weapon."

The hooker studied the logo on the card. "This the same company that makes those reality TV shows?"

"One and the same."

The hooker tucked the card into her small purse and held out her hand. "Gimme the cash; I'm Constance."

Alexis opened her purse, pulled out a hundred-dollar bill and handed it to her. "Now, is there someplace we can go talk?"

Constance put the cash in her purse. "Yeah, I'm hungry. You can take me out for pancakes and conversation."

&)CR

A few miles away, in the Mill Hill district of Baltimore, Trenda opened up the door of Dennis's car and got out. "Thanks, Fox. I'll holla at you later."

He peered at her from behind his expensive sunglasses. "When can I enjoy your company again?"

She opened the back door and pulled out her two bags. "I dunno. I got a lot of stuff to work out... A *lot* of stuff."

A patrol car approached the double-parked Porsche and chirped his siren. "Guess that's my queue to move." Dennis put the car in gear. "Be safe, Ms. Fuqua."

Trenda backed away, turned her back on the patrol car, and started walking. Thankfully, the patrol car drove off without paying her much attention. The late afternoon sun was fading fast. *Where you goin' now, parolee?* She looked across the street at the Flyin' Pig BBQ restaurant. She had heard they had good food but she needed a place to chill more than a meal at the moment.

She crossed the street and took a seat on one of the wooden picnic tables that sat outside of the restaurant. Placing her bags on the table, she unzipped her bag. A steady flow of customers went in and out of the popular eatery. Trenda avoided all eye contact with them—especially the lusting men as she took in the surroundings. *Things sure have changed over the past couple of years.*

The sight of new cars, fashions and popular slang bombarded her. To her it was New Parolee 101; adapt to the new environment. The letter the guard gave her when she was released got her attention. *Lemme see wassup with this.* Inside the envelope was a letter telling her to report to her parole officer, Keri Hope, on Monday morning at eleven in downtown Baltimore. She stuck the letter back in the envelope and back into her bag. The address to the parole office was definitely not within walking distance from where she was.

The reason she'd had Dennis drop her off so far from West Baltimore was simple in her mind; there was too much temptation to do wrong there. She flashed a phony smile at a black couple leaving the restaurant. Sunlight from the orange, half-sphere of the setting sun peeked at her over the roof of a section of row houses down the street. It was difficult for her to adjust to being free. She found herself waiting to be told "lights out" or "meal time."

Once she realized she was going to need a place to sleep, she scanned the immediate area. Not a hotel in sight. A middle-aged Asian man approached down the street. She stood and looked his way. "Excuse me, do you know if there are any hotels around here?"

He stopped and gave her a shy smile. "Well, the closest one I can think of is off of South Canton and 95. Do you know where that is?"

"Yeah." Trenda chuckled internally as the short man tried his best to avoid looking at her tits. "Thanks, honey."

South Canton and 95 is a lot more than walkin' distance from here. Trenda stood, and looked around. *I need a phone book and a phone so I can call me a cab.* There wasn't a phone booth anywhere in sight. She turned to the restaurant. *Might be a phone in there.* After gathering up her bags, she walked to the restaurant and entered.

The interior of the eatery was a lot smaller than it looked from the outside. Directly across from the front door was a wall with a three-by-three window of bulletproof glass with a stainless steel door underneath. A speaker and microphone sat directly between the cashier and customer. Above the window was a menu that featured hot wings of countless flavors, BBQ ribs, soda and sweet potato pie. That was it. Four circular wooden tables sat to the right of the entryway. All four tables were full of people gnawing, crunching, and drinking. The heavyset white woman behind the glass jotted down a customer's order on a grease-stained pad. Two elderly black women, dressed in their finest church gear, tested the cashier's patience with multiple questions about the Flyin' Pigs food preparation.

Trenda's scan of the place yielded no pay phone. Just as she turned to leave, a vaguely familiar, gravelly voice called out her name. "Yo, Trenda! Is that you?"

Oh shit! When she saw who had called her, she instantly wished she would have ignored the voice. *Fuckin' Beanie...I was hopin' your ass would be dead by now.* He was one of the shiftiest characters in Baltimore. They had pulled quite a few illegal capers together before she found out how much of a coward and snake he was. She gathered up her composure. "Wassup, Beanie?"

The medium-sized, fully bearded man wiped his mouth, stood

and walked over to Trenda. "Look at you!" He gave her a tight hug. "When you get out, Shorty?"

"Not too long ago."

He gazed at her in awe. "Wow! I heard Oprah was gonna pay you big bucks for your story. Is that true?"

His lack of discretion irked Trenda. She felt the eyes of curious customers on her. "No... Where did you hear that?"

"Everywhere! Folks here have been talking about what happened to you since they found those cops murdered. You a straight celebrity."

A couple sitting at a nearby table looked at her and whispered to each other. "That stuff is just rumors. Don't pay it no mind."

"I ain't buyin' that, Shorty." He shook his head, smiled, pulled his Smartphone out of his pocket, and held it up to his face. "Smile!" He took a couple of pictures of Trenda.

Anger bubbled up on her face. "What you doin'?"

"Just takin' a photo of the famous Ms. Fuqua for my Wall of Fame."

Panic worked its way through her body as more of the patrons eyeballed her. She glared and pointed at him. "Quit it! I don't want *nobody* takin' pictures of me."

He took one last picture, then put the camera back in his pocket. "Okay. Okay, don't trip."

The urge to grab one of the dining customers' forks and plunge it into his eye was hard to fight off. Her voice rose a bit higher than she intended. "*Don't trip?*"

Now the entire room was giving them all their attention. He held his hands up. "Slow ya roll...calm down."

Before she backslid into the "old Trenda," she dropped her glare from him and watched the crowd. They were focused on the show. She looked at him again. "Delete them pictures."

He took a step back. "What? Why?"

"Because..." The cook had opened the kitchen door and watched the action. "I don't like havin' my business out in public."

Before Beanie could reply, the middle-aged black cook pointed a finger at Trenda. "Say, ain't you that lady that was with those Baltimore cops that got killed a couple years ago?"

Her eyes swept the room. A murmur went through the crowd as they all glanced at her. She licked her lips and gave Beanie one last hard look. "Delete those pictures. If I find out you didn't—" She caught herself about to threaten this man with a ton of witnesses watching.

He chuckled. "You need to calm down."

I can't believe this stupid muthafucka. Without another word, she turned and left. She hurried away from the restaurant, desperately seeking a pay phone.

As luck would have it, a yellow cab turned the corner a couple blocks ahead. As it headed toward her, she stepped into the street and frantically flagged it down. The Persian cabbie passed her up, hung a reckless U-turn and pulled up to the curb in front of her. She opened the back door, tossed her bags inside, sat down and closed the door. "I need a ride to South Canton and Highway 95."

Sixteen

As Trenda checked into her motel room, her ace-coon-boon buddy, Constance, followed by Alexis, entered a Denny's. After taking her seat, Alexis turned her nose up at the menu and laid it down on the table. "Do you always have pancakes for dinner?"

Constance took the gum out of her mouth, briefly looked for a place to put it, then stuck it under the bottom of the table. "Yeah, I do. But anyway, what you wanna know? Your fifteen minutes clock is runnin' right now."

Alexis mentally cringed at the small gathering of blisters on the corner of Constance's mouth. "Well, let's get down to business then. I understand you and Trenda Fuqua are pretty good friends. Is this true?"

Constance inspected her neon pink painted fingernails. "Yeah, we go back like rockin' chairs. Been knowin' that girl since we were kids."

"So it goes without saying that you know what happened to her a couple of years ago with the 'allegedly' corrupt cops?"

"Kinda. I know what everybody else knows from the news and stuff."

Alexis could tell by her body language that she knew a bit more than she let on. "C'mon now, Constance, give me my money's worth. How deeply was she involved with the criminal underground?"

Sticking to the anti-snitching code, Constance simply said, "I dunno."

"I thought you guys were close?"

"We are…that don't mean I know *all* of her business."

Having been down this road to nowhere many times before, Alexis decided to cut to the chase. "Have you seen or heard from her since she was released from jail?"

A pleasantly plump waitress stopped to take their order. After ordering the "Grand Slam Breakfast" and a Pepsi, Constance said, "When did she get out? I ain't heard about her getting out of jail. I thought she had about another year to go."

"Well, it's pretty much been all over the news. She got out a couple of days ago. I was pretty sure she would want to get in touch with family and friends."

"Well, she ain't got to me yet."

"Do you know where she might be? You know of any of her old hangouts?"

"Ain't no tellin'. She hung around here sometimes. Last I heard she was on the West Coast."

Alexis sat back in her seat. *This tramp is wasting my time, telling me stuff I already know.* "Okay, Ms. Brimmer, let's cut through all the bullshit. I have another hundred bucks if you can tell me of at least one person or place where I'll have the best chance of running into Ms. Fuqua."

Constance waited until the waitress sat her food down, then spoke. "I ain't no snitch."

"Two hundred bucks?"

Constance's face told Alexis she was close to caving in. Constance nibbled on her pinky nail. "I might know of one place she might be." She shook her head and picked up her fork. "No… I can't…"

"Three hundred cash."

"Damn, woman." Constance put the fork down, put her elbow on the table and her face in her hand. After five seconds of consideration, she said, "I might know of somebody she might wanna see who could help her out."

Constance leaned forward. "Who? Give me a name."

"Gimme the cash first."

Alexis went into her purse and pulled out three more hundred-dollar bills. She laid one of them on the table. "I'll give you the other two *after* you give me the name. Let me see if it's worth my money."

Constance sucked her teeth with irritation and placed her hand on the bill. "Shit, my word is good. Ask anybody on the street."

Alexis placed her hand on the other half of the bill and shook her head. "That may be true, but I feel my offer is very generous. I'm willing to bet these four hundred bucks are a *lot* more than you have ever made in less than an hour of work. And with the economy sucking the way it is, I'd say this is a bonanza for you." Alexis sat back and read her body language. Constance was clearly overmatched by Alexis's negotiating expertise. "Take it or leave it."

She caved in. "Dennis Wilcox, that famous lawyer dude in Georgetown. She used to tell me how he hooked her up when she needed help. She called a few days after she got locked up and told me he was gonna work with her for free."

Alexis quickly processed the information. *I was wondering how she was able to afford that expensive, arrogant asshole! That makes total sense to me now. I always heard he was a kinky sex freak. That also explains how she was able to turn down the lawyer we sent to represent her.* She shuddered at the images of the kind of sexual payback he would expect of a hottie like Trenda. She lifted her hand off of the money. "And you're *sure* about this?"

"Hell yeah, I'm sure. Like I told you, Trenda is my girl."

Oh my God! Her stomach rolled as she watched Constance splash hot sauce on her eggs, grab a fork full, jab that into a syrup-soaked triangle of pancake, and stuff it in her mouth. She rose from her seat. "Good doing business with you. Take care." On her way back to the car, her phone rang. It was her assistant. "Hey, Sherry, what's up?"

"Great news! I just got word there's a guy in Baltimore with pictures of Trenda Fuqua he wants to sell. Are you interested?"

"You bet! Get his information and make sure he doesn't sell to *anyone* else until I get a look at them."

൦ൽ

This ain't too bad for forty bucks, Trenda thought as she entered the seedy, *Nite-Lite Motel.* The rundown motel, nestled conveniently behind a just as rank strip club, was the only motel in the area she was able to check into using a cash deposit instead of a credit card. She entered her room, closed the door, sat her bags on the floor and flopped down on the mushy bed. As she lay on her back, staring at the ceiling, a strong sense of déjà vu swept over her. *This reminds me of that room Lollie hooked me up with back in Oakland... I wonder how my girl is doin'?*

As the more unpleasant memories of that ill-fated segment of her life rose into her consciousness, she sat up on the bed and put her head in her hands. The memory of shoving Baby into King Gee's heart overwhelmed her. It wasn't the first time she had ended a life, but for some reason it grabbed her sense of morality and tried to strangle it. Recollections of how hard her parents preached against her type of behavior further jostled her emotions. She removed her hands from her face and found them wet.

Searching for something to wipe her eyes with, she opened the drawer on the nightstand. A black Bible stared up at her. Her hands trembled as she picked it up. It fell from her shaky hands to the floor. She picked it up and read the passage beneath her thumb:

"I am ashamed, my God. I am embarrassed to look at you. Our sins have piled up over our heads, and our guilt is so overwhelming that it reaches heaven."

—EZRA 9:6

A torrential downpour of tears fell from her eyes. That was one of the most quoted sayings her late mother had preached to her when she did wrong. For the first time since she'd heard of her mother's death, she grieved. After tucking the Bible to her chest, she fell back on the bed and had a long, cleansing cry.

Seventeen

"What are you up to, green-eyed lady?" Messy Marv said, holding the mug shot of Trenda. Sunlight contracted his pupils as he opened the shades in his small breakfast nook. He stood there in his boxers as he had done every morning for more than two decades. His Northwood neighborhood home was quiet, neat and spacious. He sat the mug shot of Trenda down next to his bowl of oatmeal, on his maplewood dining table. He added brown sugar to his black coffee and took a sip. "I hope like hell you show up to your parole officer today."

An old manila folder with the name "Percy 'Slip' Wells" sat on the table as well. He read the lengthy rap sheet on Slip. Being a serious workaholic, Marv kept almost as many of his files at home as he did in his office. "I just know this boy knows something about Trenda...I can tell by how spooked he was by her mug shot." His desire to get a simple statement from Trenda about her dealings with officer Kain had him working monstrous overtime. If he could find out what unsavory characters Darius worked with, he could greatly narrow down who had him and his partner butchered.

ဆဌ

"No!" Trenda shouted as she jumped out of bed, knocking the Bible to the floor. She had been awakened by a nightmare. She saw herself staring down the barrel of Slip's black gun, inches away from her face. In her dream, he grinned as his finger applied pressure to the trigger.

Heart beating fast as an airplane propeller, she looked around, disoriented. It took her a moment to realize the small, generically furnished motel room wasn't a jail cell. Just short of hyperventilating, she managed to calm herself down. She pulled out the chair beneath the desk across from the bed, sat down and looked at herself in the mirror mounted to the desk. *I need some stress relief before I fuck around and have a heart attack.* A knock on the door startled her. "Who the hell?"

She got up, walked over and looked through the peephole. A young Spanish woman said, "Housekeeping."

"Come back later."

"Okay."

Trenda leaned her back against the door as the housekeeper pushed her cart to the room next door. She glimpsed at the blue digital numbers on the clock radio on the nightstand. *Shit! I only got two hours before I'm supposed to see my parole officer.* She picked up her bag, put it on the bed and opened it up. "Where is that letter?"

After reading the letter from the parole office and double-checking on the address, she quickly got dressed, wrestled with her unruly, curly, reddish-brown hair into a style. Her new chain belt, Seven jeans and olive-colored princess seam blouse went together well for a hastily concocted outfit. "This is gonna have to do," she said to her reflection in the mirror. "I ain't tryin' to win a beauty contest today."

She paused and looked at the Bible lying on the floor next to the bed. Memories of the nightmare and other drama she'd faced since being released briefly rattled her. She used the toe of her shoe to push the Bible under the bed. *I swear, I feel like I'm cursed sometimes.*

In the lobby of the hotel, she stopped at a table next to the registration desk that had a few leftover pastries from the complimentary continental breakfast. After grabbing a cinnamon raisin danish and cup of orange juice, she made her way out to the sidewalk. Having run the streets of Baltimore and the surrounding areas most of her life, finding a bus to get her to her parole meeting was easy.

While sitting at a bus stop two blocks from the hotel, more eyes than normal fell upon her. Having grown up as a "fine" woman, attention was nothing new to her. But this was different; she felt like she was on display. She finished off her food, stood and tossed the napkin and cup into the trashcan next to the bus stop. *Where is the bus?* Concerned about being late, she looked around for a clock. A Brennan's Jewelers sign two doors down grabbed her attention. *They gotta have a clock in there.*

On her way to the jewelry store, a pair of African-American teenage girls crossed the street a few yards in front of her. As soon as they saw Trenda, they stopped in their tracks, mouths open. The one with micro-braids to the middle of her back pointed and said, "Oh my God! That's that lady who had those cops killed in Baltimore!"

Trenda furrowed her eyebrows. *What the fuck?*

The second girl, an excited, mulatto looking youngster, nodded her head. "Yeah! My momma showed me the *Jet* magazine that had a picture of her. I'd know those eyes anywhere. She's *famous!*"

A thousand thoughts rushed at Trenda. Fortunately, the bus turned the corner and headed her way. *These kids got shit all twisted up.*

Trenda turned around and headed back to the bus stop. Behind her she heard, "Excuse me! Excuse me! Can we get your autograph?"

Trenda quickened her pace. *This is all bad!* She dug into her pocket, pulled out a handful of cash and peeled off a couple of dollar bills. *Is that what folks think of me?*

The sound of the approaching bus drowned out the calls of the girls. Trenda hurried aboard the bus, paid her fare and sat down. Out of the window, she saw the girls talking and taking pictures of the bus with their camera phones. She exhaled deeply as the bus drove off. Thankfully, she was one of only three people riding the bus. The other passengers didn't seem to notice her.

During the twenty-minute ride to downtown Baltimore, Trenda did her best to hide her face from the entering and departing riders. She never wanted a pair of sunglasses as bad as she did at that moment. *I sure as hell hope that was a fluke…don't need to have folks hounding me over that Darius shit.*

Minutes later, she got off of the bus in front of the parole office on East Preston Street. Trenda stood outside the brick building, looking at her reflection in the glass doors. *Been a long time since I been here.*

&xecx;

Hmmm…I see Ms. Fuqua is punctual, Messy Marv thought as he sipped his cup of coffee, standing next to a granite pillar near the elevators, watching Trenda enter the building. "For a parolee, she sure looks mighty stylish." He watched as she emptied her pockets and put her purse on the scanner conveyor belt and walked through the metal detector. It was hard for his professionalism to shield him from her sexiness. Her natural walk was levels above the average woman. It was a far cry from the no-nonsense walk she'd adopted while in jail.

Even the sheriffs doing the scanning let their eyes rape the green-eyed goddess as she walked toward the elevators. Marv turned his back and took a swig of coffee as Trenda passed him by. Since he had done his homework on her, and knew exactly where her parole officer was located, it was easy for him to stake her out. His conservative gray suit and sensible black shoes blended him in well with the rest of the majority of the administrative lawmen populating the busy first floor.

After watching Trenda disappear into an elevator, he prepared for the rest of his mission; find out where Ms. Fuqua was living. He swallowed the last mouthful of his coffee and tossed the cup into a trashcan. His burning desire to crack the media-dubbed "Lighthouse Massacre" case caused him to reshuffle all his other cases and put Trenda right on top. With all the bad publicity the department got over the alleged corruption, he had all the support he needed in cracking this case.

He checked his watch. "Hopefully, her meeting won't take too long." He then walked out the building to his unmarked car parked across the street. He had a great view of the front of the building. Most notably the exit door. He picked up a copy of the *Baltimore Sun* off of the passenger seat. He opened it up and went to the financial page. "Let's see how shitty my 401K is doing today."

ഹരൂ

"Have a seat, Ms. Fuqua," Keri Hope said. "We need to go over a few things."

Trenda sat on the black, wheeled chair in front of Mrs. Hope's desk. She pulled her green rosary beads out of her purse and gently fondled them. As she counted her prayers, Mrs. Hope pulled open her bottom desk drawer and removed a small white box. She placed it on the desk in front of Trenda. "I need a urine sample from you. Can you give me one right now?"

Trenda looked into the brown eyes of her parole officer. "Yeah...where you want me to go?"

Mrs. Hope rose from her seat, walked around the desk and stood over Trenda. "Come with me. We can go to the restroom across the hall." She pointed at Trenda's purse. "Leave all of your stuff here on my desk, including that necklace you're holding."

Trenda pursed her lips. "It's not a necklace; it's my rosary beads."

Mrs. Hope turned a nice shade of crimson. "Look, missy. Don't give me any of your lip. I don't care if it's a freaking rattlesnake; put it on my desk along with your purse."

We are gettin' off to a real bad start, Trenda thought as she tucked the beads in her purse and sat it on the desk. "Is my stuff gonna be safe here?"

Mrs. Hope glared at her. "You really don't want to piss me off today, Ms. Fuqua. All I need is the smallest reason and I can have your ass locked back up." She picked up her phone handset. "If you're not going to do as I say, tell me now so I can make the call and save us both some time and trouble."

The middle-aged woman looked like her panties were wet with the thought of sending her back to The Cock. Trenda felt a wave of defiance surging through her. She closed her eyes and tried to calm herself. She searched and found a suitable Bible passage:

ECCLESIASTES 7:9 *Do not be quickly provoked in your spirit, for anger resides in the lap of fools*

She opened her eyes and took a deep breath. "I'm sorry, Mrs. Hope, I missed breakfast and had a bad start to my morning. I didn't mean to get smart wit' you."

off from Trenda. He hopped out, flashed his badge, clipped it back on his belt and looked at the gangsters. "Don't you fellas know there's a law against jaywalking?"

෴

"Never been more happy to see a cop," Trenda said as she watched the gold Crown Victoria swoop up on her harassing miscreants. "These fake-ass gangbangers are infestin' the hood like roaches." She enjoyed watching them get frisked and fish for their IDs. When she saw the cop look in her direction, she turned and continued her walk toward the shelter. On her way, thirst drove her into the 7-Eleven. After grabbing a cold bottle of Sprite, she eyed a Tracfone display on the wall behind the clerk. She set the bottle on the counter and looked at the Arab clerk. "How do those Tracfones work?"

Ten minutes later she emerged from the store with the Sprite and a pair of sunglasses, along with a new prepaid cell phone. *Can't wait 'til I can get somewhere and charge this thing up.* The closer she got to the address of the shelter, the more rundown the neighborhood became. Litter, broken glass, graffiti, and abandoned cars populated the area. Shady and unsavory characters seemed to materialize out of nowhere. *I dunno if I wanna be this deep in the hood.*

෴

After he was through detaining the pair of thugs long enough for Trenda to get out of sight, Messy Marv let them off with a warning and hurried after her. *Hope she didn't get too far*, he thought as he scanned each intersection for her. A nice, heart-shaped ass filled his vision. He kept his distance until he watched her stop in front of a large row house that had been converted into a women's shelter. After she entered, a message came over his radio telling him a dead body had been found in the back of the notorious junkie hangout dubbed the "Lighthouse." He confirmed he was on his way, turned around, then thought, *At least I know where I can find Ms. Fuqua.*

Twenty

Ain't *no way*, Trenda thought as she looked around the despair-ridden Baltimore Outreach Women's Shelter. Single women, women with children—mostly black— milled about the large family room. *These folks look like they are ready to swallow a gun barrel.*

The words coming out of Director Shannon Crowder's mouth barely registered in Trenda's consciousness. She was definitely not feeling the throngs of down-and-out residents. Many of their eyes lingered on her too long for comfort. A young Puerto Rican woman and her four kids huddled on one of the three couches in the family room, staring at the TV mounted to the wall.

"You're in luck. I just had a couple of people move out a few days ago. Would you like to start the residency paperwork?"

Trenda glanced at the water-stained ceiling, the mix-matched furniture, the coughing, elderly janitor and into the director's face. "How about I give you a call later? I need to check out a few other spots first."

"Okay, but let me know as soon as you can. This place usually fills up pretty fast."

"I'll keep that in mind," Trenda said as she slipped on her sunglasses and headed for the exit. *This spot is way too depressin'. I have got to be able to do better than this.* In order to avoid the possibility of running into the thugs again, she walked in the opposite direction.

ജൗ

In the parking lot of a Joe's Crab Shack in Houston, Beverly placed her small, wooden, penis-shaped weed pipe to her lips, flicked her lighter and ignited the bowl of high-dollar marijuana. *I need a good buzz before I make this call.*

Due to the desire to push forward with her planned destruction of Trenda's world, Beverly finally found the courage she needed and made the call to Lionel. Instead of hanging up like she usually did, she exhaled the plume of weed smoke and waited for him to answer.

"Hello?"

For a second, her finger hovered over the red END button on her cell phone after hearing his voice. *Not this time.* "Hello, Lionel. It's me, Beverly."

"Bev! How are you? How have you been?"

She tapped weed ashes out of her pipe into her ashtray. "I'm okay. Just thought I'd give you a call and thank you for your support."

"You don't have to thank me; looking after you is the least I could do...I'm sure Darius would have done the same thing for me."

She closed her eyes and recalled how close he and Darius were. They had grown up together since high school and even went through the police academy at the same time. They were even partners briefly, early on in Darius's career, until Darius pissed off his captain and sued the city of Baltimore for discrimination. As punishment for embarrassing the department, Captain Kelly arranged to have Lionel shipped to another precinct, knowing that would irritate Darius.

From that point on, he and Darius had been in a constant

pissing contest. Darius had one ace-in-the-hole that kept Captain Kelly at bay; his late, well-respected grandfather, Floyd Kain. He was one of the greatest police chiefs the city of Baltimore had ever known. Many of the most influential members of the force gave Darius a lot of rope just on the strength of his grandfather's legacy.

"Still, I want you to know I appreciate you," she said as she opened her eyes. "And I do have a favor to ask of you."

"Anything. What do you need, Bev?"

She paused before making her request. "I want to put a hit out on somebody."

"Whoa! Whoa! Whoa! Hey, Bev! What the hell? You can't be making statements like that!"

Ignoring his warning, she went on. "I want to have that tramp that had my husband killed punished."

"Bev! Check yourself! You do know I'm a cop, right? And that saying this to me is a crime, don't you?"

Rage seasoned her tone. "I'm well aware of that. I know what you cops can do… I know what kind of connecti—"

Before she could finish, Lionel jumped in. "Bev! For Christ's sake, I can't sit here and listen to this…this craziness…let me call you back."

"Coward!" she said to the dead phone connection. "Is everybody scared of that slut?" The image of her son growing up without his father motivated her next move. "I'm tired of waiting for people to solve my problems for me." She called her Aunt in Galveston and arranged for her to watch her son for a couple of weeks. Then she called American Airlines and purchased a round-trip ticket to Baltimore.

Twenty-One

A few blocks away from BOWS, Trenda caught the bus back to her hotel. Once inside, she unpacked her new Tracfone and plugged it into the wall socket. While she waited for it to charge, she squatted down by the bed and picked the Bible up she had kicked underneath it. She looked at the gold-embossed words "Holy Bible" on the black cover for a few moments before putting it back inside the nightstand drawer.

Her father's face appeared in her mind. "I can't believe how old he looks," she said as she lay back on the bed, staring at the ceiling. She allowed her conscience to take her back in time. Besides the harsh discipline she'd received growing up, she recalled a few great memories. She let her arm lay across her eyes as she thought back to the fun summer trips she went on with the church. Every summer she, her brothers, and other children members of her father's church were the envy of the neighborhood kids. She could still see the jealous looks in the eyes of the kids that couldn't go on the trips as her father drove the church's refurbished school bus to fun destinations.

The smell of his Old Spice aftershave still lingered in her mind. She remembered how the scent used to briefly stay with her after hugging him. Trips to the fair, amusement parks, church picnics and the like were interwoven into her past. Even though they had their scrimmages, she still held on to a few precious memories.

Images of her mother bled over into her thoughts. She could see the deep shade of green in her mother's eyes; the same shade as her own. Looking back now, Trenda realized how much of a burden and pain in the ass she had been. Especially to her mother. All the many nights her mother had broken down in tears, blaming herself for the waywardness of her only daughter pinched Trenda's heart.

For over an hour, Trenda stared at the ceiling, reliving some of the most embarrassing and rebellious years of her life. *I deserved a boatload more ass-whoopins than I got*, she thought, sitting up on the edge of the bed. *Might have changed this sin-filled life I'm dealin' with now.*

Instead of continuing her self-hating moment, she walked over, unplugged her phone and turned it on. Although the phone was less than halfway charged, Trenda decided to use it anyway. Ten minutes later after activating the phone, she took the dollar bill out of her wallet with Walter's funeral home number on it. "I wonder if he's still with Lollie?"

She dialed the number. Two rings later, a polite woman's voice said, "Secrease Mortuary and Crematorium, how may I assist you?"

"Is Mr. Secrease in?"

"No, he's not. Would you like me to transfer you to his assistant?"

Trenda walked over, opened the off-white drapes and looked out the window of her room. "Yeah…do that."

As she looked out onto the parking lot of the motel, a familiar voice pleased her ear. "Hello, this is Ms. Slawson, Mr. Secrease's assistant. How can I help you?"

A smile as wide as the Grand Canyon filled Trenda's face. The sound of her old friend's voice was unmistakable. "Yeah, I'd like to know how much to burn up my dead dog."

"Excuse me?" Trenda grinned as that familiar voice paused. "Wait a minute…is this who I think it is? Is this *you*, Mya?"

Trenda chuckled. *Damn, forgot she only knew me by my old alias.* "Yeah, you can call me her. How you been, Lollie?"

Her shriek made Trenda pull the phone off her ear. "*Girl!* What the hell? How you doin'? What the...where are you?"

"I'm in B-more. What about you? I see you done graduated to Mr. Secrease's assistant. Y'all must have got *real* close."

"Wow! I can't believe this shit! I mean, after hearing about what happened to you on the news...okay, wait. Be straight with me; is your name really Mya? 'Cause on the news I heard it was somethin' else."

REVELATIONS 21:8 *But the fearful, and unbelieving, and the abominable, and murderers, and fornicators, and sorcerers, and idolaters, and all liars, shall have their part in the lake which burns with fire and brimstone: which is the second death.*

That timely verse eased Trenda's mind as she thought about how many times she'd had to lie about her true identity. In an effort to change her ways, she told the truth. "My real name is Trenda...Mya was my alias. In my old life, having a fake name was a must."

"Oh...okay. I feel you. Damn, girl, we got hella stuff to catch up on. Where you at right now?"

Trenda switched the phone from one ear to the other. "I'm on the Westside. You?"

"I'm over here off Frederick Avenue and North Hilton. How far is that from you?"

After a quick calculation, Trenda said, "I'm off South Canton... about a twenty, thirty minutes' drive from you."

"Well, look girl. How about we hook up real quick? You got time?"

"Yeah, I have time but I have no wheels. I can catch the bus but it's gonna take a minute."

"Don't even trip; I'll come get you. Let me tell the secretary

I'm gonna bounce and I'll be there. Where are you? Gimme the address and I'll lock it in my GPS."

GPS? What the hell? The term GPS perplexed her for a moment until she thought back to how her former, temporary lover, Box, had described what it meant to her once upon a time ago. After giving Lollie the address to her motel, she hung up, plugged the phone back up and prepared to meet up with her homegirl.

ഽﮬ

"Enjoy your stay at the Baltimore Marriott; we look forward to your arrival," the kindly hotel employee said as Beverly hung up the phone.

Beverly dropped her cell phone on the bed next to her open suitcase. "I'm looking forward to my arrival as well," she said as she packed a few pairs of underwear sets into her bag. A couple of tears fell from her eyes as she kissed a picture of her and her son and tucked it into her suitcase. Even though she knew Darius had cheated on her, she still hated the idea that Trenda was the cause of her son not having his father.

But her exceptionally competitive, possessive and ego-driven side had a hand in her plans. Also the fact that she'd been raised in "The Hood" made her seek street justice. Unlike Piper, whose psychosis more than anything else drove her desire to kill Trenda, Beverly's sheer anger at being embarrassed and forced to leave her home fueled her rage. She went to her closet, reached on the top shelf and pulled down a two-year-old Day Planner. She opened it and scanned the middle pages. It was loaded with information on Trenda and her family she had compiled. She slapped it closed, walked over to the bed and tossed it into the suitcase. *I'm going to return the favor to her or die trying.*

Twenty-Two

Trenda paced the lobby floor of her motel as she waited for Lollie to arrive. Fortunately, the young black clerk behind the counter gave up on engaging in conversation with Trenda after she fed him a few single-word responses to his flirty attempts at small talk. More than once she caught him staring at the ass in her skinny jeans.

I forgot to ask that girl what she was gonna be drivin', Trenda thought as she looked out of the lobby doors onto the street. She caught herself nibbling on her thumbnail and stopped. *Why the hell am I so nervous? It ain't like she's a cop.*

Minutes later, she saw a new, lime-green Dodge Challenger R/T with black stripes pull into the passenger loading zone in front of the lobby doors. She could tell by the long flowing hair and deep chocolate skin the driver was her ol' buddy, Lollie. Trenda chuckled and hurried out the lobby doors. *Damn! That's a bad ass car!*

Lollie was almost at full running speed as soon as the heels of her black boots hit the pavement. "Oh my God! Come here, girl!" she yelled as she ran over and met Trenda for a tight embrace. "I'm so glad to see you!"

"It's good to see you, too!" Trenda said as they held and looked at each other. Trenda watched a single, mascara-stained tear roll out of Lollie's right eye. Trenda blinked hard to try and control her own tears. "Don't be cryin'…you gonna get me started," she said as she wiped the lone tear off of Lollie's face.

Lollie broke the embrace, took a step back and checked out her friend. "Damn, you look pretty good. Jail must not be as bad as I thought," she said with a smile. She then ruffled Trenda's wild hair. "This is the first time I've seen you with that much hair… it looks *real* good on you."

Trenda laughed and slapped Lollie on the round mound under her calf-length black denim skirt. "Looks like you either got butt implants or somebody has been ridin' you right, Lollie-pop!"

Lollie blushed and wiped her hair over the shoulder of her lime-green sweater. "I see you're still nasty as ever."

Trenda smirked. "Not hardly. I'm not that chick anymore."

"Bullshit," Lollie said as she circled Trenda, admiring her very curvaceous frame. "You still have a body that could stop a bullet train."

"Whatever," she said with a laugh. "Anyway, tell me what's up? How the heck you end up out here on the East Coast?"

"Well, it's a long story." She looked at her watch. "How about we go get something to eat and I fill you in?"

Trenda nodded. "Okay, let's do that. I sure wanna know how you got your hands on this sexy car."

Lollie grinned as she hit the remote button on her key ring and unlocked the door for Trenda. "For starters, this is a rental. I'm only using it until I leave."

Trenda opened the door, sat down and rolled down the window. "Where are you going?"

Lollie closed her door, clicked on her seatbelt and started the engine. "I'll fill you in, in a minute. First, what you wanna eat?"

"I ain't sure. Let's go over by the Harbor and see what's there."

"Okay," Lollie said as she pulled away from the curb. "I love the P.F. Chang's over there. You like Chinese food?"

"Yeah, that'll work." She watched the downtrodden, depressing landscape of West Baltimore pass by as Lollie headed for the freeway. "I haven't had any good Chinese food in a few years."

৪৩০৪

"This is not good news, Nick," Anton Ivanski, a lieutenant in the Russian mafia, said as he ground out his cigarette with his high-dollar, square-toed shoes. "I had high hopes for you."

Nick looked into Anton's cold gray eyes. They told him the Russian fellow and his bulky, quiet and rough-looking associate had seen many, many bad things happen. "Look, Anton, I know this looks bad but—"

Anton shook his head and brushed off the sleeves of his expensive dark blue suit. "I told you earlier, I don't like 'buts'. Either you can do a thing or not." He stared deep into Nick's eyes. "How do you plan on paying us back the twenty grand you 'lost?'"

Nick took a peek outside the vacant entryway into the empty Camden Yards Stadium they were conducting business in. Anton's comrade never took his eyes off of Nick. This was Nick's one and only opportunity to make it big in the underworld. Not even his former foe, Darius, had connections to the ruthless and well-funded Russian mob. He also knew that his life meant about as much as a hot pretzel to these international bad guys. "Well… if you can give me a couple months, I can scrape it up."

Both Russian men chuckled at the same time. Feeling comfortable, Nick made the mistake of joining in on the laughter. Seconds later, the backside of Anton's right hand smacked the shit out of Nick's face, knocking the diminutive cop up against the wall. "You don't have a couple of months, asshole," Anton said as his friend slid on a pair of brass knuckles. The sharp spikes on the edges of them looked extremely menacing—and painful.

After grimacing and spitting out a wad of bloodstained saliva, Nick wiped his mouth and took a step back. "What the fuck?" His eyes landed on the brass knuckles and widened. "What are you doing, Anton?"

Anton's friend grabbed Nick by the shoulder and held him tightly. Nearly a foot taller than him, and built like a Sherman Tank, Nick made little fuss. Anton stood toe-to-toe with the cop. "I'm a fair man. You can still salvage this mess. I'll give you two weeks… in that time you had better have twenty-five grand for me or else I'll be forced to let my countryman here tenderize you, got it?"

Nick's mouth fell open. "*Twenty-five grand!* I only owe you twenty. How you figure—"

Anton nodded at his companion. He then took his brass knuckle-covered fist and punched Nick square in the shoulder. The spikes dug deep into Nick's flesh. "*Owwww fuck!*" Nick yelled as he gripped his upper arm and grimaced. "*Goddamn it! What the hell was that for?*"

Anton glanced at his diamond-studded watch. "Just an incentive. I'd hate you to somehow forget about our deal. Come up with the original balance *plus* accrued interest and I can perhaps persuade my associates to go forward with our larger plans. "

Nick removed his bloody hand from his arm. The amount he had bled through his sweatshirt sleeve was disturbing. Ironically, his wound was almost in the exact same place as Slip's wound he had aggravated earlier. "This is *way* out of line, Anton. I'm your best bet at getting your foothold in the Baltimore drug trade now that the Island Boys have been practically eliminated." He looked at his bloody hand again and glared at the pair of Russians. "Ever since that bastard Darius and his partner got murdered, the department has been on the warpath, arresting and harassing everybody that so much as spits on the freaking sidewalk. I'm the *only* one on the force with the necessary connections to keep the heat off you and your people. My network goes all the way from these streets up the freaking legal ladder. So I suggest you tell your goon to keep his fucking hands to himself."

After listening in silence, Anton grinned and clapped his hands. "Nice speech, Officer Nick." He pulled a pack of cigarettes and lighter out of the inside pocket of his jacket, tapped a smoke out and fired it up. "Two weeks. If you don't have the money by then, kiss our deal, and your ass, goodbye."

As Nick watched the two mobsters walk toward their champagne-colored Bentley Continental GT, a sense of doom grew in him like an aggressive cancer. His ace-in-the-hole had just been trumped. The only safety net he had between him and Russian mob justice had been shredded. "Fuck me." He pushed down the collar of his sweatshirt and inspected his shoulder. Blood leaked from three deep holes.

As he eased his collar back up, he flashed back to his first meeting with Anton two months ago. Slip insisted on hooking Nick up with his new foreign friend. After a series of meetings behind the condemned "Lighthouse," Nick and Anton agreed on a plan to fill in the holes in the lucrative drug trade left by the disappearing Island Boys gang. Nick had one thing going for him that Darius lacked; he had the complexion to make more secure connections.

Before leaving his relatively discreet meeting spot, he looked around to make sure he wasn't being watched. Taking the risk of meeting in daylight was foolish but necessary. The Russians were ready to invest twenty-five million with Nick's "network" as seed money. But first he had to prove he could move a measly twenty-grand worth of dope. And to his chagrin, he'd loused that up. *I can still fix this damn thing, but I'm gonna need some serious help...I need somebody that knows how to move a lot of product in a short amount of time.* A pair of unbelievably green eyes and an awesome rump appeared in his mind. He grinned and hurried to his custom Harley-Davidson motorcycle, strapped on his half-helmet, hopped on, fired it up and sped off.

Twenty-Three

"How long you say he's been dead?" Messy Marv asked, looking at the corpse of a young, male Puerto Rican gunshot victim.

"Judging by the blood coagulation, I'd say about nine hours, give or take an hour," the young CSI officer replied.

He looked up from the stiff body and stared at the large, old house dubbed the "Lighthouse" years ago. The number of dead bodies found in or near the legendary crime magnet was astonishing. Tatters of the yellow and black, police "Murder Tape" still clung to the nightmarish residence. *I wouldn't feel the least bit bad if someone torched this house of horrors.* Images and the stink of the murdered and mutilated' bodies of Darius and Tyrone stood fresh in his mind. Although the city had boarded the place up, a mile of red tape kept the rundown property from being bulldozed over.

He placed his arms akimbo. He read the nametag on the officer's smock. "Well, Cliff, tag him and bag him. Forward me some pictures and all other info you find on this fella." He walked a ten-foot circle around the body. "Looks to me like he was shot somewhere else and dropped off here."

The CSI officer grinned. "Yup, according to my investigation, that's exactly what happened to this fellow."

Marv walked over and inspected the heavily boarded up house. It smelled like an outhouse, but showed no signs of having been broken into. He took a deep breath, released it and turned to the CSI officer. "Well, Cliff, I'm out. Chat with you later."

Cliff took three quick photos of the body. "Okay, Messy. Take care." As he walked down the driveway, Cliff called out to him. "Hey, Messy! Did you hear one of our guys found a bloodstained screwdriver over in the alley next to the old hardware store where that girl got shot a few days ago?"

Marv paused and ran that info through his mind. He turned toward Cliff and said, "Is that the place across the alley from the old burned out Wing Wong Chinese Café?"

"One and the same. They found it yesterday. They're gonna run tests on it and see if they can find any prints. Results should be back in a couple of weeks."

"Thanks again, Cliff. Later." After getting in his car, he made a few calls and managed to get ahold of the lead investigator on the former, deceased, Jane Doe now identified as twenty-two-year-old Letty Paul. After a little further digging, he found that the blood type on the screwdriver matched that of gang member Percy "Slip" Wells. After ending his call, he started his car and pulled away from the curb. "I hope visiting hours aren't over yet."

&0C&

"I can't believe it's been almost three years!" Lollie said as she sped toward the Baltimore Harbor. "Walter ain't gonna *believe* it!"

Trenda turned in her seat toward Lollie. "Speaking of Walter, what's really goin' on with you two? How did he—and you—end up out here?"

Lollie smirked. "After you disappeared, Walter and I continued to kick it. After about a year, we got kind of serious." She held up her hand and showed Trenda the two-carat solitaire ring on her right index finger. "We got engaged!"

"I'll be danged!" Trenda took Lollie's hand and inspected the brilliant-cut ring. She had the look of a well-kept woman. A lot of the "Hood Flava" Trenda saw in her when they first met had been transformed into straight "High Society Swagga." "Congrats!"

Lollie beamed. "Yeah, I told him I'd put it on my left ring finger *only* after he came up with an official wedding date."

Trenda let go of Lollie's hand. "Okay, I got that—and I'm not real surprised y'all hooked up, but how did you end up out here on the east coast?"

Lollie exited the freeway. "We got to talking about you one night and I mentioned to him that I had family out here in Maryland. I saw a light bulb go off over that crazy man's head. He told me he was thinking of expanding his business and felt Baltimore would be an ideal place...we both knew there was plenty of death going around out here—especially in West Baltimore." She stopped and waited at a red light. "That next weekend, he got us plane tickets to B-more. We came and he met some of my family. After that, he checked out a few funeral homes in the area and found this place called Richfield Crematorium that was a dollar away from bankruptcy. After talking his brother and sister into it, he managed to buy Richfield out."

Trenda stared at a trio of streetwalkers doing their business a few blocks away from the Harbor. *I'll be damned! That's my girl Constance! And I bet that black chick in the middle is Cherry.* Lollie drove past them too fast to be absolutely sure, but Trenda was confident those were her buddies. *Ain't another white woman in the state that has as much ass as Constance.* "Where is Mr. Man at anyway?"

Lollie slowed down and entered P.F. Chang's parking lot. "He's back in Oakland. He had to go back and handle some business stuff. He left me here to help get the new staff hired and get things moving smoothly."

"How long you been here?"

"I've been here about three months now." She zipped into a prime parking stall ahead of a couple in a sleek, red Cadillac STS. She turned to Trenda. "But I'm getting a little homesick, though."

Trenda checked out her friend's new look. Her makeup and hairstyle had vastly improved. She had the look of a well-to-do woman. *She even talks more proper than she used to,* Trenda thought as she inhaled the scent of Lollie's pleasing perfume. "How long before you go home?"

"Not sure...I still have a few more things to get straightened out at the crematorium."

"What exactly do you do for Walter? I get that you are his boo and all that, but are you *really* his assistant, too? You *can't* be still workin' at the hotel if you been out here this long. Did you quit?"

Lollie blushed, then checked her glossed lips in the rearview mirror. "Well, let's see..." She brushed her hair off of her shoulder and pulled the keys out of the ignition. "Walter and I continued to kick it after you disappeared. As a matter of fact, we spent damn near every day together after that 'special' weekend the three of us had in your suite."

Trenda grinned as she recalled the hot threesome they'd shared a few years ago. She could almost taste the sweetness of Lollie's pussy and creaminess of Walter's warm sperm. "Yeah, that was the *business!*"

Lollie chuckled as she opened her door. "Yeah, sure was. A couple months later, Walter got tired of all the shit I had to put up with at the hotel and insisted I quit and work for him. After I told him I didn't wanna work with any dead bodies, he offered me a position as his personal assistant."

"That's cool! Bet the pay is way better than at the Water's Edge."

"At first it wasn't, but once he saw I was hesitant to quit, he offered me double my pay *and* benefits. That nut even called and told my boss and fired *them*; can you believe that?"

Trenda laughed as she opened her door and got out. She smiled at Lollie over the roof of the car. "I can believe it; he is one hard-headed, gotta-have-it-his-way, dude."

"You got that right." She blushed again. "But he's my baby...I love my Wally."

"*Wally?*" Trenda cracked the hell up. "You call him *Wally?*"

"Yes, but only his close family calls him that...don't you *dare* tell him I told you. He gets *so* embarrassed."

Trenda met Lollie in front of the car and began walking with her toward the restaurant entrance. "Ya secret is safe with me. I'm the last person that wants to mess up y'all's good thang."

After being seated in a booth with a nice view of the Harbor, Trenda and Lollie continued playing catch up. Trenda placed the menu on the table after deciding on the shanghai shrimp with garlic sauce. Lollie took a sip of her Asian Pear Mojito and said, "So, what's your plans, girlfriend? Are you going to stay here in B-More?"

Trenda sat back in her seat, trying to keep eye contact with the other patrons down to a minimum. "I dunno, yet...I'm pretty much stuck in Maryland for the next eighteen months until I'm off parole. Besides that, just gotta try and survive. Not gonna be easy to find a decent job with my record." She sighed and stirred the ice in her Sprite with her straw. "But things could be worse, I guess..."

Lollie cocked her head and smiled at Trenda. "This is *so* weird; it's like déjà vu."

Trenda gave her a puzzled look. "Huh? What you mean?"

"Remember when we first met? You were fresh in town looking for a room?"

"Yeah...yeah, I remember you straight hooked me up."

"You know, every now and then I miss that old hustle." Lollie paused as a pair of police cars sped by, sirens screaming, lights flashing. "I wish I had a gig for you, but I just finished hiring the staff I need."

Both women sat back as their food was delivered and placed in front of them. Dejected, Trenda stared at the bubbles, struggling to get past the cubes of ice in her soda, in a quest to rise to the top. *Woulda been cool if she had a job for me...that way I'd have a fightin' chance at making a legal living.* Reaping the harvest she had sewn in her life sucked hard at times like this. But after spending the past few years locked up, Trenda learned to let *"Coulda, Shoulda, Woulda"* thoughts go. "Thanks for thinkin' about me anyway...I'll find somethin'..."

Lollie reached her hand across the table and placed it on top of Trenda's. "Don't give up yet." She gave Trenda's hand a squeeze. "I'm sure as hell not. I owe you big time. If it wasn't for you, I wouldn't have met the man of my dreams and gotten the job of my dreams."

"You mean you always wanted to be Walter's assistant?"

"No...I don't know if I ever told you but I went to college and got a degree in Business Management. It's just an AA degree, but I always hoped it would somehow help me get a foot in the door."

Trenda smirked. All the time she'd spent partying with Lollie, she had no idea she was a college girl. Looks had certainly deceived her. "Looks like it got you a *whole* lot more than a foot in the door."

Blushing, Lollie unwrapped her chopsticks. "I'm working on it."

Again, Trenda was amazed at how much Lollie had changed. She carried herself in a much more dignified fashion; nothing like the "hoodish" Lollie that was ready to help her kick the late

King Gee's ass back in that Oakland club. A small part of her envied Lollie's ability to change for the better. *The hell with all this self-pitying bullshit; let me just enjoy this meal with my friend.*

An hour later, after finishing off her Harvest Spring Roll appetizer, half her order of Singapore Street Noodles and plenty of girl talk, Trenda had to push back from the table. "Dang...I feel fat as Jackie Gleason," Trenda said, unbuttoning her skinny jeans. "But that sure was *good!*"

Lollie laughed. "You need to quit it; you ain't even *got* a belly and you got the nerve to be unsnapping your pants! Bitch, *please!*"

Trenda chuckled. "Not *that* sounds like the old Lollie!"

As the laughter subsided, Lollie checked her watch and sighed. "Shoot, I have to get back. Walter's going to be calling me in a little bit for an update on things and I need to be at my computer." She opened her expensive black leather clutch, removed her wallet and placed a platinum AMEX on top of the bill for their meal. "I had a *great* time Mya; I mean, *Trenda.* My bad! I'm still trying to get used to your real name."

"It's all good," Trenda said as she wiped up a small spill of soy sauce. "I guess that's gonna take a lil' gettin' used to."

"I still can't wait to tell Walter I ran into you; he is gonna freak out."

As the waiter picked up the bill and credit card, Trenda asked him to bag up her leftovers to go. She looked out the window just in time to see the last flicker of sunlight wink out. "Where are you livin'? In a hotel somewhere?"

Lollie stifled a burp with her hand. "Heck no! I'm staying with my aunt and uncle over in Rockville. They have a six-bedroom house and no kids. The only thing is they're too old fashioned to let Walter and me stay in the same room without being married. You know how old folks are."

The mention of "old folks" tweaked Trenda's heartstrings again. The persistent image of her feeble father popped back up in her mind. "Yeah, I know what you mean."

"Thanks, hon," Lollie said to the waiter as he handed her card back and sat Trenda's doggy bag on the table. She fished her car keys out of her purse. "You going back to your hotel?"

Trenda stood up and grabbed her bag of food. "Yeah…I guess I'll go chill for a while."

They rode in relative silence back to Trenda's motel. A layer of sadness covered the friends. They both realized they were on two totally different paths. Lollie pulled up in front of the motel lobby and said, "Do you mind if I give Walter your number? I'm sure he'd love to say hi."

"Yeah, girl! I'd love to speak to 'Wally.'"

Lollie's eyes bugged. "Don't you dare call him that! Gonna get me divorced before I get married!"

After a little shared laughter, Trenda grabbed the door handle. "Thanks for everything…not just the food; your friendship and everything. You're one of the best friends I have… That's on my momma."

A tear leaked from Lollie's eye. "Trenda…"

Feeling a wave of emotions heading toward her, Trenda leaned over and hugged her buddy. No words were necessary. The held each other for a minute, then composed themselves.

"Okay, I'm out." Trenda wiped her eyes, grabbed the handle again and opened the door. "Don't forget to have old Walter call me."

"I won't," Lollie said, voice cracking a little. "And save some time for me; I don't work all day. We can still get together before I head back to Cali."

"That's a done deal. You know how to reach me. Be safe, hon."

She closed the door and watched the sexy car pull off. Even after that welcome reunion, her heart was as heavy as an anvil. Her conscience yelled in her ear. "You know you need to go see your daddy!"

Twenty-Four

"And you're sure of that blood type, Brian?" Marv asked as he pulled into the parking lot of Baltimore County Hospital.

"Yes, sir—O-Positive."

Marv parked in one of the stalls reserved for police officers, opened his glove box, removed a mug shot of Trenda, tucked it into his inside pocket and got out his car. "Thanks a lot, Wendy. I'll be in touch."

He ended the call and put his phone inside his jacket pocket as he entered the emergency room entrance. *Looks like a busy night,* he thought as a cluster of humanity suffering from a range of ailments from the flu to broken bones filled the waiting room. Nurses scrambled to triage them as fast as safety allowed. At the nurses' station, he found out what room Slip was in and headed for the elevators. On the third floor, in the ICU ward, he entered Slip's room. The privacy curtain shielded him from Slip's view. He rounded the curtains just as Slip changed the TV channel to ESPN. "Cool, I'm just in time to see how my Red Sox are doing."

"*Huh?*" the shocked Slip said. "What you talkin' about?"

Marv pointed at the commentators giving sports score updates on the screen. "I've been wondering how they are doing against the Yankees."

Unease filled the young thug. His eyes darted around the room. "Ummm...okay..."

Marv stuck his hands in his pockets and turned his attention to Slip. "How you doin', Slip?"

He placed his hand on the bandages on his belly. "How you think I'm doin'? Muhfucka stabbed me and shit. I'm hurtin' like hell!"

"Sorry to hear that." Marv walked over held onto the bed rail. "Hopefully, we can catch who did this and get you the justice you deserve."

Slip's eyes ran away from Marv's. "Yeah…I hope y'all do."

Marv looked at the IV machine feeding into Slip's arm. The bandages on his arm looked like they'd recently been applied. "Slip, do you happen to know what your blood type is?"

"Hell no! How I'm supposed to know that? I ain't no doctor."

Marv glared at him. "*Hey!* Quiet down. Have some respect for the other patients." He went into his pocket and pulled out the picture of Trenda and held it up in front of Slip. "Do me a favor; tell me if you know this person."

Slip's eyebrows and mouth twitched. He rubbed his freshly re-bandaged arm that Nick had aggravated. "Nah…never seen her before."

He exhibited all the classic body language of someone avoiding telling the truth. Marv had spent a long time studying the psychology of liars. *I hate having to play these games with these macho-filled punks.*

"Okay, fair enough." He put the picture back in his jacket pocket. "But let me leave you with this; we found a screwdriver stained with O-Positive blood on it in an alley next to a building where a young lady was found shot to death the same night you got attacked. That's one hell of a coincidence, huh?" He took one of his business cards out of his pocket and put it on the tray next to Slip's bed. "If you have a memory jolt and something about that night comes to mind, give me a call. I'd hate to see a perpetrator get away with a crime."

He could tell the vague information he fed to Slip had hit the mark. Nervousness covered him like a quilt. Being a two-strike felon, he knew his last strike was close enough to spit on. He grabbed the remote next to him and pressed the call button for a nurse. "Man, it's time for me to get my medication...I can't talk no more."

₮℞

I can't stand that trick! Slip thought as he watched the husky detective disappear around the privacy curtain. He heard another set of footsteps approaching.

"How can I help you, Percy?" a Korean nurse asked. "Are you in pain?"

"Hell yeah! Why you think I called you?"

She fought to keep a pleasant smile. "I'm sorry to hear you're hurting. On a scale of one to ten, with ten being the worst pain, what number is your pain?"

"What you mean, what number? This ain't *Sesame Street*. Get me some pain medicine!"

She walked over and injected a dose of Fentanyl into his I.V. line. "This should take care of your pain in a few minutes. Can I get you anything else?"

He used the bed remote to raise the head of his bed a little. "No...I'm good."

"Okay, your dinner will be served in about an hour. Try and get some rest."

The feel of the painkiller entering his body relaxed him a little, but not enough to make him forget his troubles. *Who was the green-eyed bitch? Why Messy Marv keep askin' me about her? Did he bust her and she tell him what went down?* He turned down the TV volume a bit. "Naw...if she had snitched, Messy woulda cuffed me to this bed." His eyelids drooped as the pain in his arm and abdomen weakened. *I need to try and find out who that broad is that jabbed me...she's gotta be known in the hood if Messy's lookin' for her...* The remote slipped out of his hand. *If he catches her before I do, she's liable to cut a deal with him and snitch me out...*

The Fentanyl took hold. He no longer heard the voices in the PA system, the constant clicking of his I.V. machine or the infrequent moans or yells of pain from the neighboring rooms. *And Nick...how the fuck am I gonna pay him back the twenty Gs I owe? Had to hustle damn near three months to make that...*

Twenty-Five

"Hi, baby!" Lollie said to the image of Walter on her laptop screen. She loved the sound quality of the wireless Bluetooth headset Walter had sent her. It was exactly the same as the one he wore. She had been trying to connect with him ever since she'd dropped Trenda off several hours ago. The clock in the lower right corner of her laptop read seven minutes to midnight. She took off her bra and put on a peach-colored silk robe. "How are things going on your side of the world?"

"A little stressed, but okay. Having to deal with family as business partners can be a real pain in the ass." His web-cammed image looked at Lollie as she brushed her hair. "Sure is good to see a friendly face...not to mention the rest of you."

Her loose robe allowed her right tit to show itself. "Speaking of friendly faces, guess who *I* ran into today?"

He removed his polo shirt. "Who? One of your country cousins?"

"No, smart-ass." She recovered her tit with her robe. "One more guess...make it count."

She watched as he stroked his goatee, pretending to be in deep thought. She loved the look of his freshly dyed, jet-black beard. It gave him a rugged yet youthful appearance. "Santa Claus...I don't know...I give up."

Lollie grinned and leaned closer to the built-in webcam on her laptop. "Mya."

Too stunned for words, Walter sat staring at her, mouth agape. "Not *the* Mya? Not green-eyed Mya?"

"Yes, sir! *That* Mya."

She could see the combination of lust, joy and shock on his face. He stood up, clad only in his maroon boxers, and paced the area behind his large desk. "Are you bullshitting me? How? Where?"

She spent the next half-hour filling him in on her reunion with Trenda. "I'm still having a hard time believing the whole night. It still hasn't sunk in that it was *her* they were talking about in the news a few years ago when we heard about those cops that got murdered out in Baltimore. I cannot believe it was *our* Mya—I mean, *Trenda*, that was involved. That's crazy, ain't it, baby?"

Walter placed his elbows on the desk, then lowered his face into his hands. A few seconds later, he looked up, readjusted his headphones and shook his head. "That girl is a real piece of work! I *knew* there was something about her...something out of the ordinary."

Lollie smirked at him. "You mean something extraordinary like her hot sex?"

He lifted his eyebrows and showed her his bright, white teeth. "Now, what makes you think that, dear?"

She shifted in her seat and gave him a good look at how hard her nipples were under the silky fabric of her robe. "I can tell by how you licked your lips and lowered your eyes when I mentioned her name. That's the same look you get when I get on my knees in front of you."

Like one of Pavlov's dogs, he licked his lips again after Lollie mentioned Trenda again. "You pay much too close attention to detail." He rolled back in his chair far enough for her to see his crotch. "Tell me; what kind of details do you see here?"

Lollie's hair fell over the side of her face as she leaned closer to the screen. She paid no mind to the fact that her left tit had popped out of her robe. "I need a closer look."

His lips formed a wicked grin. He reached inside his boxers and fetched his swelling penis. "Can you see this?"

She slid her laptop closer to the edge of her nightstand and scooted back on her full-sized bed. From that position, the webcam was focused directly on her midsection. Her hand lazily made its way to her gold boy shorts. "Ummm...how about you give me another look?"

His hand surrounded his stiff cock and caressed the shaft. "How much do you wanna see, ma'am?"

Lollie's hand found a warm, moist spot several inches beneath her fuzzy navel. The fabric of her boy shorts deterred her fingers from exploring her slick slit. The split-screen picture of her fondling her vaginal area on the left side and Walter holding his piece on the other screen turned her fire up. She decided to take him down Memory Lane. "Honey, remember that night when me, you and Trenda hooked up in her hotel room?"

His eyes closed as he massaged his dickhead slowly. "Ummmm, hmmm...that was off the charts...that was the first time we fucked..."

Lollie slowly rolled her head as she recalled the first time she'd felt his dick. How she'd climbed on top of him and eased down on his concrete hardness. Her finger found the edge of her panties as she reminisced. The image of Trenda rubbing Walter's balls and her nipples made her breath catch in her throat. "Yessss...mmmmm, wish we could do that again right now..."

Walter's stroking pace increased. "Me too, baby... I have only felt you cum that hard a few times. I felt your pussy juice spill all over my balls." He slowed his stroking. "Let me see your titties..."

Lollie let her robe slide down her right arm, exposing her right breast. She pulled on her erect nipple. "Hmmmm…I'll give you a sample." She slipped a finger behind her panties and touched her swollen pussy lips. She used her middle finger to circle her wet clit. "You remember how good she ate me out?"

He stopped stroking and held his dick. "Mmmmmm, hmmmm. I can still see how you laid back while Trenda sucked your clit."

Lollie moaned as she continued stimulating her pussy. The sight of Walter working his man on the screen sent a shiver through her. She longed to suck the fat head of his knob. She inserted two fingers inside herself. "Pretend you're fucking Trenda, baby…let me see how hard your dick gets," she whispered sensually. "Stroke it, baby…mmmmm, stroke it faster…"

She stood and slowly eased her panties off and held them up to the camera. In reaction to Lollie's sultry command, his pace quickened. "Shit, girl…you know those are my favorites," he moaned.

"Imagine Trenda pulling them off me while you watch." The chocolate middle finger of her right hand eased between her pussy lips. She loved seeing herself on camera. Her exhibitionist fetish was free to act up. That, coupled with her love of pleasing her man, kept a line of orgasms waiting for their chance to explode. Each time she heard his moans in her earphone, her fingers slipped deeper inside her. "Mmmmm…you want her to suck your dick while you eat my pussy, baby?"

"Ohhhh fuck…mmmmm shit, Lollie…" he moaned, jacking off faster. "I'm gonna cum…"

Lollie sat back on the bed, spread her pink lips apart with two fingers and showed him her swollen clit. "Give it to me, honey… nut all over this pussy…" She inserted three fingers inside. "Cum with me, baby…let…me…seeeeee…"

Three orgasms erupted inside Lollie, soaking her hand. Walter was shown her ability to squirt her orgasmic fluid. That triggered his own eruption. *"Ooooooooooooohhh fuckkkk, Lollie!"*

After a fifth orgasm, she sat up and rubbed pussy juice on her hard nipples. "Yessss, baby...there you go, let me see you cum... Shoot it for me." A jumble of guttural words and grunts escaped his mouth as he stiffened up and moved closer to the camera. At that point, all Lollie could see on her screen was his genitals. He moaned loudly as a gusher of creamy cum shot out of his dickhead and onto his laptop. A drop obscured him from her vision momentarily before running down the screen, off the camera lens. She covered her mouth with her hand and her eyes bulged. "Oh my *God*, baby! You made a mess all over your computer!"

"Hmmmm?" he said, eyes half-closed, as he held his twitching organ. "What you say, hon?"

She wiped a sweaty lock of hair out of her face and laughed. "Baby, you just skeeted all over your laptop. *Look at it*!"

ₛℐℂ℣

As Walter desecrated his laptop, Nick the Dick prowled the streets of West Baltimore. His quest to locate the best drug runner in the city took him into the seediest sections of town. Getting his hands on the drugs to sell would be no problem. He had an inside man with a major gambling problem who happened to work in the confiscated evidence department. He was always down to make a few bucks on the side.

Although he had a decent network of underworld hustlers, the drug trade was his weakest area. Darius and his former minions ran that side of the cities cop corruption. Moving stolen merchandise and extortion was more his forte. Even with Darius and his partner eliminated, others from his clique quickly filled their spots. *I'd have better luck getting a picture of Bigfoot riding a unicycle than getting any of those bastards to help me*, Nick thought as he rode around a section of Baltimore famously called "The Block." It was a section of Baltimore famous for its selection of more than thirty strip clubs.

Being single with no kids, him visiting a gentleman's club wasn't out of the ordinary. But this trip to "The Block" wasn't for pleasure. He parked his motorcycle and hopped off of it. To many, seeing a white man walking in this section of Baltimore was highly unusual. But the populous most likely to cause harm to a stranger in their land knew this particular Caucasian was off limits. To many of them, he was a coworker.

Still hurts like hell, Nick thought as he rubbed his aching shoulder. Earlier he'd stopped by a Rite-Aid drugstore and bought a bandage for his wound. A few yards from the Kat Tale Klub he spotted a group of young black men loitering near the club entrance.

"Bingo!" Nick said as he saw one of them was one of his most reliable informants. He stopped a few yards short of the group. He gazed at them until he caught the eye of his intended target. He read the look of recognition in his informant's eyes. Nick nodded his head toward the club, and then entered. After paying his cover charge, he looked over his shoulder and saw his guest behind a couple of other patrons paying to get in.

Nick walked over to a nearby table, the furthest away from the stage, and pretended to be interested in the mulatto beauty making love to the brass pole onstage. The seductive music playing for the stripper filled his ears. He barely heard the skinny but hot waitress ask him if he'd like a cocktail.

"Yeah...get me a Bud Light."

As he watched her wiggle away from him, his acne-scared guest took a seat next to him. "The fuck you doin' here, Nick?"

Nodding his head offbeat to the music, Nick kept his eyes glued to the stage and grinned. "Looking for a pussy."

The young man shifted in his seat, looked at the chick on stage, and then back to Nick. "You mean, lookin' for *some* pussy."

Nick turned to his guest. "No, Beanie. I said *exactly* what I meant, Pussy."

Beanie pursed his lips and looked around the dark club. "You keep disrespectin' me like this and I'm gonna—"

Nick ground the heel of his hard, black motorcycle boot on the toe of the grimacing Beanie's thin sneakers. "Shut up, you piece of shit and listen." He leaned over and spoke into Beanie's ear. "All you're going to do is what the fuck I say. Got it?"

Pain contorted Beanie's face. "Yeah, I got it! Get off my foot!"

Nick leaned back and lifted his foot. "Good, glad we have an understanding. I need some info." The waitress returned with his beer. After taking his drink and tipping her, he returned his attention to Beanie. "And I need it right now."

Beanie mean-mugged the cop. "Yeah?" He wiggled his sore foot. "And I need pay...*serious* foldin' money." He pointed at his aching foot. "I think you broke my goddamned toe and I ain't got no medical insurance!"

"Cry me a river." Nick scanned the sparse crowd. He didn't see any of Beanie's contemporaries. "You know my rules; I only pay for what I can use."

Beanie scratched his jaw. "Man, c'mon with all that drama...I ain't got time for all this chit-chattin'. I got business to handle."

Nick watched a few men stuff the g-string of a coffee-colored stripper with dollar bills as she spread her legs for them on the edge of the stage. "I need you to make a delivery for me."

"A delivery? You know I don't do that transportin' shit no more."
Nick poured half his beer into his glass and took a swallow.
"Guess what? You just started back."

Beanie shook his head. "Nah, man. I'm outta that business.
Too risky for me."

I really don't have time for this bullshit, Nick thought. He recalled
how well known Trenda and Beanie were in the underground for
their transporting skills. If you needed something moved—no
matter how big or small—those two were the best. That was
until she and Beanie fell out for reasons unknown to Nick. The
sound of *Drake's* latest hip-hop hit assaulted the room. "Beanie,
I have so much shit on you, I feel like a pigeon sitting on a statue.
Not to mention shit that some of your 'associates' would be
unhappy to hear. Like the time you turned in Jamaican Mike for
the reward on his head." He looked over and saw Beanie's jaw
twitch with stress. Jamaican Mike was third in command of the
notorious Island Boys gang. Even though they were practically
disbanded after the murder of Officer Darius Kain and his
partner, they still had ways to reach out and touch you if
necessary. And punishing a snitch was *very* necessary. "Well?"

The mixed facial expressions told Nick he had touched a nerve
in Beanie. Beanie ran a hand down his face and leaned back in his
chair. "That's fucked up, Nick...you told me you wasn't gonna
bring that up no more. I thought we was through with that
business?"

Nick took another swallow of beer. "Beanie, you know what
you signed up for the first time I let you off after catching you
with a gun used in the murder of that beloved jeweler, Mr.
Gluckstein... An *unsolved* murder at that. Just imagine what would
happen if by some chance that gun—with your prints still on
it—turned up."

Pressure, Nick knew, could bust a pipe. He leered at the chocolate dancer as she hung upside down on the pole. Beanie exhaled loudly and leaned on the table, on his elbows. "Look, Nick; I ain't got no car or driver's license. Plus, all the contacts I had are dead or locked up. I ain't made no runs since me and Trenda used to get down a few years ago."

Nick continued to ogle the dancer. "Well, the car and license I can take care of. The connections are in your hands. Do what you need to do. I'm sure you know that your former partner is back in town."

"Yeah, I know she here, but I ain't fuckin' wit' her no more…"

Nick's heel found Beanie's toe again. "You better kiss and make up, friend; your freedom depends on it."

He removed his foot and poured the last of his beer into his glass. Beanie grimaced and massaged his aching foot. "You need to quit all that bullying shit!" Anger mixed with the pain in Beanie's face. "You *way* outta line!"

"Oh really?" Nick stood, took a few swallows of beer and splashed the rest in Beanie's face. "Meet me at the Lighthouse at midnight tomorrow or your ass will be grass and I'll be the mower."

A short time later, he put on his helmet and straddled his bike. *Even if Beanie doesn't manage to connect with Trenda, I'll make Slip his new partner.* A relieved grin stretched his lips. *Slip might be a careless prick, but he is damn near as good a hustler as Trenda.*

As he rode off, deep inside his psyche he knew Trenda was his best bet to get the job done in time. And getting it done in time was a bet he could not afford to lose.

Twenty-Six

"Yeah, I know it's check out time and no, I'm not gonna pay for another night," Trenda said as she hung up the hotel room phone. She yawned, stretched and pulled open the basic, floral-patterned drapes. Outside, sunlight peeked in and out of the scattered clouds. Despite her unsettled living arrangements and other drama, she was in a good mood. She looked out at the cars traversing Interstate 95, half a mile from her window. A growl escaped her belly. "I wonder if they have a Mickey D's around here? I'm starvin'.."

After a hot shower and putting on one of the sexy outfits Dennis bought for her, she grabbed her bags and went down to the lobby to check out. As she walked past to the rack of newspapers, magazines and brochures, she froze. Her bags fell to the floor. *What the—?* A picture of her sat on the bottom corner of the *Talk-of-the-Town* tabloid newspaper. It was a new, lesser-known competitor of the *National Enquirer* owned by StarShine Entertainment.

"How the hell?" She walked over and picked up a copy of the magazine. The young Muslim woman behind the counter gave her a brief glance, and then went back to counting her cash drawer. Trenda read the caption superimposed on the four-by-three inch picture: *Trenda Fugua: Green-eyed Goddess or Murderous Ghoul?*

Muthafuckin' Beanie! I can't believe that punk sold those pictures!

The photo of her inside the Flyin' Pig restaurant was unmistakable. A scowl identical to that in the picture spread across her face. *I should have known…can't trust that fool as far as I can throw a hippo.* Memories of how he'd bailed out on her while they were getting carjacked in Philadelphia surfaced. The events of that night replayed in her mind. Half-past three in the morning, less than a mile from the drop off point for the three thousand Ecstasy pills they carried, a pair of southwest Philly thugs in a souped-up Ford Bronco came out of nowhere and rammed the back of the plain, unassuming Mercury Sable Trenda and Beanie were in.

With Trenda behind the wheel, they did their best to shake their pursuers. Using Beanie as her navigator, since he lived there most of his life, he managed to lead them to a particularly rundown section of town. The damage muffler screeched and sparked for blocks before falling off of the Sable. The Bronco stayed on their asses the entire time. To Trenda, it seemed they weren't trying as hard as she thought they should have been to catch them. She also noticed that Beanie was a lot calmer than usual under the circumstances.

Ten minutes into their chase, he managed to lead them into a cul-de-sac that dead-ended into a large housing project. Less than a minute separated them from the Bronco. Trapped, Trenda reached into her boot and pulled out "Baby" and prepared battle.

I can still see the shifty look in his eyes as he grabbed the gym bag full of pills and jetted out the car. Punk-ass bitch didn't even bother to tell me to follow him…hopped out before I stopped the car good and ran off into the projects.

The tension she felt as the Bronco sped up and stopped inches short of the Sable's damaged rear bumper gave her goosebumps.

Her heart thumped like a kick drum as the Bronco driver flashed the high beams into the interior of the car. A few seconds later, the Bronco reversed, did a three-point-turn and sped off into the night. Weeks went by before Beanie resurfaced. His excuse for abandoning her was almost as weak as his explanation of what he did with the pills. She had to suck a lot of dick and move a lot of merchandise for free to pay off her client. Although he did manage to come up with her cut of the money they would have made, she'd heard he had set her up from the get-go. *That's why the chase ended the way it did.* The only reason she didn't carve him up was the fact that everyone in the state knew she was looking to hurt him, and she could ill-afford for him to come up dead while the spotlight was on her. Instead, she ended their partnership and suggested he stay as far away from her as possible.

While the cashier was busy counting cash, Trenda took the magazine, rolled it up and quickly stuffed it into her purse. After hastily checking out, Trenda walked toward the tall red and yellow McDonald's sign three blocks away, conveniently located next to the freeway entrance. *I wonder how many folks saw my picture on that damn magazine?*

Her appetite waned as she calculated how many people read that smut-ridden magazine. She put her hand on the door handle and looked inside before entering. *I ain't feelin' this*, she thought as she peered at the diners inside. *I'm gone.*

She turned and walked toward the freeway. Two blocks away, she stopped, sat on a bus stop bench, pulled her sunglasses out of her bag and put them on. The fact that she was in a mostly industrial area gave her a bit of comfort, but not enough. She understood now that no matter where she went in Baltimore— especially West Baltimore—she was going to be under a micro-scope. Depression took a seat next to her on the bench and put an arm around her soul. A bus arrived and dropped off a young woman who was more interested in her phone conversation than anything else. Trenda waved off the bus driver as he waited for her to board the bus.

The warm rays of sun that bathed her helped her mood a little bit. She closed her eyes, leaned back and let her mind drift. Images of all the drama she'd been through so far after getting released flashed like billboards. Somewhere deep in her subconscious, a completely unexpected thought bubbled to the surface: Get out of Baltimore!

She looked up at the bus stop sign and did a quick calculation. *I'm about three bus transfers and an hour-and-a-half away from Randallstown.* A bus lumbered toward her from a couple of blocks away. Moisture gathered in her palms as she gathered up her bags and stood up. Unaccustomed nervousness gripped her. The bus pulled up and the doors opened. Her half-minute hesitation felt more like a half-century. She sought strength in Luke 10:10:

But when you enter a town and are not welcomed, go into its streets and say, 'Even the dust of your town that sticks to our feet we wipe off against you. Yet be sure of this: The kingdom of God is near.'

"I gotta get going, lady. Are you taking this bus?" the chubby black bus driver said.

Trenda's paralysis broke. She climbed aboard, dug some money out of her pocket, paid her fare and carried her bags to her seat. Ignoring all the eyeballs around her, she focused strictly on her destination.

&⊃C&

"You sure that's where he's at?" Bruno "Do-Dirty" Grant, former enforcer for the Island Boys gang, asked local gangbanger, Vincent "Stitch-Giver" Riles.

"I'm positive," Vincent said, recalling how he and Slip had gotten into a heated argument the night Slip ended up shooting and killing Bruno's little sister in that abandoned hardware store. "I told you he was there when I first talked to you the other day. His bitch-ass is there fa sho; my broad's brother is a janitor at the county hospital. He said they got him in ICU. I even got his room number; D104."

Bruno took a puff off of the fat joint hanging on the corner of his mouth. Smoke filled the inside of his midnight blue, top-of-the-line Jeep Commander. The tinted windows helped keep their meeting private. He reached inside his center console and pulled out a silencer and a Walther PK380 pistol. He passed the joint to Vincent, then screwed the silencer onto the gun. "It's time to make a house-call."

Vincent watched the tall, bald, chocolate thug pull a combination cap and dreadlock wig off of the backseat and put it on his head. The fake dreads hung to the middle of his back under the red, black and green cap. After Bruno put on his dark sunshades, Vincent said, "*Damn!* You look like a whole new person!"

Bruno laid the gun on the dashboard, opened his glove box and pulled out a plastic bag with a fake beard inside. He then looked in the rearview mirror, put it on and smoothed down the fake, jet-black goatee. "If you gonna do ya work, you gotta be equipped." He then reached in the console and pulled out a set of gold fronts and put them on his teeth. He looked like half of the current rappers. "*Fully* equipped."

Vincent tapped ashes from the blunt into the ashtray. "Since we talkin' business, don't you have a reward on the head of who shot your sister?"

Bruno stared him down behind his glasses. "You'll get your money after I confirm he's the right person." He started the engine and put the gun in the center console. "You want your money, ride with me."

Vincent knew he couldn't punk out if he wanted to maintain

his street credibility. He did his best to hide his nervousness as he broke eye contact with the killer seated next to him. "Let's roll."

Twenty minutes later, Bruno parked a block away from Baltimore County Hospital and left the engine running. He then pulled out his cell phone and looked at his call history. "Is this your cell number, 267-555-0977?"

Vincent nervously picked at a hangnail on his thumb. "Yeah... that's it."

After pulling a pair of black leather gloves out of the pocket built into the bottom of his door panel and putting them on, Bruno reached over and gripped Vincent by the back of his neck and grimaced at him. "Look here, youngsta; don't go all pussy on me now. I can smell fear comin' off you like a skunk-sprayed dog." He leaned over, inches away from the cringing Vincent. "I want you to listen *very* carefully. I'm gonna walk to the hospital, pay a visit to your boy and call you to come pick me up at the Wawa store down the street from the hospital. You got that?"

Vincent swallowed hard as he fought off breathing in Bruno's marijuana-scented breath. "Yeah...yeah, man...I got you."

Bruno gazed at him for a moment longer before letting him go, taking the pistol out of the console and opening the door. His baggy, blue, Champion sweatsuit fluttered in the mild breeze. He looked around, and then tucked the gun in his waistband, behind his back. He looked back inside the jeep at Vincent after closing the door. "Remember what I said; as soon as I call, have your ass ready to pick me up at Wawa. If you ain't there a minute after I call, guess whose momma I'm gonna go visit..."

Vincent knew Bruno's threats were not to be taken lightly. Rumor had it that he had killed enough people to fill a Greyhound bus. He nodded his head and straightened out his yellow, New Jersey Devils cap. "I'll be there."

§⁊◌⅋

This food tastes like straight garbage, Slip thought as he tossed the dry turkey sandwich back on his tray. *Wish I had a cheesesteak from the Explorers Den in Philly instead.* He pushed the tray away and picked up the TV remote. He turned to the *Steve Wilkos Show* and laid the control on his belly. Earlier, he'd gotten word that he was going to be moved to a step-down unit from ICU now that it was determined his injuries were not life-threatening.

As he cheered on a fight on the show between two hillbilly-looking fellows, he heard the click of the door closing. A tall, dark stranger emerged from behind the privacy curtain separating his bed from the vacant one next to him, holding a pillow in his hand. Slip glared at the looming figure. "Who the fuck are you, housekeepin'?"

"Is your name Percy Wells?"

Slip's mouth went dry. *Nobody* called him Percy—let alone a stranger. "Man, how you know my name? Who the fuck are you?"

"Do you remember a young lady named Letty Paul?"

The stranger's calmness bothered Slip tremendously. "Hell naw. Who the hell is that bitch?"

The stranger reached behind his back and pulled out a black, silencer-equipped pistol and walked to the edge of the bed. "That 'bitch' was my baby sister. You shot her in the heart a few days ago."

Slip frantically reached for the remote to call for help but the tall stranger got to it first. He tossed it over the bed railing, out of Slip's reach. Recollections of the night he and his boys were going to have an orgy inside the old hardware store in West Baltimore with a couple of skanks flashed inside his head. He did his best to scoot away from the stranger. As he opened his mouth to yell for help, the stranger swiftly placed the pillow over his face, pressed the muzzle of the silencer into the pillow and fired three whispered shots. Slip's struggles ceased seconds later.

In the stairwell of the hospital parking garage Bruno had scouted out the day before, he removed his gloves, beard, gold fronts, wig and sweatsuit and stuffed them into a nearby garbage can. Now dressed in an army fatigue T-shirt, matching camouflage pants and black boots, he looked like a clean-cut American soldier. Next, he unscrewed the silencer from the pistol and put both that and the gun in the large pocket on the side of his pants. Afterward, he calmly walked away from the hospital and called Vincent. "I'm ready."

By the time Bruno got to the Wawa parking lot, his jeep was there waiting for him. Approaching police sirens filled the air as he hopped in the passenger side and grinned at his panicky driver. "You aight, son? Looks like you about to jump out ya skin."

"No…I'm good…just," He watched as a trio of police cars sped past the store. "I'm just, you know, ready to go."

Bruno chuckled, reached into the large pocket behind the driver's seat and emerged with a banded stack of cash. He tossed the ten-grand bundle into Vincent's lap. "Get me outta here."

Twenty-Seven

A day after dropping her son off at her aunt's house, Beverly touched down in her former hometown. *This city is even more depressing than I remember*, Beverly thought as she drove her Enterprise rental car out of BWI airport. Not even the brightness of the sun-filled late afternoon improved her mood. Her Bruxism had gotten markedly worse. Not using her tooth guard had contributed to her malady. She had worn a small hole in her left real molar. The minor toothache it produced added to her bad attitude. She did her best to ignore the pain as she thought of ways to take care of Trenda. *I sure wish I could have brought my gun with me.*

A traffic jam slowed her progress to the Baltimore Marriott. While sitting in the fast lane, waiting for traffic to move, she called Lionel. Her call went straight to his voicemail. Before she could leave a message, a horn blared behind her, urging her to move up. She decided against leaving a message and instead gave the driver behind her a disgusted wave and crept up. In the distance she saw signs that there was construction work going on ahead. A Maryland State Police car sat in the fast lane, behind the construction cones, half a mile ahead of her, red, yellow and blue beacons flashing.

For a moment, fear shrouded her. Being stuck in the middle of that traffic congestion made her an easy target. She tightly gripped the wheel of her mid-sized Ford and sunk down in her seat a bit.

The voice of the serious-faced detective who'd tried desperately to get her to accept their offer to put her in the witness protection program spoke to her. *"You would be wise to stay away from here. Take advantage of this chance to put your life back together and raise your son. No amount of compensation can bring back your husband, but you can at least get away from bad memories and bad people."*

Her lack of trust and disgust in the Baltimore PD made her turn down his offer. She wasn't fully convinced her husband hadn't been murdered by other cops. "He had a funny nickname but I can't remember it for shit," she said and winced after grinding down on her damaged tooth. She rubbed her jaw. "I need to go find me some Orajel or something...damn, this tooth is *killing* me!"

Fear seeped into the car with her, accompanied by paranoia. A late model sedan occupied by four rough-looking black men pulled up alongside her to the right. A BMW with a Rastafarian-looking driver pulled up behind her. A large 4x4 truck sat a foot from her front bumper. To the left was the center divider. The anger that blindly drove her to coming back into enemy territory all of a sudden gave way to sheer terror. "Oh my God! *What am I doing here?"*

Her hands trembled as she pressed the automatic door locks, even though the doors were already locked. Her mouth went dry when she looked to her right and saw the driver, and the passenger behind him, in the sedan, peering at her. The driver winked at her. She cringed, fully expecting him to pull out a gun and blast her. In her unbalanced psyche, the vehicles surrounding her were all working together to assassinate her. A pair of tears dribbled down her face. Her bottom lip trembled. The interior of the car heated up and windows began to fog from her rapid breathing. She looked in the rearview mirror. The BMW seemed to be inches off of her rear bumper. The driver appeared to be staring into her eyes. "I've got to get out of here!"

She looked around frantically for an escape route. All four passengers in the sedan were now watching her freak out. After seeing the men chuckling, she stepped on the gas pedal, turned the wheel and drove down the emergency lane next to the center divider. In her haste, she sideswiped the 4x4 truck that was ahead of her as well as two other cars. "Help!" she yelled as she sped through the orange construction cones. "They're going to kill me!"

Horns honked all around her as she sideswiped a couple of more cars and missed others by inches. A terrified highway worker frantically waved his orange flags for her to stop. Seconds before she smashed into him, he hopped over the concrete center divider, narrowly missing being struck by traffic on the other side.

The other five men working in the lane scattered like thieves in the night. Fifty yards from the patrol car, the screaming Beverly slammed on her brakes. Fifty yards wasn't enough brake room. She slammed into the back of the patrol car as the Ford's airbag slammed into her face.

ℴℂ

"What in the world is she doing here in Baltimore?" Detective Jim Watson asked his coworker, Detective Messy Marv. They both spoke to the officer outside Beverly's room. "You ever figure out why she turned down our offer to put her in the witness protection program?"

Messy stuck his hands in the pockets of his dark brown slacks and shook his head. "According to her, she couldn't trust us or Trenda. She told me Darius used to always complain about the department being out to get him after suing them for discrimination. She was convinced that Trenda *and* the Baltimore PD were responsible for his murder." He walked closer to Beverly's hospital bed and looked down at the sleeping woman. Since she was admitted as a 51/50 patient, she was strapped to her bed. With both her eyes blackened by the impact of the crash, she looked like a cute raccoon. Fortunately, that and a broken nose were the extent of her injuries. "She's been in Houston for the past couple of years. I guess we're going to have to wait until her sedative wears off before we can question her."

Both men looked in the direction of the door as Dr. Moyer entered the room. The young Caucasian doctor looked young enough to have just graduated high school. He looked from one detective to the other. "Gentlemen, how are you?"

Jim offered the doctor his creamy, mitt-like hand. "Doing great, doc. What's the status of Mrs. Kain?"

The doctor adjusted his glasses. "Well, she's in stable condition. Besides some assorted bruises and the trauma to her face, she's doing okay."

Messy Marv pointed at the leather straps wrapped around her wrists. "What's her *mental* state?"

The doctor looked across the bed at Marv. "Judging by her behavior when she was admitted, I'm recommending we place her under a seventy-two-hour evaluation."

Jim's gray eyes fixed on the doctor. "Did you find any drugs in her system?"

"She had a significant amount of THC in her system; it appears she was a heavy marijuana smoker. Besides that and her teeth showing signs of constant grinding, she's a very healthy woman."

Jim scratched his head. "Would that explain the eyewitness accounts of her erratic behavior?"

"No...not really. The test results only showed signs of THC, none of the bad hallucinogenic drugs like PCP or LSD that alter behavior to the degree hers reportedly was."

Messy looked from the wedding ring on her finger to the doctor. "Did she say anything particular when she was admitted? Anything out of the ordinary?"

The doctor pondered his question, and then said, "The only thing in the reports that I recall that was sort of peculiar, was her babbling about wanting to shoot someone named Trenda in her green eyes. Does that mean anything?"

Both detectives looked at each other at the same time. Messy looked at the doctor and said, "Thanks for your time, doc. We'll check back with you a little later."

As Marv and Jim left Beverly's room and headed toward the elevators, Jim popped a piece of Nicorette gum into his mouth and said, "So, what you think about that last statement? You think she *really* risked coming back here looking to find Trenda?"

Marv pushed the elevator button for the lobby. "I can see it." He reached inside his jacket and pulled out his phone and checked the time. "Love can be a monster, Jim...a ruthless, heartless, careless monster under the wrong conditions."

"You got that right."

As they rode the elevator, Marv stared at the elevator doors. *Something nutty's going on...first Slip gets executed in his bed, in a hospital, in broad daylight, then here comes Darius's looney wife looking to get a piece of Trenda. Everybody associated with Trenda these days seems to have bad things happen to them.*

Twenty-Eight

"Wait a minute now, Nick. That's a little *too* risky," Barney Marks said. As the officer in control of the evidence room, he was very useful to Nick. "I'm a year away from retirin'. I can't afford to take chances like this anymore."

In the coolness of that spring night, both men stood next to a railing in the famous Baltimore Harbor, having a conversation. A mirror image of the illuminated Baltimore skyline looked back at Nick in the smooth, still water. He spat at it. *This miserable old fart is going to make me hurt him...he's been lending and selling me stuff out of evidence forever; now he wants to chicken out. I'm gonna have to call bullshit on that.* "Barney, what's the friggin' big deal? All I need you to do is get me a little heroin, take your pocket money and be done with it. Why are you chickening out now?"

The gray-haired, sixty-seven-year-old man shook his head. "Sorry, Nick. Things have been tight around there ever since I got those last keys of cocaine for you a couple months ago. When they came up short on the inventory, all hell broke loose. They installed some new cameras in the evidence room. A few of them, I heard, are hidden. I'm out the business, Nick. Sorry."

For years Barney had a foolproof system. Barney had the inventory incredibly well-maintained. After many years of pinching off pieces of confiscated drug evidence before it was catalogued, he managed to put together his own supply of dope.

On the week that he was out on vacation, the department, for the first time in decades, decided to do inventory without him being present. The discrepancies in the evidential quantities were difficult to explain. But Barney managed to barely convince his superiors they had calculated wrong. As a safeguard, they beefed up the evidence room surveillance.

"C'mon, Barney. You've been running that evidence room for almost thirty years. I know you have a few tricks up your sleeve." He placed an arm around the stocky, elderly clerk. "What about the fifty keys that got confiscated yesterday in that raid on South Charles? I *know* you can move some of that around. How about this one last time? I'll even throw in an extra couple hundred bucks per kilo, deal?"

The old man angrily shrugged Nick's arm off of his shoulders. "What the fuck? How hard is it for you to understand that I am *done... Done!*" He backed away from Nick. "Find another hustle."

The urge to shoot the old bastard in the back surged through Nick. Instead, he yelled, "Hey, Barney. Remember that cookout at your house a few years ago? I sure do. I went to use your upstairs bathroom and walked past your bedroom. I recall seeing a bunch of naked boys on your computer screen. You forgot to log out of your pedophile site. I got all your account information, you sick fuck. And I have saved screen shots with your face and information all over it."

Barney froze in his tracks as if he'd run into an invisible wall. He turned around slowly. "Fuck..."

Nick grinned as the old man looked back at him. All the color had run out of his face. "I guess you *do* remember."

Five years ago, Nick got word that Barney had an affinity for boys. No one could prove it, but Nick figured that knowing the truth could work in his favor. Besides being a pure asshole, Nick was also a very competent cop. He spent many hours researching and watching Barney. Finally, after two years of surveillance, he struck pay dirt. While attending a barbeque at Barney's house, Nick found the downstairs bathroom occupied. He then went upstairs in search of a second restroom and found one. Before taking a much-needed dump, he discovered there was no toilet paper. Instead of walking all the way back to the backyard to ask Barney if he had more, he went to the linen closet down the hall in search of some toilet paper. As he walked past Barney's bedroom door, a picture on his glowing computer screen got his attention. The picture of a nude boy, no more than ten or eleven, looked back at him. As he watched, other pictures of nude boys rotated on his screensaver. He then went inside and clicked around his computer and discovered that Barney was a member of NAMBLA. He found an eight-gigabyte USB drive next to the computer. He used it to download as much incriminating information he could—including a screenshot of nude boys— and pocketed the drive. Armed with that info, Nick was also able to track down Barney's membership information, more photos of him with underage boys and a host of other sinful information.

Barney walked over and stopped a few feet in front of Nick. His eyes begged for mercy. "Please don't do this."

Nick leaned back against the railing. "Why shouldn't I? You abandoned me in my time of need; why in the hell should I spare you?"

Barney was almost in tears. "Nick...you're gonna ruin me. What about my kids?"

Nick couldn't help but wonder if Barney's ex-wife of almost thirty years had left him because of his boy-love issues. It would certainly explain why his two daughters never visited him. He smirked at the distressed man. "I'm not an unreasonable man,

Barney." He watched the old man's eye twitch from stress. "I think you know what I need to keep this hush-hush."

Barney's face turned to stone. He was stuck like a rat on a glue trap. "If I do this, I want my fucking drive back."

Nick shrugged his shoulders. "Get me what I want, you get what you want. Deal?"

Defeated, Barney looked away from Nick and stared at the Baltimore skyline. "Meet me here tomorrow night at ten…"

My daddy always said pressure could bust a pipe. "Ahhh, this has been a productive meeting! I'll be here at ten sharp." He held his hand out to his unhappy partner. "Good doing business with you, buddy."

Barney declined to shake his hand. Instead, he gave him a cold glare and headed toward his beloved, restored 1948 Ford pickup truck. As Nick watched him storm off, his walkie-talkie squawked. He adjusted his cap and walked toward his patrol car. He was dispatched to a robbery in progress call, a mile or so from him.

A sense of relief made him almost float to his car. *Good! Now all I need is to get my couriers rounded up and get my package sold.*

An hour later, he wrapped up his investigation of a hoagie shop robbery. He feigned concern as the Turkish owner of the store recanted the story to him. He closed up his notepad and put it in his breast pocket. "Okay, Mr. Yilmaz, we'll be in touch with you. Don't hesitate to call that number I gave you, if you recall any additional information."

The old man used the burning butt of his current cigarette to ignite a fresh smoke. "I hope you catch that rat-bastard…I've been here over twenty years and never had a problem." He dropped the butt and put the newly lit cigarette in his mouth. "Do me a favor, Nick; once you find that asshole, give him a good ole 'wood shampoo' for me."

Nick almost chuckled at that old school term for when an officer beats someone with their club. "I'll keep that in mind. You go on inside, or better yet, shut down and go home. I'll see you around. Mr. Yilmaz."

As he cruised the Baltimore streets, Nick's criminal mind went to work. He searched his databanks for possible places where Trenda could be found. He pulled into a Wawa store for a cup of coffee. As soon as he entered the store, the cover of the *Talk-of-the-Town* tabloid stole his attention. He pulled the magazine off of the rack and glared at the picture of Ms. Fuqua on the bottom corner. "Come out, come out, wherever you are..."

Twenty-Nine

his is stupid, Trenda thought as she brushed her teeth and looked at herself in the mirror. *What are you gonna do? Go broke tryin' to afford this freakin' hotel while you build up some courage?* She rinsed her mouth out and wiped her face. For two days straight, after catching the bus out of Baltimore and talking Lollie into booking a room for her at the Randallstown Radisson Hotel, she wrestled with her emotions.

The ninety-five dollar a night hotel was well out of her budget, but was the cheapest in the area. With no credit card of her own to use to book the room, she connected with Lollie and paid her in cash to use her card to book a room for her. Lollie agreed and booked Trenda a two-night stay. Trenda promised to pay her back if she needed to stay any longer. The fact that it was only a mile away from the house she was raised in had a bit to do with her decision. For the past two days she'd isolated herself from the world. She turned off her phone, didn't watch any TV nor listen to the radio. She spent the majority of her time reading the Bible, rubbing her rosary beads and occasionally standing on her fourth-floor balcony people watching. The clock on her night-stand read a quarter past eleven. "No turning back this time," she said as she pulled on a pair of tan, high-waist linen pants and a black, Hatchi sweater. "No more excuses." The conservative outfit was a must for her next stop.

After slipping into her black boots, Trenda grabbed her purse and cell phone and then left her room. Butterflies swarmed her belly as she left the hotel lobby and stepped onto the sidewalk. The unseasonably warm weather made her question wearing her sweater. *Too late to go change now; no turning back.* She walked to one of the two cabs sitting in the designated zone outside the entrance and hopped in the backseat. "Where to, young lady?" the middle-aged female cabbie asked.

"3780 Fieldstone Road." Just speaking that address out loud raised goosebumps on her arms.

The cabbie started the engine, flipped the fare flag down and pulled from the curb. "Gotcha. Be there in about fifteen minutes."

This area has changed a lot over the years, Trenda thought as she looked out of the window. It had been over a decade since her last viewing of her old neighborhood. Her former high school, best friend's house, and favorite doughnut shop whizzed by. Judging by all the expensive cars in the driveways of the expensive houses, the neighborhood had graduated from middle class to upper-middle class.

A block from her destination, Trenda tapped the cabbie on the shoulder. "You can let me off here."

She paid the cabbie, got out and took a deep breath. The prospect of seeing her father after running away and all the other drama on her plate made the little girl inside her whimper. *Get moving, feet.* She pulled her sunglasses out of her purse, put them on and started her journey. Six houses from home, she slowed her pace. "Okay, this is it."

That said, she trudged on. Past the Watsons' house. Past the Hurleys' house. Past the Seymours' house. Memories of her former neighbors helped keep her mind off of what was coming up. As she approached the light-pink, stucco-walled house she'd grown up in, she spotted an ancient 1955 Mercury Montclair.

The teal and white, slightly weather-beaten vehicle sat under the carport next to the two-car garage. *Wow, he still has Grandpa's old car!*

A sense of nostalgia filled her as she looked at the antiquated vehicle. Over twenty years ago, under that very carport, she'd lost her virginity in the backseat of that old Mercury during a thunderstorm. After having her sweet sixteen party canceled because she'd missed curfew the night before, she'd let her boyfriend, Rod, talk her into giving him the pussy. To spite her parents, she met him in the car at one in the morning; hours after her parents went to sleep.

She chuckled as she approached the gate of the three-foot-high, white picket fence. *Good thing that car has vinyl seats, would have been a nightmare tryin' to clean up after he popped my cherry if it would have had cloth seats.* Summoning up her courage, she didn't hesitate; she unlatched the gate and walked up the brick walkway. Weeds sprouted between many of the bricks. *Daddy would never let the weeds get outta hand like this back in the day.*

She choked up as she glimpsed the dying roses in the flower garden that ran along the perimeter of the house. Her mother used to spend almost every Saturday tending to them. She climbed the half dozen stairs and stopped in front of the white security gate. It looked brand new. *Damn, never had one of these on the house while I was livin' here. I know the ol' hood ain't changed that much.*

Her hands shook as she placed her finger on the illuminated doorbell button. *God, I hope this is the right thing to do.* She pressed the button and waited.

A gravelly, deep voice she hadn't heard in a long time greeted her from deep inside the house. "Comin'…give me a minute."

Trenda shifted from one foot to the other. Nervously, she removed her shades and put them in her purse. *Chill, just chill… it's gonna be okay.*

From the time she heard her father's voice, to the time she heard the door open, felt like a lifetime. The sound of him sucking in oxygen as he stood behind the security gate was as loud as a gunshot. "*Trenda*? Is that...really...*you*?"

The sound of his voice cracking spread to her own vocal chords as he unlocked the security gate. "Yeah, Daddy...it's...it's me."

She stood back as he pushed the gate open. For a few seconds, neither of them knew how to proceed. They sought direction in their eye contact. Once found, Trenda opened her arms and her tear ducts. The man she'd despised for so long looked smaller, kinder and much frailer than she remembered. He still had those big, calloused hands, but the curvature of his spine kept him from being able to stand fully upright. Even through his cataracts, his love for his daughter showed clearly.

His arms surrounded her as his cane fell to the floor. "I have prayed for this moment for so long...so...long."

They hugged and cried, hugged and cried and hugged and cried. Finally, face waterlogged, Trenda stood back and held her father's shoulders and took inventory of his physical being. "Daddy, how you doin'?"

He used one hand to hold onto the doorframe and the other to wipe his tears away. "I'm fair to middling," he said with a smile. His dentures were as white as fresh snow. "But by the grace of God, I'm in heaven now that my baby girl's back home."

"When did you put this up?" She rapped on the white metal gate with her knuckles. "Looks like you the only folks on the block a security gate."

"I had it installed about a year ago. I got tired of all the news people and other nosy people coming to bother me. You would be surprised at how many folks come by looking for you, or to talk to me about you."

"That's crazy!" Trenda watched him attempt to bend over and get his cane. "Wait, Daddy, I got it." She picked it up and handed it to him. "Let's go inside so you can sit down."

"I'm fine...I'm fine," he said as he took the cane and rubbed her back. "I still can't believe it!" He looked at her and wiped a tear out of the corner of his eye. "Wish your mother could be here to see how grown you are."

Trenda sighed and dropped her eyes. "Yeah...I know..."

She followed and sat her purse on the small table by the front door. He hobbled over and picked up his black cordless phone. "I have got to call everybody and tell them you're home! Your brothers will certainly be glad."

Trenda placed a hand on his forearm. "Please Daddy, don't... I'm not ready...for everybody yet," she implored him. "*Please?*"

He nodded slowly as he put the phone back on the cradle. "I understand."

"Thanks, Daddy."

The house still held a mountain of memories. The walls of the dining room were filled with photographs. She saw herself in many of them. Family members she hadn't seen in decades looked back at her. The large picture of her parents taken at Coney Island, in front of the famous Ferris wheel, in the mid-sixties, made her heart flutter. The look of love they had for one another was undeniable. Her mother looked remarkably like the woman Trenda now saw in her mirror. He walked over and took a seat at the long dining room table. He then waved at the seat across from him and smiled. "Sit down, honey. Let me have a look at you."

"Okay." She pulled out the chair, folded her hands and looked at her old man. "You've probably got a lot of questions for me so go ahead."

He chuckled, reached across the table and placed his hands on hers. "First, how about you go in the kitchen and fix us each a bowl of that rainbow sherbet in the freezer?"

Trenda almost fell out her chair. The memory of how they used to eat her favorite, rainbow sherbet, together when she was a child moved her. Only she and her father liked that flavor, so to her it was a *very* special bond. Most times they shared that treat in order to cheer her up. Like the time when her parakeet died while they were on vacation in Florida. The six-year-old Trenda was devastated. Or the time she got cursed out, a year later, by her mother for playing hide-and-go-get-it with the next-door neighbor's son in their basement. "You still remember we used to eat that together...*wow!*"

He grinned. "Yes, every time I eat a bowl, I think of you."

Trenda walked into the kitchen and paused. *Besides some new appliances, still looks the same in here as it did the day I left.* Before memories of that ugly day, over ten years ago, when she'd fought with her mother and ran away messed up her mood, she opened the cupboard and grabbed two bowls. The mint-green, ceramic bowls had been in her family as long as she could remember. After filling both bowls, she walked back in the dining room and placed a bowl in front of herself and her father. "I can't remember the last time I had some of this."

Before Trenda could put the first spoonful into her mouth, her father stopped her. "Wait, how about you grace the table for us?"

She paused with the spoon halfway between her mouth and bowl. "Huh? Oh...uh...okay." Awkwardness sat between her and her father as she searched her mind for a suitable prayer. During the rebellious teenaged years before she'd run away, Trenda had begun resisting the heavy religious theme of her household. That included refusing to say grace at the table. Her father sat with his head bowed, waiting for her. *Shoot...here goes.* She closed her eyes and said,

"*For this and all we are about to receive, makes us truly grateful, Lord. Through Christ we pray. Amen.*"

"Amen," her father said. He lifted his head and looked at Trenda. "That was real good. Sounds like you've been practicing."

Trenda swallowed a spoonful of sherbet. "A little..."

Halfway through their sweet treat, he said, "Are you out for good?"

"Yeah. Well, I'm on parole for a while."

He ate a couple more spoonfuls. "Where are you staying?"

"I'm staying in a hotel right now. Just until I get on my feet."

He pulled a napkin out of the triangle-shaped, chrome napkin holder. "How long will that be? Do you have any job prospects?"

Tension coursed through her. This line of questioning was far more annoying than she'd anticipated. "I haven't had a chance to do much job huntin' yet, but I'm workin' on it." She grabbed a napkin and wiped her mouth. "I'll be all right."

"But it's expensive staying in hotels, isn't it?"

"Kind of, but I have a few bucks to hold me."

His spoon rattled as he dropped it into his empty bowl. "How about you stay here? Your bedroom is still the same as the day you..." He paused as if recalling that dark day when his only daughter ran off. "You left..."

Trenda swallowed hard. The pain in his face was hard to look accept. She looked from his eyes to the medical alert ID bracelet on his wrist. *You could and should do this...and you damn well know it.* Images of the harsh restrictions she lived under in her parents' house were hard to shake. Unsure of how to answer him, she stood and collected their bowls. "Let me think on that...thanks for the offer."

A phlegmy cough rattled his thin frame. He pulled a dingy handkerchief out of his pants pocket and spit into it. After wiping his mouth and tucking it back in his pocket, he unhooked his cane off of the chair next to him and stood. "You take as much time as you like. No rush." He walked into the kitchen as Trenda put their bowls into the dishwasher. "When you finish that…" Winded, he paused to catch his breath. "I want you to come upstairs with me."

Trenda closed the dishwasher. "What's up there?"

He gave her a mischievous grin. "You'll see when you get there."

"Now, Daddy, you know I don't like surprises."

He walked away from her. "I think you're going to like this one."

Halfway up the stairs, he had to lean against the wall. His breathing was short and labored. *He doesn't look too good.* She tentatively touched his shoulder. "Daddy?"

He gave her a weak wave. "I'm okay…just get a little tired… climbing these…stairs some…times." He gave her a reassuring wink. "I'll be all right. I got my second wind."

"You sure? You looked kinda pooped."

"I'm positive; God gives me strength."

Trenda pursed her lips. *You still on that kick?* Her parents' belief that God would do more for them than modern medicine used to irk Trenda to the bone. But now that she had grown spiritually, she didn't feel the need to condemn him for it the way she used to. "Yeah, God is good."

At the top of the stairs, he turned to the right and headed toward his bedroom. Once there, he pushed the door open and waved Trenda inside. "Go on in."

She walked in and looked around the peach-colored room. Heartbreak and sadness grabbed her. A vacant hospital-style bed sat next to the queen-size bed her parents had once shared. A string of pearl rosary beads with a silver crucifix hung on the bedpost. *Momma had those rosary beads since I was a kid.* The only other new addition to the bedroom was a strange looking machine on her father's nightstand. It sat next to a bottle of water and three bottles of pills. She walked over and picked up what looked like a small scuba mask. "What's this do?"

"That's a CPAP machine." He scratched his gray head. "Helps me sleep at night...I went to the doctor's office last year and he told me I have sleep apnea."

The term was foreign to Trenda. She smirked at him. "I don't know what that is, but it must be kinda serious if *you* of all people are usin' somethin' a doctor told you to use."

He ignored her comment and pointed at the walk-in closet. "Open that up for me."

She walked over, slid the white doors apart and looked inside. The rack was full of fashionable women's wear. The floor of the closet was littered with dozens of pairs of women's shoes. "Momma was a straight fashionista!"

"A what?"

"A fashionista...you know, she loved clothes...fashion, get it?"

He shrugged. "I guess you could say that."

"Never mind, Daddy." She snickered, explored further in the closet, then turned to him. "Where are your clothes? These all look like Momma's."

He smiled. "I had to put most of my stuff in your brother's old room across the hall. Your mother evicted my clothes a long time ago." He walked behind her and tapped her leg with his cane. "It's all yours now."

She spun around and gazed at him. "Say what?"

He nodded. "All her clothes, jewelry and what-nots are all yours."

The reality of having lost her mother had never been so clear to her. Her mother was *very* picky about her clothes. Even more so about her jewelry. Cheap wasn't in her vocabulary. Everything from her colorful assortment of leather coats to her formal gowns and pantsuits were designer garments. Admittedly, although nice, most of her mother's clothes were not Trenda's flavor. Her mother prided herself on being one of the best-dressed women in church. Trenda could barely bring herself to touch a single item.

She fought off a rush of emotions as she fingered one of her mother's silk blouses. "You *sure*, Daddy? I'm surprised her sisters didn't come jump on this stuff after she…"

"Over the years, she softened up her stance on what happened between you two." He walked over and sat down on the bed. "I think she finally admitted she saw a lot of herself in you."

Trenda's eyes ballooned. *"What?"*

"Yes, your mother was a pistol back in her day." He closed his eyes and chuckled. "Yes indeed…your mother *and* her sisters. They *still* have a reputation back in Shreveport. *Nobody* messed with those Hopkins girls…*nobody.*"

Trenda's head spun with the impact of this previously unknown revelation. All her life, all she knew about her mother was the fact she was a hardcore Christian. That was until she converted to Catholicism after she got pregnant with Trenda's oldest brother. She let go of the sleeve of the blouse she was holding and stared at her father. "C'mon, Daddy…you tryin' to tell me my mother, your wife, was a bad as—" She covered her mouth. "Ooops, I mean, she was *fast?*"

"Now, don't get me wrong; she wasn't a floosy, but she was… colorful." He slowly stood and walked over to the foot of the bed. He pointed to the antique locking cedar chest. "Come here for a minute. I need you to open this for me."

Her childhood ran back to her. As a child, she and her brothers had tried like hell to open that cedar chest, trying every combination of numbers on the combination lock their kiddie minds could think of. Although it had a keyhole in the center of the dial, none of them ever found the key. And they'd spent years looking for it, she could hardly believe she was about to be given the secret password. "You want me to open Momma's cedar chest?"

"Ummmm-hmmm."

"You got the key?"

He shook his head. "Nope...never had a key, but I know the combination."

Trenda got on her knees in front of the chest. "Okay, what is it?"

After a brief coughing fit, he grinned. "You mean you kids never figured it out? After all your trying?"

Trenda was red-faced. Back in the day, her and her brothers *did* spend a lot of their time trying to access the chest. They used to sometimes sit around and pretend it was full of treasure. Instead of denying his claim, she said, "How did you know?"

His smile grew. "Your mother was as sneaky as you guys were. She used to always leave the dial set on a particular number after she closed it. She'd remember it or sometimes write it down and check it every day. When it was changed, she knew one of you was trying to get in it."

Damn! She was slick as Vaseline! Trenda stared at the light-brown, oak wood-finished chest. "Why'd she never tell us?"

"To her, it was a game she enjoyed. She liked it so much, she would sometimes find a reason to leave the house just so you kids could try your luck."

"And you knew about it?"

"Yes, I did, but I promised your mother I wouldn't let on...I got a kick out of the whole thing, actually."

A ray of sunlight broke through the gap between the cream-colored drapes. It landed on the chest as Trenda stared at the dial. She had no idea her no-nonsense mother had a playful side. *She sure didn't play with my ass.* She turned the knob a few times. "What's the combination?"

"It's very simple; it's the number of the month of each of your kids' birthdays."

"Are you kiddin'?" She laughed as she spun the dial. "What number comes first?"

"She set the order of the numbers in the same order you three were born."

Trenda grinned, closed her eyes and shook her head. "Momma was a *trip!*" She dialed in the combination and opened the lid. For the first time in her twenty-eight years on earth, she was going to get a look inside the mystical, magical cedar chest. The smell of mothballs almost knocked her on her butt. "Dang, Daddy." She fanned her face as she stood up. "When is the last time you opened this thing?"

"Been a long time." He pointed his cane at the quilt folded on top of the other contents. "Take that out and set it on the bed. That quilt was made by your mother's grandmother. It's been in the family for almost a hundred years."

The aged quilt had more colors than a box of crayons. For a quilt its age, it was in pretty good shape. Besides a few tattered squares and frayed threads, it had held up well over the years. Trenda gently sat the heirloom on the bed. "I remember Momma used to lie this across y'alls bed in the winter. I ain't seen it since I was around eight or nine years old."

"She stopped using it around that time because it was getting too fragile. She wanted to keep it in shape for when she handed it down to you kids."

This tender side of her mother was shifting, rocking and distorting Trenda's world. She looked back inside the chest. An old sewing kit, two shoe boxes full of antique ceramic figurines, three pairs of bronzed baby shoes, a locked, black strong box and four picture albums were the extent of the contents. "Is any of this your stuff?"

"Nope...all that belonged to your mother. Hand me that blue photo album."

She moved the bamboo sewing kit, set it aside, picked up the album and handed it to her father. "That Momma's, too?"

He laid his cane on the bed, sat down, opened up the album and patted his hand on the bed. "Sit down; I want to show you something."

Trenda sat down and watched him open the album. Pictures of relatives she hadn't seen since she was a child looked back at her. "These are some old pictures."

"You got that right." He placed his hand on Trenda's hand. "Your mother made me promise not to show these next few pictures to you kids...but now I guess it's okay."

Trenda turned her body to get a better look at him. "What pictures?"

He let his eyes fall from hers to the album. "These."

When he flipped the next page, Trenda sucked in a deep breath and held it for what seemed like a century. An 8 x 10 photo almost sent her into shock. "Whoa! Whoa! Whoa! Is that *Momma*?"

A pair of sexy legs, protruding from a short, short red mini skirt grabbed her attention. Further up, a pair of awesomely perky tits, covered by a tight white cashmere sweater and a pair of deep green eyes hypnotized her. There, sitting cross-legged on a couch, holding a can of Colt 45 malt liquor, smiling seductively at the camera was Thelma Hopkins—aka—Thelma Fuqua.

Her father rubbed the picture affectionately. "I still get the same reaction when I see this picture. As you can see, your mother was a pistol."

The shock held Trenda like a steel shackle. As her father turned the pages, pictures of her mother in some of the sexiest outfits of her day made Trenda blush. She had only known her mother to wear the most conservative of outfits. *This is like somethin' out of the* Twilight Zone! *Momma was a straight hottie!* The uncanny resemblance between her and her mother was unsettling. Her stomach churned when she saw a picture of her mother, on a beach, in a black and white, polka dot bikini. Her long red hair rested on her shoulders. Her nipples were embarrassingly erect. The confidence in her face added to her natural sexiness. Just like her daughter, her eyes said it all. They could lure a fish out of water. "This is crazy, Daddy. I mean... how...when did..."

He interrupted Trenda's befuddlement. "I know this has to be a shock to you, but I felt you needed to know."

She looked up from a picture of her mother, in a tight, yellow dress, looking back over her shoulder, provocatively. Her ass was spectacular. Trenda had no doubt now where she'd gotten her great buns from. "What do I need to know?"

He looked away from a picture of his wife in a black mink coat and what appeared to be nothing else. "I wanted you to know where you came from."

His words barely registered with Trenda. The twenty or so photos of her mother's hottie days had her staggered. *Can't believe how much I look like her...damn...that's me.* "How old was Momma in these pictures?"

He glanced back at the picture of his fur-wrapped, young, future wife. "She was in her teens to early twenties in most of them." He tapped the picture of her in the mink coat. "She was about your age in this one."

Trenda looked closer at the picture. A silver cross dangled from her mother's neck, just above her impressive cleavage. "How did, I mean, I thought Momma was raised in the church. It sure don't look like it in these pictures."

"She was…but she didn't always live in the ways of the church." He smirked at Trenda. "She had what you would call a 'rebel' side. She could shake a leg Saturday night and sing in the choir on Sunday morning."

According to the pictures Trenda saw, her mother did a lot more than just shake a leg. Trenda looked down and waited for her father to turn to the last page. His hand lingered on it. "Turn the page, Daddy."

He closed his eyes. To Trenda, it looked as if he was praying. He sighed and placed his free hand on her back. "Honey, like I said, your mother had a 'rebel' side…well, actually a dark side." His eyes drilled into Trenda's. "But deep inside, your mother was a good woman. No matter what—"

"Daddy, why are you stallin'? What you tryin' to tell me?"

He stared at her for a moment and then turned the page. "This was taken a couple days after your mother's twenty-first birthday."

Trenda grabbed the album out of his hands, jumped to her feet and said, "*What the hell?*" She glared at her father. "Is this a *joke?*" An old mug shot of her mother, heavily made-up in the Atlantic City County Jail, holding up a sign under her chin with her booking ID on it, chilled Trenda's blood. It also featured a profile picture of her as well, on the same photograph. She paced the room while looking at the picture.

Her father stood up. "Honey, this was from a very dark time in your mother's life." He grabbed his cane and leaned on it. "A time she...*we* wanted to keep from her children."

A tear leaked from her eye. "What did she get arrested for?"

He walked over, opened the drapes and looked outside. "Prostitution."

Thirty

While Trenda reeled from the revelations about her mother, Nick the Dick entered the precinct four hours before the start of his shift. The stress of coming up with Anton's money made it a necessity. He sat down at a desk in the department library. *Time for a little detective work.* He logged onto the computer and Googled the *Talk-of-the-Town* tabloid website. "What a bunch of crap," he said after skimming through a few pages of scandal-ridden gossip. "Pure bullshit."

Minutes later, he found what he was looking for. After reading the entire article about the release of Trenda Fuqua, he sat back in his seat and stared at the screen. Blood rushed to his genitals as he looked at her picture. His desire to stick his dick in her almost made him forget the real reason that he needed to find her. *There'll be time for that later.*

Trying to chase her down in the streets of Baltimore would be as hard as moving a mountain with a moped. She was much too skilled to be captured easily. "I need to make her come to me...I don't have time to play cat-and-mouse-games right now." After digging through several pages of information on her criminal past, he found something of value. He tapped his ink pen on his notepad after scribbling down the address of Father Fuqua. "Sounds like a logical place to look for a newly released convict with nowhere to go."

With a full three hours before his eight-to-four graveyard shift began, he logged off of the computer. *I have plenty of time to pay the Father a visit and get back here.* The ache in his shoulder reminded him of just how urgently he needed to find his soon-to-be courier. The idea of having all the rest of his body menaced by Anton's goon was not appealing. Not even a little bit. He rubbed the wounded shoulder as he stood and walked away from the desk.

Outside in the employee parking lot, he paused before getting into his customized, burgundy Nissan Armada and ran a finger across the tinted window. *Geez, my truck is filthy.* His below-average frame was in complete contrast to the bulky SUV. It served to appease the appetite of his Napoleon complex. Being one of the shortest cops on the force kept him bombarded with "short guy" jokes. The need to feel "bigger and badder" fueled his über-machismo. He opened the door, hopped behind the wheel of his urban tank and sped out of the parking lot.

ഇരു

Wonder what that little bastard was doing here so early? Messy Marv thought as he exited the lobby restroom and watched Nick leave the building. *Just as well, it's always better to see him going than coming.* Dismissing his nemesis, Marv took the elevator up and went into his office. The investigation of Slip's murder had taken priority over his elusive green-eyed query.

Not a soul on the nursing staff was willing to discuss the photo of the tall, dark, gold-toothed visitor who was the last person to see Slip alive. Of all the people that entered Slip's ward that day, the dreadlocked man jumped out to Marv. He pursed his lips as he looked at the photo of the man. *I can tell none of those nurses wanted to talk; I'm willing to bet they were scared he was part of the*

Island Boys. Their reputation for taking out entire families of snitches is well known.

The more he examined the film and the photo in his hand, the more he was convinced the man had on a disguise. After an hour of normal investigative procedures, Marv stood up, walked across the room to his Mr. Coffee machine and poured himself a cup. The Rasta suspect in the photo from the hospital reminded him of the unsolved murders of officers Kain and Dash. And that, in turn, brought Trenda back into his thoughts.

"I just know she has the info I need to close this case." He stirred a spoonful of Splenda into his coffee. "Kind of makes me wish for the good ol' days when you could 'creatively' interrogate a suspect without worrying about getting sued or fired." He had to be honest with himself; there had been more than a few times when he had engaged in the old school way of questioning a suspect. And at that moment, he had already decided that Trenda was worth some special questioning.

₭₩

Let love be without hypocrisy. Abhor that which is evil; cleave to that which is good.

—ROMANS 12:9

"Wait a minute...*prostitution?*" Trenda almost vomited at the thought. "What the hell you mean prostitution?"

He held up a hand. "Hold on...calm down. I'm going to tell you." He pulled out his handkerchief, coughed up a wad of phlegm and put it back in his pocket. "It's not easy to talk about. I don't know how I managed to hold it in this long."

Trenda locked her eyes on him. All the years of being persecuted by her holier-than-thou parents sent a tidal wave of anger through her. *This is fucked up! He better have a real good reason for doggin' me so much.* The pain of having been called everything from a Jezebel to a tramp during her teenage years resurfaced. "Y'all crucified my ass for *way* less than that!"

"Trenda...honey...give me a chance to explain."

She turned her anger down to a simmer, stopped pacing and tossed the photo album down on the bed. It landed spread open and face down like a large, square, blue butterfly. "Go ahead... I'm listenin'."

He removed his glasses and rubbed his weary eyes. "Trenda, when your mother and I first met, we were high school sweethearts. Loved each other to death. So much so, as sophomores, we considered running off and getting married. Luckily, we weren't fool enough to try it." He clasped his hands together and sat them in his lap. "A couple of years after graduating from high school, we broke up. Me, being a baseball star at the time, left her in search of fame, fortune and...well...women."

Trenda glared at him. "So? Folks break up all the time. What's that got to do with Momma turnin' tricks?"

He pointed a finger at her and returned her glare. "Don't you talk ill of the dead; *especially* your own mother! Don't you *ever* disrespect her memory like that again. I know you had your differences with her but I will *not* allow you to bad talk her."

The fire in his cataract-covered eyes reminded her of the strong, respect-demanding father she was raised by. She eased back on some of her saltiness. But not *too* much. "I'm just sayin', I was called everything but a child of God for some of the stuff I did..."

"Trenda..." He broke eye contact with her and looked down at his hands. "Try and understand. We were both young and young people sometimes make mistakes. Your mother was devastated after I left her. She moved in with her cousin, Marlene, in New Jersey. That's when things got out of hand. From what I found out from her relatives, she decided men were too deceitful to trust and began making them pay for me breaking her heart. For three straight years, she ran the streets; nobody could slow her down. She managed to make enough money, dating different men, to live high on the hog. Her parents got so desperate, they called my folks and asked them to see if I could talk some sense into her."

Trenda folded her arms across her chest. "Let me guess; you swooped in and saved the day...I hope you don't think that makes me feel any better."

"Trenda, please." Flabbergasted at his daughter's insolence, he shook his head and continued. "Since my baseball dreams didn't pan out, and I was in a funk and looking for a job, I thought that seeing my old flame would cheer me up. I scraped up money for a bus ticket to Jersey and took off. Took me almost a month to find your mother. I found her working as a high-priced call girl in Atlantic City. Once I confronted her, she cursed me for old and new. She even tried to brain me with an empty gin bottle. But after two weeks of persistent pleading, she agreed to have dinner with me. She didn't spare my feelings at all. She told me all about her filthy, nasty world. I think she did it to hurt me as much as I had hurt her—and it worked. After finding out the things she had done with men for money, I was devastated... destroyed. My spirit was in bad shape. I remember it was a Saturday night and we had stayed up 'til sunrise taking turns blaming each other for our break up. Finally, out of desperation, I suggested we go to St. Monica's Church across the street from where we were, and let the good Lord settle our argument. Being as stubborn as she was, she didn't back down; she accepted my offer and off we went. No sleep and all. By the time the first service was over, we were both bawling like babies. The sermon seemed to have been written for us. We ended up joining that church and getting saved together. A year later we got married."

Trenda watched him pick up the album, turn it over and close it. Her patience with his explanation was wearing thin. "Where are you goin' with this drama?" More and more images of her childhood played out in her head. Being dragged to church almost every single day, being falsely accused of all manners of sins and being physically beaten by them—mostly her mother—made her fuse burn hotter and faster. "Am I supposed to be impressed by this bullshit?"

Shock registered on his face after hearing his daughter curse for the first time. "I'm not telling you this to impress you." He grabbed his can and got to his feet. "I feel it's my duty as your father to—"

"No!" She angrily wiped a tear off of her left cheek. Her mind educed the memory of how he had once beaten her with her brother's Hot Wheels race tracks for throwing up in church. He'd accused her of putting her finger down her throat when, in actuality, she had the stomach flu. After beating her into convulsions, her mother took her temperature and found out she was running a temperature of 103. The most hurtful part of that awful incident was the fact he never apologized. Her rage resurfaced. She had received nearly twice as many beatings as her brothers combined. "I'm *not* gonna stand here and let you try and white-wash the fact that y'all fuckin' abused me. Mentally *and* physically!"

"Wait…stop all that—" He grimaced and rubbed his sternum. He took a few deep breaths and sat back down on the bed. His shaky hands picked up one of the bottles of pills on his nightstand, shook two white tablets out and tossed them down his throat. Then he opened the bottle of water and took a swallow, wiping a dribble of water off of his chin.

Moments later, his breathing returned to normal. "We have to talk about this like adults."

I can't believe this shit... The fact that she had broken her promise to stop cursing helped her blood pressure rise. "You know what?" She closed her eyes, shook her head and walked away from him. "I gotta go."

Thirty-One

Twenty minutes after Trenda stormed out of her father's house, Nick exited the freeway and entered Randallstown. While sitting at a red light, he rubbed his aching shoulder. The amount of money he stood to make off of allowing the Russians to peddle their dope in the city was impossible to turn down. *I can make enough money off those Ruskies in two months to pay for my dream-spread in Montana in cash*, he thought as the light turned green. "And I'm not about to kill this golden goose."

He slowed down as he turned onto Fieldstone Road and looked for Father Fuqua's address. *Here we go.* He parked a few houses down, across the street from the Fuqua house. He slipped on his dark sunglasses and hopped out of his truck. The upscale neighborhood was quiet. From the lack of vehicles parked in the driveways, he deducted that most of the residents were at work.

After making sure he wasn't being watched, he crossed the street, opened the gate and walked up to Father Fuqua's door and rang the bell. Impatient after no response, he pressed the bell again. *Sure hope I didn't drive all the way over here for noth—*

Before he could turn to leave, he heard a gravelly voice. "Who is it?"

Good, he's home. "Mr. Fuqua?"

He listened as the front door opened. "That's me, who are you?"

Nick fixed him with a fake smile. "Hello, Mr. Fuqua, I'm Jeff Wilson; a good friend of your daughter."

"Okay, Mr. Wilson, how can I help you?"

Nick strained to see the man's face behind the wire mesh design of the security gate. "I'd like to talk to Trenda if I can. Have you seen her? I heard she was back in town."

"Hmmm, I'm sorry, Mr. Wilson, but I can't answer that without her permission. You want to leave me your information? If I hear from her, I can pass it on."

Nick rubbed his itching shoulder wound. "I would *really* like to speak to her... I have a job opportunity for her that I can't hold onto much longer."

"That's nice, Mr. Wilson, but still..."

This old bastard is really getting under my skin. "I totally understand your position, Mr. Fuqua, but I'd *really* like to help her out...she and I were good friends before her...you know, troubles began." He took a step closer to the gate. "Can I trouble you to use your restroom? I have a long drive back to Jersey."

For a moment, he thought the old man was going to deny him, but then he heard the deadbolt unlock. "Okay...I guess that's a long way to go between rest stops. I'll get you some paper and a pen so you can leave her your information;"

"Thank you, sir," Nick said as he fixed the elderly man with a plastic smile. *Looks like he's been crying.* "This sure beats stopping at one of those filthy gas station bathrooms."

"Any friend of my daughter is a friend of the family." He pointed down the hallway. "It's the second door to your right."

Nick, using his cop's observation skills, noticed a black purse on the table next to him as he entered the house. When Mr. Fuqua turned his back, Nick took a peek inside the open purse. *Interesting...that deserves my attention. It can't belong to his dead wife.* A brown wallet sat inside among a set of green rosary beads and a few other items. In one quick motion, he pulled out the wallet and tucked it under his red and black, plaid, lumberjack jacket. "Thanks a million for your hospitality, sir."

"No problem, son." He pointed to the dining room table. "I left a pad and pen here so you can write down your phone number."

Nick nodded. "Thanks again, sir." After locking the bathroom door, he quickly pulled out the wallet and opened it up. He grinned. *Nick, you are one awesome cop!* Inside the cash-packed wallet was a parolee ID card from BCDC. Trenda's unforgettable face was embedded in it. "Got you, convict." He removed her ID and cash and then put it in his pocket. After that, he closed up the wallet, laid it on the sink and took a leak. His confidence soared because of his good luck. That fact that he had stumbled upon Trenda and was able to get Barney to cooperate had him on a natural high. After washing his hands, he tucked the wallet back inside his jacket, under his arm. Father Fuqua was in the kitchen on the phone. Nick walked to the dining room table and wrote down his cell phone number.

He then stuck his head inside the kitchen door and said, "Thanks again. Tell your daughter I said hi."

Father Fuqua took a few steps in Nick's direction as Nick opened the front door and gate. "Hey, did you leave your number for her?"

Nick slipped on his dark shades. "I sure did."

ଛୠ

"This is some *bullshit!*" Trenda said as she walked onto the playground of St. Mary's Catholic School. She hadn't been there since she was a child. After bursting out of her father's house, she'd walked aimlessly for three blocks until she stopped at her old school. She sat down on the two-foot-high perimeter wall surrounding the sandbox. She looked up at the figure of St. Mary etched into the tall clock tower. *I bet you ain't ever had to go through all the crap I'm goin' through.*

After getting no response from the silent sculpture, Trenda put her head in her hands. The sound of the cars driving by the deserted school began to fade, replaced by an echoed sound of her father saying "Prostitution" in her head. The more she tried to shake the image of her mother issuing blowjobs and being screwed by strange men, the more it soured her stomach. *I need to call me a cab and get the hell out of here.*

Her head snapped up out of her hands. She realized she didn't have her cell phone with her. "Where is my purse?" after a moment's thought, she recalled leaving the house so fast that she had forgotten to pick it up. "And just my luck, my phone's inside my damned purse." With no alternative to facing her father again, she stood, brushed sand off of her ass and began walking back to the house. The few fond memories she had of the old neighborhood were dulled by her anger. She was so lost in her thoughts that she failed to recognize the pale-faced, red-haired man in the customized SUV that had pulled over a few yards ahead of her.

೫ಛ

"*Unbelievable!* I need to go buy a friggin' lottery ticket," Nick said as he pulled over and watched his prey walk his way. He quickly took her wallet and put it under his seat. Recollections of how Darius used to brag about how good she was at moving dope surfaced. *He used to say the only thing better than her trafficking skills were her blowjobs. Once she gets me my money, I'll take a sample of that as well.* Before she could recognize him, he got out, walked around the rear of his truck and waited for her. "Hello, ma'am."

Startled, Trenda stopped and took a step backwards. "What the...what you doin' out this way, cop?"

He stepped onto the sidewalk, a few feet away from her. "Oh, just visiting a friend. How about you?"

Trenda took an additional step back from him. "Minding my own business. Why you askin'?"

God, she has some nice tits, he thought as his eyes devoured her. "Hey, no need to get defensive. All I want to do is talk..."

"About what?"

He did his best to make his smile sincere. "Trenda, look; just give me ten minutes of your time...I promise it'll be worthwhile to you."

She held off on answering until the engine noise of a passing bus subsided. "You got me mixed up with one of those street walkin' chicks back in the hood. I'm not the one. You need to go somewhere with that mess. I'm gone."

He held up both his hands. "Hold up! Hold up!" He shook his head and took a step toward her. "I'm not propositioning you, Ms. Fuqua; well, not for what you're thinking anyway."

ঠব্দ

What is this fool up to? Trenda wondered as she kept a few feet between them. She looked around at the thinning traffic. Not more than a handful of people were within half a block of them. Behind Nick, the sun sought the horizon. Her simmering anger was on its way to being reheated. "Look, Officer, I'm not lookin' for *any* kind of trouble. Not even a little bit. So, you might wanna step to the side so I can go about my business."

A shade of red seeped into his pale, Irish complexion. "The only way you would run the risk of trouble is if you *don't* calm your ass down and listen to what I have to say."

Oh, this fool is on one! She glared at him. "Excuse me? What makes you think I wanna hear anything you have to say? Man, if you not arrestin' me, I'm gone."

He looked around, then locked eyes with her. "Enough of this bullshit." He reached in his pocket and flashed her parolee ID. "This get your attention?"

Her eyes widened. "*Hey!*" She attempted to snatch it out of his hand, but he jerked it back just in time. "Gimme that! How'd you get my ID?"

He tucked it into his back pocket, walked over and opened the passenger door. "I found it while I was having a nice chat with your dad."

Her heart almost stopped. She glared and pointed at him. "What the *fuck* you doin', talkin' to my father?"

"Easy, lady, easy." He opened the passenger door of his truck. "I'll tell you more once you get inside."

Her first inclination was to walk away and see what he would do. But after finding out that trying to walk the path of the righteous wasn't all it was cracked up to be, she reconsidered. While glowering at him, she walked over and got inside. *If he tries to drive off with me in here, I'm bailing out.*

"Now, that wasn't that bad, was it?" he asked after closing the door. "This won't take long."

She watched him walk around the vehicle and get in. She tried to lower the window, but it was locked. Instead, she just kept her hand on the door handle. The overwhelming aroma of pine flooded her nostrils. She looked over her right shoulder and saw a trio of tree-shaped air fresheners hanging from the coat hanger clip. She turned away and looked at him. "What you want with me, Nick?"

His eyes strip-searched her. He then grinned. "You're not wearing a wire, are you?"

Unmoved by his attempt at humor, her cold reply was, "No."

"Okay, just kidding...I'll cut straight to the chase. I need you to move some ingredients for me."

She shifted in her seat in order to get a good look at him. "You must be high; how you gonna ask me to do some shit like that, *knowin'* I just got out of jail? Either that or you think I'm stupid." She pointed at him. "*You* must be the one wearin' a wire. And just in case you are, my answer is 'hell no!'"

"Let me assure you..." He took off his jacket and handed it to her. Then he lifted up his shirt and showed her his lean, pale midsection. "I'm not wired."

She tossed his coat back to him as if it was covered in feces. "What you doin'? Put your clothes on!"

He took his jacket and tossed it onto the backseat. "I'm just trying to make you comfortable. We're going to have to learn to trust one another."

She gripped the door handle tighter. "What you mean by that? I ain't agreed on a damn thing. And to be honest, I have no desire to get involved with you or any other cop." She pulled the handle and prepared to get out. "Good luck findin' a new recruit."

His mood changed like a cash register. "Close that door and sit your ass *down!*"

Oh hell no! Time for me to cut out. She saw a high level of anger in his crimson face. "You need to—"

Before she could finish her statement, his hand was around her throat. "Look, convict, I don't have time to play—"

She caught him by surprise with a left uppercut to the chin.

Due to her poor positioning, it didn't pack much punch. *Gonna kill this muthafucka!*

She fought back as much as she could, but he had leverage and strength on his side. With the tinted windows, and lack of traffic, no one could see what was going on inside the truck. After she managed to scratch the side of his neck, he wrapped both hands around her throat and squeezed tighter. "*Bitch!* If you…don't stop…struggling…I'm going to…kill you…" He put his face inches from hers. "…*and* your father."

As if someone had hit her off switch, Trenda's hands fell. She read truth in his eyes. From what she'd heard about him in the streets, he was responsible for more than a few missing persons. It took every bit of her restraint to keep from fighting him to the death. *Fuck! If only I had Baby!* Realizing she was in a no-win situation, she slowed her breathing and did her best to calm down. "Let go of me, trick!"

"If you try and run off when I let you go, I'll keep my promise. You got that, *trick*?"

Trenda said nothing as he let go of her neck. She breathed hard through her nose with anger. From somewhere deep within, *Psalm 40:12* leaped into her mind:

For troubles without number surround me; my sins have overtaken me, and I cannot see. They are more than the hairs of my head, and my heart fails within me.

The fact that she was face-to-face with a certified killer who was a direct threat to her father helped calm her down. *This ain't the time to feel sorry for myself.* She rubbed her sore neck. "What the fuck you want wit' me?"

Thirty-Two

"How you feeling, baby?" Beverly's mother, Sylvia, asked. She gently rubbed Beverly's forehead. "Did you get enough to eat?"

Beverly scratched her handcuffed wrist. "I'm fine, Mom." She then looked at her barely touched hospital dinner. "I'm just not crazy about hospital lasagna."

Sylvia opened her large gold purse and pulled out a PayDay candy bar. She smiled and held it out to her eldest daughter. "I know you like these."

Beverly moved her hair out of her face with her free hand, careful of her bandaged nose, gave his mother a slight smile and accepted the treat. "Now *this* I can eat anytime."

After hearing about her daughter's accident and the suspected reason for the crash, Sylvia decided against telling the rest of her family what had happened. She wanted to see what state of mind her daughter was in for herself. After talking to Dr. Moyer, she found Beverly was doing better than he'd expected, but wasn't ready to be released yet. As Beverly opened the candy bar, Sylvia moved the dinner tray to the side. "DJ misses you..."

Beverly paused before taking her first bite. "I miss him, too..." The image of his cute baby-face reminded her of her dead husband. A whirlpool of emotions swirled inside her. Before it could send her off into a panic, her Ativan medication wrestled it to the ground. She took a bite of the candy bar. "I can't wait to get home to him."

Sylvia placed her hands in Beverly's hair and began braiding it into a ponytail. "We all hope you can get home soon."

Beverly stared at the candy bar as she slowly chewed. The dull pain from her broken nose increased with each bite. An uncomfortable silence sat between them. She couldn't find a way to explain her situation to her prudish mother. Never had anyone in her family ever been admitted to the psych ward. That embarrassment was all the more reason to want to see Trenda in a pine box. A whisper escaped her. "Dirty cunt."

Sylvia paused her braiding. "What did you say, Bev?"

Oh shit! Almost forgot she was here. Beverly regained her composure. "Nothing...I was just thinking out loud."

She resumed braiding. "Do you feel like talking about what happened?"

Beverly took another bite. "Not right now...I'm still trying to process everything..."

Sylvia finished the ponytail and let it go. "Okay, honey." She walked back over to the side of the bed and looked at her watch. "Visiting hours are over. I'm going to head back to my hotel. I'll come see you tomorrow."

Beverly looked her in the eye. "You have a room?"

Sylvia smirked at her. "Of course! Did you think I was going to leave my baby here all alone? Your nurse told me they were going to move you to a new location tomorrow. It's supposed to be better suited for people in your...condition. Doesn't that sound good?"

Even through the fog of her drug-induced calmness, a piece of her was still terrified at the idea of being in Baltimore. Fortunately, her medication kept her panic in check. "Yes...I'm looking forward to it."

A male nurse stuck his head in the door and frowned. "I'm sorry, folks. I really hate to be the bad guy but visiting hours are over."

Beverly nodded. "That's okay. We were just saying our goodbyes."

ဆာ

As Beverly toiled with the idea of how to satisfy her homicidal appetite, Trenda was in the middle of a dance with the devil. Nick lifted his eyes from her tits to her face. "All I need you to do, friend, is find me a buyer for some high-grade horse."

She glowered at him. "Why you need me for that? I'm sure you have plenty of workers in the hood that can hook you up."

"Okay, maybe I didn't make myself clear; I need this to happen *yesterday*. And from what I understand, you have a knack for getting deals like this done."

Her facial expression didn't change a bit. She knew her reputation as one of the best dope transporters on the east coast was well-earned. Her many transactions put her in close quarters with some of the most connected hustlers in the criminal underworld. "That was true a while back. Did you forget I've been locked up for the past couple of years? I've been out the game too long."

"Well, guess what?" He leaned closer to her. "That just means you have to get to work ASAP. I'm sure there are enough dope-dealing scumbags out there for you to move my goods."

God must really hate me! She continued to stare Nick down. Her options were nil. Even though she was pissed off at her father, he didn't deserve to be harmed by this crooked asshole. "What if I don't?"

He chuckled and turned away from her. He looked out of his window at a group of well-to-do looking teenagers walking across the street. "I guess I'd be forced to make you an orphan," he said and turned back to her. "And I'm sure you'd hate to have to add making funeral arraignments for your feeble old man to your list of things to do."

A part of her knew she was going to have to acquiesce to his demands, but needed to hear his threats out loud. "If I do this, you know you're gonna have to cover me. I don't wanna be harassed by none of your pig friends."

A confident grin spread across his face. "Done. As long as you play by my rules, you won't have to worry about anybody on the streets but me." He pulled an ink pen and an old gas receipt out of his center console, and then scribbled a phone number on the receipt and held it out to her. "That's my private line. Use that number to contact me. And don't call me unless it's important."

She snatched the paper and stuffed it in her pocket. Internal warning signals blared at her, but she knew what she had to do. She was also well aware that once one of these street sharks got their teeth into you, they seldom let go. She'd learned that firsthand from her dealings with Darius. Early in her hustling career, during her third drug-running assignment, he'd pulled her over for not signaling during a turn. While questioning her, he spotted an empty pack of Zig-Zags on the floor of her car. The car belonged to a local mid-level cocaine dealer who had talked her into delivering an ounce of coke to a client in Georgetown. Darius decided to search the vehicle. After feeling her up in the guise of searching her, he went through the car and found the dope hidden in a box of tampons in her purse. Instead of arresting her, Darius gave her the option of going to jail or sucking him off. She chose option number two. In the process, he let her go and talked/threatened her into being his personal illegal merchandise courier and sex provider. She was so scared and relieved, she agreed. For nearly six years he owned her.

Shaking herself out of that memory, she bravely faced her new devil. "So when, and how, is this supposed to go down?"

"Meet me at the Harbor tonight at eleven. I'll fill you in then."

Trenda saw lust building in his eyes as he struggled to keep from looking at her tits. She knew that look and just how to use it. Even after two years of hibernation, she was impressed at the power of her sexual magnetism. She took a deep breath, giving him a nice look at her breasts. "Whatever...I'll be there," she said, rubbing her sore neck. "We gotta get one thing straight right now; I don't like nobody puttin' hands on me...*nobody*."

He looked up from her chest. "Well, as long as you do what you're told, you won't have that problem." He went into his breast pocket, pulled out a City of Baltimore police officer business card with his name and info on it out and handed it to her. "If you do happen to get pulled over by one of my fellow officers, give him this and ask them to give me a call. You got that?"

Her eyes locked on his. "Yeah, I got it... Can I go now?"

He hit the unlock button and freed her. "Sure! Give my regards to your dad."

"Oh, and can I get my ID card back?"

He snapped his fingers. "Oh, sure." He then pulled it out of his back pocket and dangled it in front of her. "Anything for my new employee."

She snatched it out of his hand, ignored his last statement, opened the door, and got out. *No wonder everybody calls him a dick.*

ಸಾಧ

What a hot slut! He reached under the seat, pulled out her wallet, let the window down, started the truck and backed up to her. "I guess there's no harm in giving her back her wallet...sans cash." After he caught up with her, he yelled out the window, "Did you lose this?" He tossed the wallet out and drove off.

ಸಾಧ

"What's that?" she said as she stepped out of the way of whatever it was he threw at her. After looking at it for a moment, she seethed with anger. She picked up her new wallet and brushed it off. "Awww, shit." She grimaced with anger as she opened her cash-free wallet. "Bastard even took my check…"

On the way back to her father's house, she rehearsed what she was going to say to him. After being robbed by Nick, she could no longer afford the hotel. And until she found out what the deal was Nick had in mind, she couldn't count on him paying her right or at all. Having cussed her father out didn't help matters much. If she couldn't reconcile her differences with her father, she would be homeless. The thought of having to move into a shelter like *BOWS* didn't appeal to her at all. Not even a little bit.

She stopped in front of the house. A motion sensor security light came on. Even in that light, the house looked dark, lonely. The only interior light shining came from the upstairs bathroom window. *Why I gotta feel so guilty? I ain't the one who lied.* Her sense of fairness kicked in. She had to admit that she hadn't been the most saintly child. Her transgressions ran as deep, if not deeper, than her mother's. *I'm pretty sure Momma ain't killed nobody.* The walk from the gate to the front door seemed like a death march.

As she lifted her hand to ring the bell, her father's voice startled her. He was completely cloaked by the downstairs darkness. "I'm glad you came back." He unlocked the security gate and opened it. "When the motion light came on, I looked out the window and saw you standing by the gate. I was watching and praying you would come in."

Thirty-Three

Outside United Airlines, in the passenger loading zone, Lollie wrapped her arms around her fiancé. "Hi, baby!" Walter gave her a quick kiss. "Hello to you. Sure glad to finally get to hold my chocolate treat. It's been *way* too long."

Lollie tingled as his hand slid down her oversized t-shirt and rubbed her round butt. The tight, lavender yoga pants underneath her white t-shirt accentuated her ass magnificently. They hadn't touched each other in over six weeks. Her coochie twitched with sexual anticipation. She separated from him, smiled, and pointed at his one suitcase. "Is that all you packed?"

He collapsed the telescopic handle, lifted the bag and tossed it into the trunk. "Yup. Didn't have time to pack anymore. I literally ran away from home. I know my sister is gonna kill me. We are supposed to meet in the morning and go over the bids she received from contractors who want to replace the roof on the Compton building."

Lollie handed him the car keys. "Ohhhh! You know she is gonna be extra pissed at you! That girl—"

Walter placed a finger to her lips. "Shhhh, no shop talk; get in the car so we can go play 'house.'"

She grinned and opened the passenger door. "Aye, aye, Captain!"

As he navigated out of the airport, Walter placed his hand on Lollie's thigh. "What's for dinner?"

"What you wanna eat?"

He showed her all of his teeth. "That's too easy." He eased his hand up her thigh, and down to her treasure chest. "I haven't seen you in over a month; take a wild guess what I want to 'eat'."

She smirked and took his hand from between her legs. "You're right; that was too easy. I think I'm going to make you wait a bit longer."

He entered the freeway. "Wait a minute, I was just kidding! You can't hold out from me...not now!"

She laughed. "I don't see why not? You should be nice and empty."

"How do you figure that?"

She reached over and stroked his jaw with the back of her hand. "Why don't you ask your laptop that question?"

He shook his head. "Oh no-the-hell-you-didn't go there!"

"I sure the hell did." She rubbed the back of his neck, admiring the neatness of his freshly-lined haircut. "I hope you were able to run that thing through a dishwasher or something."

His genitalia shifted with thoughts of their last webcam episode. He was amazed at how much the mention of Trenda had added to their session. "I'm afraid the dishwasher won't work. It's going to need a steam cleaner, a car wash *and* Jesus."

It was her turn to laugh. "You are a bona fide fool!"

"I hear that a lot. By the way, did you book us a room?"

"No...I thought we were going to my uncle's house. Aren't we?"

"Not tonight." He looked at her out the corner of his eye. "The way I'm going to fuck you tonight would definitely get us kicked out of their house."

"You are *so* nasty."

"Yes, I concur."

"Speaking of nasty, Mya—I mean, *Trenda*, gave me her number. She wants you to give her call."

"Wha? Are you serious? Did she say what she wanted?"

"Far as I know, she just wanted to say hi. You wanna talk to her?"

Walter's mind went into overdrive. The look on Lollie's face told him that she was reading his mind. They were slowly coming to grips with the fact that they both got turned on by threesomes. Although Trenda was the only live version they had tried, so far, they'd had numerous conversations and cybersex bouts laced with ménage à trois scenarios. "Yeah...give her a call."

ဆဝ္ဆ

After a couple of hours of confessions, prayers and soul-baring, Trenda and her father managed to come to grips with the wrong on both their parts. Things were far from perfect in her book, but she at least found enough solace to accept his offer to move in. He nodded off for the tenth time while sitting in his recliner, holding his Bible. Trenda, once again, called his name to wake him. "Daddy...*Daddy*." She got up from the loveseat, walked over and shook his shoulder. She cringed. His bones, even under his robe and white thermal shirt, felt too close to the surface. "Wake up and go to bed."

"Hmmmm?" He blinked his eyes and wiped a string of saliva off of the corner of his mouth. "I'm not sleepy."

The grandfather clock in the far corner of the dining room chimed nine times. A commercial promoting the newest hybrid vehicle by Chevrolet played at low volume on the TV. It was an upgraded model from the old TV that had sat there in front of her father's favorite chair for decades. She gazed at her father and sighed. The thought of Nick putting hands on him kept a stress knot in her belly. "It's two hours past your bed time. Get on up and go to bed."

He sat his Bible on the small, marble table next to his chair, wrapped his gnarled hands around the arms of the chair, leaned forward and got to his feet. He looked at her. "Okay...I'm going. What are you going to do tonight?"

"I need to get back to my room and get my stuff..." She furrowed her eyebrows and looked away from him. *How am I gonna get back to the hotel? That trick took all the money I had!*

"What's the matter?" He picked his glasses off of the table and put them on. "What were you saying about getting your stuff?"

She ran a hand through her hair. "Yeah...I need to go check out but." She had to force herself to look him in the eye. "I'm broke...I think I left the money I had back at the hotel. You got a few bucks I can borrow so I can catch the bus?"

He pointed toward the wall between the living room and dining room. There, she saw the brass key-shaped key holder that her father hung there when she was a child. "Get that key ring with the blue rabbit's foot on it and bring it here."

Rabbit's foot? She walked over and looked at two sets of keys. One set had several keys on it and a strange-looking black remote control. She grabbed that set of keys and inspected the odd key fob. She turned it over and stopped in her tracks. On the other side, she saw the unmistakable Mercedes Benz emblem. "Ooo-oohhh wee...must be nice." She then put that set back and grabbed the rabbit-footed set. It had only three keys on it and a remote control. Unfortunately, there was no Mercedes emblem on it. She walked over and held the keys out to her father. "Here."

He pushed the keys back to her. "You said you need a ride; take your mother's car. It's in the garage."

A thousand thoughts ran through her head, the first was that she had no driver's license. "Wait, Daddy. You want me to drive Momma's car? Maybe I can just wait and have you take me in the mornin'."

He shook his head and then coughed up into his trusty hand-kerchief. "There's no need for that. You can drive yourself; she left the car to you, too."

Tremors went through her body. Emotion after emotion hopped on and off her heart. The woman she had detested for most of her life, had yet again that day, reached out and touched her. "Daddy..." She stared at the keys in her hands. "Why—"

He held his hand up and stopped her. "Trenda, how about you just go get your things and then we can finish this discussion in the morning?"

She looked at the smile on his face. "Okay...I'll be back in a little while."

"Wait a minute; follow me." He grabbed his cane, walked over to the mantel, picked up his wallet and pulled out a few bills. "Here you go. I don't know how much gas is in it."

"I don't need this much," she said as she looked at the pair of twenty-dollar bills in his hand. "I ain't gotta drive that far."

"Take it. Go have a little fun. When's the last time you went to the movies or visited one of your friends?" He pressed the money into her hand. "*Take it.*"

Her hand slowly curled around the bills. She still battled with the anger over their sordid past, but it was beginning to lose its hold on her. "Thanks, Daddy. I'll try and not wake you when I get back." She then wrapped her arms around him. "Get you some rest."

"I will." He paused and pointed at the ceiling. "Oh, did I tell you your friend Jeff stopped by? He left a number for you to call on the table; he has a job offer for you."

After a few moments of questioning, It only took her a minute to deduce that "Jeff" was really Nick, and the number was actually the same number he had given her earlier. The urgent need to meet up with him on time far outweighed the need to check out of her room. The responsibility of protecting her family from her drama swirled in her head as well. *I'm gettin' sick of these dirty cops.* "Thanks, Daddy. I'll give him a call later."

‟ксә

"Wait a *minute!*" After unlocking the garage door and turning on the light, she lost her breath. Underneath the glowing fluorescent lights was a white Mercedes Benz. It looked brand new and was as sexy as soul singer, Sade. "Oh shit..." She whispered as she walked over and peeked in at the black leather interior. A silver cross hung from the rearview mirror. "Looks like this is the show-off-for-the-church-folks car."

Next to the Benz was a silver Buick LaSabre. She inspected the three-year-old car. A thin layer of dust coated it. *This is definitely Momma's style; plain and simple.* The fact that she didn't have a driver's license made her hesitate before getting in. *No need in worryin' about that, considerin' what you about to get into.* She hit the unlock button on the remote and opened the door. The smell of the burgundy leather interior and stale air rushed past her nose. She sat behind the wheel and started the car. It cranked slowly. "C'mon, baby, start for me." After one slower crank, it fired up. Lights filled the dashboard and chimes filled her ears. She studied the dash. The car had half a tank of gas, low windshield wiper fluid and according to the small sticker on the top left of the windshield, was due for an oil change.

When she grabbed the mirror to adjust it, the eyes of her mother stared back at her. A silver cross similar to the one in the Mercedes hung from the mirror. For a fleeting moment, she accepted just how much she favored her late mom. A touch of anger returned. *At least I'm not a hoe.* She pressed the garage door opener on the visor, put on her seatbelt and backed out. Thirty minutes later, after allowing the final charges to go onto Lollie's credit card and checking out of her room, she sat in the car, staring at the dangling cross. In less than an hour, she was due to meet up with Nick. That fact filled her with anxiety. She knew this meeting was akin to becoming roommates with the devil.

‽℞

As Trenda checked out of her room, Nick watched Barney's truck pull into the alley behind the Barnes & Noble bookstore. Nick walked over before Barney could get out. He tapped on the passenger window. Barney let the window down, leaned over and said, "Let's make this quick. I'm not crazy about being out in public under these circumstances."

"You must be reading my mind." Nick looked down at a box of Alta Gracia Irish Crème Cigarillos on the floor, then back at Barney. "I thought you said you quit smoking cigars last summer?"

Barney's face soured. "That's yours."

"Well, now." Nick opened the door, sat down and picked up the box. Underneath the first layer of cigars in the fifty-count box, he saw a rectangular, plastic-wrapped brick of dope. "This all you could get?"

Barney scowled. "I told you moving that crap out of evidence is harder that pushing an elephant through a needle eye. But you should be happy to know that, that's a kilo of pure Afghani Heroin; after it's cut, it's easily worth over a hundred grand."

Holy smokes and Jesus! Nick thought as he gazed at his goods. *This will take care of a lot of problems.* "This'll do...for now."

"For now?" Barney's eyes narrowed. "What do you mean, *for*

now? This is it; we made a deal. You said you would gimme back that USB drive you stole from me. Where is it?"

He smirked at the stressed old man, reached into his breast pocket and handed him the drive. "Here you go."

Barney looked at the drive, then into Nick's face. "And you didn't copy any of the data, did you?"

He has to know I copied every bit of information on that drive, Nick thought as he grinned, took one of the cigars and inhaled the sweet aroma. "You know how these things work. You'll just have to 'trust' me."

Cigar box in hand, he got out of Barney's truck and watched him drive off. "Sick old bastard." He walked back to his squad car, put the box on the passenger seat, pushed in the lighter and waited for it to heat up. He checked his watch. "Ms. Fuqua should be here shortly." The cigarette lighter popped out. He fired up the cigar and looked around. "She sure as hell better not flake out on me."

The dull ache in his wounded shoulder reminded him of just how badly he needed her. He took a few puffs off the cigar. Normally he didn't smoke on duty, but his nerves needed calming. The fact that Trenda had been off of the streets for a while posed a bit of a problem for him. He couldn't help but wonder what he would do if she wasn't able to move his smack before the Russians' deadline. A tugboat's horn sounded in the distance. *I better move someplace where she can see me, especially since I don't have a phone number for her.* He flicked his cigar down the alley, started the car and moved to the main road.

Thirty-Four

Where is this fool? Trenda thought as she drove past Camden Yards. Although a lot of the faces had changed on the area streets, she saw much of the game remained the same. Hustlers, pimps, whores and dope addicts still did what they did for a living. Some of them she knew; some of them looked like fresh faces.

A dangerous sense of excitement crept over her. The lure of the streets was fighting to control her thoughts. Yeah, she had a seething hatred of Nick, but she had to admit, she was more at home in the street life than anywhere else.

Watch and pray so that you will not fall into temptation. The spirit is willing, but the body is weak.

—MARK 14:38

"Yeah, I feel you, Mark." She saw a police car cruising along the street, a block ahead of her. She started to speed up to see if it was Nick but hesitated. *What if it's not him and I get pulled over?* After a moment of indecision, she let her credo, "if you scared, buy a dog," decide for her. She followed until a red light caught both of them. She then pulled next to the squad car and looked at the driver. *Yup, that's him...lookin' like a broke Michael Rapaport.*

He motioned for her to follow. They drove for about ten minutes, in and out of various West Baltimore neighborhoods. Finally, in a particularly rundown section of town, he pulled over in front of a boarded-up brick building. One-third of the structure had been damaged by a fire long ago and never repaired. Both sides of the street had nothing but vacated premises. Due to copper thieves stealing the copper wire from the street lights, the area was bathed in darkness. With no residents to call and complain, the city didn't put a priority on repairing the lights. She pulled up next to him and rolled down the passenger side window. "We stoppin' here?"

"Pull up in front of me and park."

She rolled her window up, pulled in front of him and shut off the engine. Seconds later, Nick turned off his lights. It was as dark as a tomb outside. "What the hell?"

He walked over, tapped on her window and motioned for her to let it down. "Step out the car and bring your purse."

Accustomed to unusual dealings with cops, she did what he said. After she took a seat in the back of the squad car, he got in the driver's seat and turned on the dome light. On the floor, she saw a black, insulated lunch bag. "So, what's up?"

He turned down the volume of his two-way radio. "Open that lunch bag on the floor."

Trenda sat her purse next to her, picked up the bag, unzipped it and opened it up. The brick of heroin, two sandwiches and a red apple sat inside. The brick took her back to a dark time in her life. A time when she handled merchandise like that on a regular basis. A time filled with thrills, cash and danger. A time she secretly loved. *You know as soon as you touch this dope, you back in the game.* She ignored the pleas of her conscience. The reality of the danger her family would be in if she refused overrode the unlawfulness of the situation. She picked up the plastic-wrapped package. "What you wanna do with this?"

"I need you to go and turn that into fifty-grand for me."

She inspected the brick. *Looks like some high-grade shit.* "I dunno…gonna take a while. Don't know who the money players are these days."

He turned off the light and looked at her through the mesh screen dividing them. "Here's the thing; I need it done by next week."

She snapped her head around to face him. "You must be high! How you expect me to do that? I told you, I don't have my same connections no more!"

He looked at his watch. "Well, I suppose that means you need to get your ass to work, ASAP." His mouth twisted into a cold grin. "That is, unless you don't care much for your family's good health. That reminds me; have you seen your new niece? I heard from a good source that she looks *just* like you."

The threatening, anonymous letter she'd received while in The Cock flashed in her mind. Mention of her niece was also made in that letter. So was the term "family's good health." Before exploding with anger, she analyzed the information. She locked eyes with him and imagined how much he would bleed if she got the pleasure of severing his jugular. She flipped the script and cooled down. "We ain't gotta talk about my family; this is strictly business."

To her, he looked to have been knocked off kilter by her calmness. His hardened face cracked and shifted. "Good…good…no need in messing up our friendship over misunderstandings."

Ignoring his sarcasm, she continued her coolness. "I'm gonna need some stuff to even have a chance of gettin' this done."

"Stuff like what?"

"For one thing, cash. You robbed me for all I had."

He chuckled. "Oh that." He went into his pocket, pulled out her check, rolled it up and pushed it through the mesh screen. "There you go."

She took the check and unrolled it. "What about my cash?"

He shrugged. "What cash? I didn't take any cash. Maybe your pops 'borrowed' it from you."

Again, she had to restrain her temper. *Okay, I see this asshole is gonna be extra difficult.* "Fuck it." She took the brick and tucked it in her purse. "What am I gonna get out of this?"

"Well, besides being able to sleep peacefully, knowing your family is safe, I'll pay you the going rate; five percent of the sale price."

"Wait a minute; you know it's always been at least ten percent. Don't even try and tell me you didn't know that."

He turned up the volume on his radio after hearing a call for him. "Times are hard, sweetie. I would say take it or leave it, but we both know that's not an option. I pay on delivery."

She shook her head. "You know you wrong. Plus I'm supposed to get half up front and half on delivery."

He returned a call to dispatch and started the engine. "The game has changed. I'm not Darius. Get used to it. Also, give me your number. Don't forget to *only* call me on my private line number I gave you. We need to stay in touch. I expect to hear from you on a daily basis. You *really* wouldn't want me to have to come looking for you."

"555-4386." She glared at him as he wrote down her number. After snapping her purse closed, she waited for him to open the door so she could get out of the car. *This is the whackest deal I ever agreed to,* she thought as Nick turned on his headlights. She jumped as a pair of scrawny black cats scurried from underneath her car. *Wish I could run off from my problems like them cats.* She went to the trunk, opened it, lifted the cover off the spare tire and stashed the brick underneath it.

As she got inside her car, Nick pulled from behind her and sped off. Before starting the car, she opened her purse and got her cell phone. "Got a lot of work to do…gonna need some help." She searched her memory for the number of one of her very best friends, Mai Tai. She was a Filipino hooker from the Bronx she had met fifteen years ago. Twenty years older than Trenda, she had taken Trenda under her wing and schooled her in the ways of the streets. Even more importantly, she had given Trenda her first butterfly knife she affectionately called "Baby."

Thirty-Five

"Now that we're settled in, time for me to call up our friend, Trenda," Walter said as he kicked off his loafers. The Pier 5 hotel he'd booked for him and Lollie was his favorite place to stay in Maryland. He picked his phone off of the desk as Lollie sat on the gigantic bed and pulled off her shoes. A bottle of champagne sat in a silver bucket of ice next to the bed. He walked over and twisted the bottle around so he could read the label. Veuve Clicquot Ponsardin...*it's not Cristal, but it'll do,* he thought as he made the call to Trenda.

಄಄಄

"I don't know who this is," Trenda said as she stared at the phone number on her cell phone display. "Hopefully it's a money call... Hello?"

"Well, hello, stranger! How have you been?"

A small smile grew as she turned on her headlights and pulled off. "I just know this ain't Mr. Secrease."

"The one and only! I guess it would be pointless to ask what you've been up to."

Trenda made her way out of the ghost town Nick had led her into. "I see you still know how to charm a girl."

"I'm glad to see it still works on you."

She pulled her phone off of her ear as a police car crossed the intersection in front of her. I better pull over. *Can't afford to get caught on this phone without a headset and get a ticket; not to mention I don't have a license. I'm way too dirty for that.* "You wild. Never thought I would see you out here on the East Coast."

"Neither did I until Lollie inspired me. I heard you guys got together for a little chit-chat."

Trenda merged into traffic. "Yeah, it was good to see my ol' girl."

"I see, so when do I get the pleasure of seeing you again?"

She could almost see the lust dripping from his words. "What are you talkin' about, Mr. Secrease?"

"Just what I said; how come Lollie gets all the fun? I'd like to join in."

Her "Time-to-fuck" alarm went off. Sex, making money and smoking some good weed were her favorite methods of stress relief. Sex was the easiest and only attainable of the three at the moment. His was the last dick to enter her pussy. And the way her clit was fluttering, she was in need of a repeat. "What ya woman got to say about that? I don't wanna break up a happy home, you-know-what-I'm-sayin'?"

He chuckled. "I know exactly what you're saying, but you should know that you are very special to us."

The conversation suddenly got very interesting to her. Instead of taking a chance on getting caught driving while talking, she pulled into a Citgo gas station and parked next to the air and water station. "How special we talkin', Mr. Man?"

She heard the sound of a muffled conversation, as if he had put his hand over the mouthpiece. A moment later, he came back and said, "How about you come by and we talk about it?"

She twisted a lock of her wild hair. "When?"

"Right now sounds good to me."

I really need to get to work findin' a home for this dope instead of socializin', she thought. The stress of her recent adventures influenced her final decision. "Aight, where y'all at?"

"Great! Do you know where the Pier 5 is?"

Trenda recalled having spent a weekend there with a well-known Washington Wizards basketball player several years back. "Yeah, I know the place. I'm about twenty minutes from there."

"We're on the third floor, in suite 35. We'll be waiting for you."

After disconnecting the call, her body warmed with the thought of some stress relief. While driving to the hotel, her criminal mind went to work. She tried to recall her most reliable underworld contacts. After sifting through them, she decided the best place to start would be with Mai Tai. She smiled with memories of her old buddy. *Yeah, that bitch got her hands in everything.*

Half an hour later, Trenda knocked on Walter and Lollie's suite door. The aroma of expensive perfume pleased her nose as the door opened. "What up, girl?" Lollie said as she embraced Trenda. "Sure glad you could make it!"

After they separated, Trenda followed Lollie inside to the L-shaped wet bar. She admired the way Lollie's yoga pants showed off her hips and ass. "So am I. Where's that man of yours?"

"He went to get some ice. He'll be back in a minute." She waved at the three brown leather bar stools. "Have a seat; make yourself at home."

Trenda looked around the plush room. The hues of purple, yellow, red and green worked well. A gigantic bed sat behind the sofa section. The premium suite also featured a full Jacuzzi and impressive entertainment center. The view outside the glass patio doors, although beautiful from that vantage point, masked the dirty world underneath the glow of the city lights. She turned away and watched Lollie open a box of snack mix. "This is a nice spot. You guys come here a lot?"

Lollie poured the contents into a bowl on the bar. "We usually stay here when Walter comes to town. He ain't too crazy about staying at my uncle's house. He says they're too old-fashioned for him."

Trenda chuckled. "I bet."

They turned their heads to the sound of the door opening. "Hey now!" Walter said as he closed the door behind him. "Is that Ms. Fuqua I see?"

Trenda returned his grin, walked over to him and gave him a hug. "What up, stranger?"

His eyes browsed her body like a secret-shopper. "Just you, my red-headed friend!" He carried the bucket of ice to the bar and set it down. "I've never seen you with that much hair. It looks good on you."

Trenda ran her hand over her rapidly growing mane. "This wild stuff? Please..."

Lollie walked over, stood behind Trenda and laced her fingers in Trenda's hair. "You oughta let me flat iron it for you. I bet it's down to your shoulders now."

The feel of Lollie's long fingers massaging her scalp made her eyes droop. "Mmmmm, might have to take you up on that." A cork popped. She opened her eyes. "What you doin', Mr. Secrease?"

Walter set three glasses on the bar and half-filled each with champagne. "I'm pouring us a toast. We need to celebrate this family reunion."

Lollie dropped her hands to Trenda's shoulders. "Good idea!" She took Trenda's hand and walked her to the bar. "C'mon, let's celebrate."

The constant eye contact between Lollie and Walter didn't go unnoticed by Trenda. *Yeah, I can see these folks have plans for my ass.* She grinned internally at the lusty thoughts surrounding her.

Lollie's erect nipples and Walter's wandering eyes told her just how much the couple desired her. A ship's horn blast outside the Port of Baltimore added to the seductive ambiance. She picked up her glass and held it up. "Aight, Let's toast."

Lollie and Walter lifted their glasses. Walter looked from one lady to the other. "To freedom, friendship and fun."

They clinked glasses. The taste of the champagne invigorated Trenda. After the past couple of years being dry, she reveled in the tingly, bubbly taste of the celebratory nectar. She looked at her empty glass. "That was the *bomb!*"

Walter grabbed the bottle, walked over to her and refilled her glass. "The second glass is even better than the first."

Lollie smiled as he refilled her glass. "I can sure vouch for that."

Trenda found her own nipples growing with recollections of the last time the three of them were together in a similar setting. The stress from the dangers surrounding her began to fade, albeit temporarily. Her ability to compartmentalize situations had taken hold. She took her eyes off of the bulge in Walter's crotch and looked into his face. "How's the death business goin' out here?"

He sat on the bar stool between the two ladies. "I prefer to call it the 'human recycling business.'" He smiled and took a sip of champagne. "And sadly, it's doing rather well."

Trenda swirled her glass. "Why you say sadly? Ain't you in it to make money?"

He sighed. "Not at the expense of watching my people kill each other."

Trenda sat in silence, recalling how she'd shoved the blade of her knife into King Gee's heart that fateful night before she went to prison. *Guess he's talkin' about people like me.* She held her glass out to him. "Hit me up."

An hour later, after finishing off the bottle and catching up with her friends, Trenda loosened up considerably. She stood up, stretched and turned to Lollie. Pussy juice seeped from between her twat lips as she looked at Lollie's tits. Lollie smiled and wiggled them for Trenda. "You remember these?"

Trenda lowered her eyes and cupped Lollie's soft jugs. "Sure do...thought about them a lot while I was locked up."

Walter got up, went to the fridge and pulled out another bottle of champagne. He was barely able to keep his eyes off of the caressing women. "I assume you ladies need refills?"

Trenda gave him a seductive look. "I could use a different kinda refill..."

Lollie gripped Trenda's hips, spread her legs while sitting on her bar stool and pulled Trenda between them. "Oooohhh, I like the sound of that!"

Trenda looked at Lollie's soft, full lips. Many a night while in her cell, she had imagined the taste of them. She turned her head slightly to the right and pressed her lips to Lollie's. As she did, Lollie's tongue snaked into her mouth. Trenda grabbed a handful of Lollie's long black hair and kissed her deeper. Walter set the bottle down, walked around the bar and watched the sexy spectacle. Trenda opened one eye and winked at him as Lollie sucked her tongue. "Oh shit..."

Trenda reached out and rubbed the crotch of his black slacks. To her pleasure, an extremely hard penis greeted her. She gripped it hard as Lollie continued to kiss and lick her mouth. *This what I'm talkin' about.* She backed out from between Lollie's legs, pulled off her black sweater and tossed it on the floor. Lollie followed suit and removed her T-shirt. Trenda smiled, unsnapped her bra and dropped it on her sweater. "Mmmmmm, much better."

Lollie walked over to Walter, dropped her hand to his hard-on and gave him a long, passionate kiss. "I didn't forget about you, baby."

He placed his hands on her dark-chocolate tits. "I was wondering if you two were having a private party."

Trenda slinked over, rubbing her nipples. All the suppression of her horniness was a thing of the past. The sight of a semi-nude Lollie and rock-hard Walter lit her freak pilot light. *Gonna get me some dick* and *pussy tonight.* She got behind Walter and started unbuttoning his shirt. "You are way overdressed."

Lollie joined in. She unbuckled his belt, lowered his pants and got on her knees. "Mmmmm, I see you got something for me."

Trenda assisted Walter in pulling off his shirt. She then looked down at Walter's swollen root. "Yeah, he sure does." She got on her knees alongside Lollie. "And I want some of that, too."

Lollie swept her hair back and gripped the shaft of his dick. She looked at Trenda and giggled. "Wanna share with me?"

Trenda cupped his balls in one hand and grinned. "Share? As thirsty as I am, I might want it all."

Walter flung his shirt across one of the bar stools. "Well, Ms. Trenda, drink all you want!"

Lollie slowly rubbed his stalk. "She's going to have to wait in line; I've been waiting on this treat *way* too long."

Trenda traced Lollie's lips with her finger. "Practice on this."

Lollie slowly performed a blowjob on Trenda's finger. She licked, sucked and slobbered on it. Walter grabbed his dick. "What about this?"

Trenda let go of his balls, wrapped her free hand around his stiffness and looked up into his eyes. "I got you." As Lollie continued sucking her finger, Trenda rubbed his dick across her lips. *Mmmmmmm, yes, almost forgot how good a dick can feel.* Her freak kicked in. She used the tip of her tongue and licked his pee-hole and dick head.

Lollie took her mouth off of Trenda's finger and moved closer to the action. She rubbed her tits. "I want some."

Trenda took her mouth off of the head. "Come on, baby. Work wit' me."

With no need for further instructions, Lollie began licking and sucking the shaft. Walter groaned and moaned as the two mouths worked on his piece. He reached down and played with both of their tits. Lollie stopped sucking, stood and took off her pants and hot-pink G-string. She then put a hand on Trenda's shoulder. "Get out of those pants."

As Trenda let Walter's dick pop out of her mouth, she licked her lips. The familiar feel of a pulsing rod in her mouth broke the dam of pussy juice she'd been holding back. After almost three years of no real sex, her beast was ready for release. She slowly and seductively got out of her pants and panties. "This is the kinda welcome home party I'm talkin' about."

Walter and Lollie exchanged mischievous grins. They sandwiched Trenda between them, Walter behind her, Lollie in front. Lollie rubbed Trenda's flat belly and eased her hand down to the reddish-brown racing stripe of hair on Trenda's snatch. "We have a special night planned for you, sexy."

Trenda leaned her head back as Walter kissed her neck and Lollie massaged her clit. The combination of sensations made her nipples hard as iron. She rubbed her own tits and moaned, "Mmmmmm…shiiiiiit…"

Lollie took her wet finger and put it in Trenda's mouth. "Taste how sweet your juice is."

Trenda sucked and licked every bit of her moisture off of Lollie's finger. Walter grabbed her chin and turned her head sideways. "Give me a taste."

He stuck his tongue in Trenda's mouth and licked the interior. Lollie watched for a moment and then stepped back. "Take her to the bed. I'll join you two in a minute."

Walter took Trenda by the hand. "Time for a little fun."

Trenda, in a trance-like state of arousal, followed him without question. The prospect of a multitude of orgasms drove her. Out the corner of her eye, she saw Lollie, bent over, digging through a small suitcase. *Damn that girl got a pretty ass.* Walter pulled all the covers off of the bed and tossed them on the floor. "You got somethin' against fuckin' on covers?"

He smiled and looked past her at the approaching Lollie. "Not exactly. It's just that they don't fit into our events for the night."

"What you mean?"

Lollie walked over and dropped a large, folded square of plastic and three bottles of massage oil on the bare mattress. She then gripped Trenda's award-winning ass. "We about to have a whole lot of fun."

Thirty-Six

"This shit has got to stop," Marv said as he finished his second beer.

"What's the matter, hon?" Bridget, his long-time girlfriend and hottest meter-maid in the city, said. She sipped from her glass of chardonnay. "Who pissed you off now?"

"Dirty cops!" On the TV mounted to the wall of his favorite watering hole, the local news played. A report stated that a member of the Baltimore police department's Internal Affairs Division, along with two other cops, was arrested and charged with a host of crimes including murder, embezzlement and money laundering. He waved the bartender over. "Those bastards make us *all* look bad."

She rubbed him between his shoulder blades. "Don't let them get to you." She then leaned over and kissed him on the cheek. "As long as we have good cops like you, they won't be around for long."

Ever since Darius and Tyrone's demise—what had been dubbed the "Acid Massacre"—Marv had seen over a dozen arrests associated with bad cops. "Another beer for you, Marv?" the Swedish bartender asked.

Marv nodded. "Yeah, Olof; keep'em comin'." Between the problems in his own department and the regular bad guys, he also got wind of a new troubling rumor. He sighed as he recounted his earlier briefing downtown. A number of major Russian thugs were reported to be in town. *That can only be bad news. Now that most of the Island Boys gang is disbanded, that leaves a huge crime vacuum that needs to be filled.* "Thanks," he said after Olof placed the glass of beer in front of him.

Bridget finished her wine, turned and rubbed his thigh. "Hurry up and finish that so we can go back to my place. We need to work off some of that stress."

The look in her brown eyes told him that he was in for a treat. He gave her a half-smile, put his hand in her curly hair and kissed her full lips. "I could sure use some of that." After taking a swallow of his beer, he pulled out some cash, paid their tab, took her by the hand and headed for his car. During the walk, his mind was still on the news story. Not only did the thought of the Russian invasion trouble him, so did the reports that Nick had been seen hanging around the areas the Russians had gravitated to. Coincidentally, there had also been a spike in the number of unsolved, brutal homicides. *If I find out that weasel is mixed up with those Russian thugs, I'll be his judge, jury and executioner.*

ॐ

"Y'all somethin' else!" Trenda said as Lollie and Walter spread the plastic sheet over the huge mattress and tucked it in. "Straight *freaks!*"

Walter grinned and tossed her a bottle of massage oil. "Takes one to know one, freak."

Lollie pinned her hair up in a bun on top of her head, sashayed over, stood behind Trenda and kissed the back of her neck. "It's about to go down, baby."

Walter flipped the top on his bottle and squirted a generous amount of oil onto the plastic cover. He then waved Trenda over to the bed. "Hop aboard."

Trenda stood at the edge of the bed and spread the oil with her hands. As she did, Walter squirted some oil on her back and ass and rubbed it in. She shivered as a dribble of oil ran down the crack of her ass. *Been too long since I kicked it like this.*

Lollie meanwhile, went to the bar, popped another cork and brought the bottle back to the bed. She took a swig and passed it to Walter. He traded her the massage oil for the champagne. "Your turn for some lubrication."

Trenda lay on her back and watched Lollie pour oil on her tits and rub it in. The track lights on the ceiling reflected off of her glistening chocolate skin. Trenda rubbed her oily hands between her thighs as Lollie oiled herself down in front of her. As Lollie oiled her bald pussy, Trenda said, "Let me see the pink."

She walked over, put her foot up on the bed and spread her lips, exposing her hard clit. "Like that?"

Walter took a swallow of champagne and sat the bottle on the nightstand as Lollie showed her goods. "I *swear* pink is becoming my favorite color."

Trenda grabbed Lollie by the hand and pulled her down on top of her. They locked lips and touched tongues. Walter poured oil on the pair as they fondled each other. The plastic had a nice coat of oil on it. They slipped and slid all over the bed. Lollie eased Trenda down on her back. She then looked at Walter and smiled. "You take the top, I got the bottom."

He winked at his lover. "Yes ma'am!"

Trenda looked from one to the other as Lollie gripped her knees and pushed her legs apart. Her head lay at the edge of the bed. "What's this? A tag-team?"

Walter stood next to the bed and let his dick dangle in her face. "Feeding time."

As Lollie held Trenda's pussy lips open and teased her clit with her tongue, Trenda swallowed Walter's dick. The more he fed her, the more she took. The more she took, the wetter her vagina got. Lollie ate Trenda with a vengeance. Walter looked down at Lollie as Trenda sucked his balls. She rose, grinned and wiped cunt-juice off of her mouth. "Let's switch."

Trenda's wet oven pulsated with pleasure. Her mouth longed to be refilled with more penis meat. She sat up and fingered her pussy as Lollie lay back on the bed. She then ran her hands over Lollie's slippery, sexy thighs. *Been wantin' to eat this for a long time.* Lollie bent her knees and spread wide open. Trenda slid between those dark thighs and licked Lollie's fat pussy lips.

As Trenda feasted, Lollie moaned with extreme delight. Trenda ate her into multiple orgasms.

Walter got up and went to the same suitcase Lollie had gotten the plastic out of. He grabbed a couple of condoms and went back to the bed. After rolling a rubber over his dick, he got on the bed, crawled behind Trenda and rubbed his dickhead up and down between her oily booty cheeks. Walter, teasing her asshole with his dickhead, turned her on to no end. For the first time in years she let herself go with the flow instead of taking charge of the fuckin'. She tossed her head back with pleasure as Walter entered her back door.

"Give it to her right, baby," Lollie said as Walter dug into Trenda's ass. "Tear that ass up!"

Ohhhhhhhhhhhhh, shit…I forgot how good that feels, Trenda thought as she pushed back on his rod. The exquisite pain/pleasure mix made her eyes roll back in her head.

Lollie got up, went back to her suitcase and came back with a long, hot-pink, double-headed dildo. Sweat leaked off Walter as he ravaged Trenda's bottom. He glanced at Lollie while pulling Trenda back to him. Lollie licked one of the pink heads. "Slow down, don't cum yet."

He slowed down, grinned and slapped Trenda's ass. "Whew! Good thing you said something." He pulled out, stood up and wiped sweat off of his forehead. "Take over for me."

Trenda rolled over, spread her legs and massaged her clit. She hadn't even broken a sweat yet. Her entire body tingled with desire. She fingered herself into an orgasm, watching Lollie suck on the dildo. "Gimme some of that."

Lollie sat on the bed and rubbed the toy between her tits. "I'll do better than that. We can both get some."

Trenda reached over, got the bottle of champagne and took a long swig and put the bottle back. She then reached down and held her kitty lips open. "I'm ready."

Lollie sat down facing Trenda. She scooted up, opened her legs and laced them in Trenda's. She then rubbed one head of the dildo on Trenda's sopping wet lips and slid it inside. "Mmm-mmm, you are creamy as hell." She then took the other head and put it inside her own twat.

"Dreams *do* come true," Walter said as he pulled off his condom and watched the girls fuck each other. He grabbed his dick and walked closer to the bed. He stroked his meat as the girls moaned and boned.

Trenda took nearly half of the twenty-four inch toy inside her. A layer of her creamy cum coated it. She watched Lollie thrash and grind on the other end. The contrast of the bright pink against her dark skin heated her up even more. She braced herself up with one hand, rubbed her hard nipples with the other and gazed at Lollie. "Yeaaaahhh...take it...take it all...mmmmm."

"Dammmmmmmmmmmmmmmn that's *hot!*" Walter said as he jacked off. He was so caught up, he could barely stand. He braced his knees against the bed for stability.

Lollie opened her eyes and saw he was close to climax. She

slowed down her thrusting and said, "You ready to let go, baby?"

"Mmmmm...yesss...'bout...to...nut..."

She eased off of the dildo, grabbed it and fucked Trenda with it. "Give it to our friend."

Trenda arched her back as a massive orgasm approached. As she was about to cum, Walter leaned closer to her. She saw the first drops of pre-cum ooze out of his head. *Mmmmmmmmm... yessssss...* She opened her mouth for him. The taste of his sweet, sticky cum filled her throat as she busted her own nut. The combination of all that sensual stimulation nearly gave her a seizure.

Thirty-Seven

M arv wasn't the only one watching that newscast. Beverly watched intensely. However, the story that followed interested her a lot more. The reporter segued into a story about the release of one of Baltimore's most intriguing criminals. The report stated that the whereabouts of recent parolee Trenda Fuqua were in question. He went on to say how most people were baffled at the fact that she hadn't sold her story yet. A number of media outlets stood ready and willing to shell out big bucks for her testimony. They then rolled tape of a female reporter interviewing Father Fuqua in front of his church. Beverly turned up the volume. The interview had taken place several weeks prior to the rumored release of Trenda. She memorized the name of the church, got out of the bed, got her purse out of the drawer next to her bed, pulled out the photo of her and her son and stared at it. *Time to pray, Father.*

Thirty-Eight

"Thanks for the welcome home party," Trenda said after putting on her sweater. Her vagina, ass and mouth were still sore from the previous night's escapades. "Sorry I can't stay for lunch, but I got some appointments to keep. Oh, and thanks again for helpin' me out with my room. I'll get you back real soon."

"Don't sweat it, girl, consider it a welcome home gift." Lollie then sighed and rested her head on Walter's bare chest. "You sure you can't reschedule?"

Walter stroked Lollie's wild hair. "Yeah, Trenda; sure would be nice to keep this party going. How about it?"

Trenda finger-combed her hair and looked at the long pink dildo lying at the foot of the bed and grinned. *Still tryin' to figure out how she was able to put one end of that thing in my ass and the other in my pussy...* She hitched her purse up on her shoulder, walked over the wadded up plastic cover on the floor, to the bed and kissed them both on the lips. "Can I get a rain check?"

After several attempts to break away from her friends, she finally succeeded. The bright sun made her squint. As she walked to her car, she realized fun time was over. She opened her trunk, lifted the mat and saw her contraband was still intact. The urge to close the trunk, walk away and disappear was hard to resist. *You already lost your mother. You gonna be able to live with the murder of your father on your hands?* "Shit." She closed the trunk, got in the car and headed to the far side of town.

Almost an hour later, a little past noon, she entered Annapolis. *I hope she still got the same number.* She turned on her phone and searched her memory for Mai Tai's number. As she punched in the number, her phone rang. At first she didn't recognize the number, then she grimaced with recognition and answered. "Hello?"

"Hello to you, doll. Did you forget to call me?"

She exited the freeway and pulled over in front of a Target store. "No...I didn't forget. Just ain't had time."

"Don't make that a habit. I'll be checking with you periodically. Go make me some money."

Ain't that a bitch? She tossed her phone on the passenger seat, pissed off she didn't get a chance to respond to his last statement. It took a few minutes, but she managed to calm down enough to try calling Mai Tai again.

After four rings, a voice she recognized said, "Hello?"

"What up, girlfriend?"

"Wha?" A long pause. "Who is this?"

"It's the one that knows how you got that scar on your left ass cheek."

"Trenda? Wait a minute; is that you, bitch?"

Trenda chuckled. She thought of the night she and Mai Tai had to run for their lives. The jealous wife of a banker Mai Tai was sexin' confronted them outside of a massage parlor Mai Tai managed. After a scuffle with the enraged wife, she pulled a pistol out of her purse. Trenda and Mai Tai took off running. Good thing the wife was a poor shot. Of the five shots she fired, one grazed Mai Tai's left ass cheek. Instead of going to the hospital, they went back to Mai Tai's apartment and patched her up. "Yeah, it's me; I'm that bitch."

Mai Tai squealed so loudly Trenda had to take the phone off

her ear. "What the hell? Where you at, girl? You betta be close by!"

That is the most ghetto-soundin' Asian chick I ever heard, Trenda thought with a smile. "I am if you still in the last place you was livin' before I went on vacation."

"I ain't went nowhere. How long before you get here?"

Trenda read the time on the dashboard. "I think I'm about ten minutes away. You got company?"

Mai Tai had a mild coughing fit. "Naw, just me and my dog."

"You still got Joe-Joe?"

"Yup, still got his stank-ass."

"Put him up; I don't wanna get dog hair all on my clothes. You know he likes to jump on me."

She had another coughing fit. "Don't worry 'bout that dog, just get yo ass over here."

"Okay, peace." Trenda yawned as she continued into Annapolis. She entered a section of town populated with expensive homes. Her nondescript sedan stood out like an oak tree in a Dixie cup among the high-dollar machines parked in the neighborhood. "There it is," Trenda said as she pulled up to the intercom, feet from the gated entrance to Mai Tai's massive house. She pressed the button and looked into the camera mounted above the keypad. Seconds later, the gates parted. She followed the smooth, asphalt driveway to the rear of the half-million dollar home. *Still can't believe she hustled her way into this bad ass house.*

As she approached, one of the four garage doors opened up. She pulled inside and parked next to a jet black, Audi sedan. It had all the bells and whistles. Parked next to it was a convertible purple Corvette. Its custom paint glistened as though it was wet. The copper Hummer next to it looked ready to handle any terrain or weather. Trenda grabbed her purse, got out and inspected Mai Tai's fleet. *This girl still got major swagga.*

The side door of the garage opened and a huge Alaskan Husky ran to her. His demonic blue-gray eyes belied his gentle nature. "Get down, dog!" Trenda yelled as Joe-Joe hopped up, placing his paws on her belly. "Gonna have dog hair all over me, *get down!*"

A short whistle got both of their attention. Joe-Joe got off of Trenda and sat on his haunches. "Leave her alone."

Trenda brushed the front of her sweater off. "I told you about siccin' that mutt on me."

"If I had sicced him on you, you would be bleedin' by now, bitch."

Awwww, man.... She took a good look at her old friend and cringed. The once hot and vibrant Filipino hottie was a shell of her former self. The sister-booty she once sported had dwindled. She looked like an Auschwitz survivor. Unsure how to respond, she simply said, "Hey, girl..."

Mai Tai placed her arms akimbo and smiled. Fortunately, her luminescent smile was still intact. She held her arms out for a hug. "What up, Ms. Fuqua?"

Trenda hesitated and then accepted the hug. "I'm cool." She broke the embrace. "Tryin' to make a dollah out of fifteen-cents."

"I heard that." Mai Tai looked at the Buick. "What you doin' drivin' that bucket?"

"Don't worry 'bout my bucket; it gets me where I need to go."

Mai Tai turned and had a mini cough-attack. Joe-Joe whined and licked her hand. She wiped her hand on her lemon-yellow robe. "Whatever. I ain't seen you rollin' like that since you first hit the streets back in the day." She looked Trenda up and down. "I'll give you a pass since you just got out the jailhouse."

Damn, what happened to my girl? The white blemishes in her mouth were disturbing. "Thanks...I could use all the passes I can get right now."

"Is that right? What's goin' on wit' you, momma?"

The rapid-fire events of the past few days bowed Trenda's steadfast resolve. In the face of the woman that had practically raised her, her chest hitched as she fought off tears. *Psalm 119:143* rang in her ears:

Trouble and anguish have taken hold on me: yet your commandments are my delights.

"I'm *tired* of bullshit…" She wiped her eyes defiantly. "*Tired*…"

Mai Tai nodded slowly, walked over and patted Trenda on the back. She then gave two short whistles and the dog walked over and stood by her side. "Let's go inside."

An hour later, sitting at Mai Tai's enormous dining room table, Trenda finished her second cup of calming herbal tea from Mai Tai's collection of imported, all natural teas. "So that's what I'm workin' wit'. Sounds like some kinda TV drama, don't it?"

Mai Tai, after remaining mostly silent—except for the occasional coughing fit—during Trenda's confessional, removed a steeping teabag out of her gold-trimmed tea cup and placed it on the saucer beneath it. She laced her fingers together and leaned on the table. "Sounds kinda fucked up, momma."

Trenda looked into Mai Tai's skeletal face. "*Kinda?* Thanks for that. Was hopin' you could tell me somethin' I *didn't* know. A little support woulda been nice." Trenda waved her hand around Mai Tai's vast, wood paneled room. "We ain't all able to kick it like this."

Mai Tai maintained her eye contact with Trenda. "You feelin' sorry for yourself now? Boo-hoo."

Trenda lowered her eyebrows and huffed. "*What?* I ain't asked for all this shit! How the hell you gonna come at me li—"

In the midst of Trenda's rant, Mai Tai silenced her. "I'm dyin' from AIDS."

Trenda's mouth hung open like trap door. She fished for words but found none. She stared at her emaciated friend as reality kicked in. The loose fit of her robe, constant fatigue, and unhealthy color chilled her core. She finally managed to say, "Oh…"

Mai Tai rubbed her bony hands together. "Yup, I got the 'Monsta.' Been livin' with it for a few years now; not sure how much time I got left."

Time went backwards as Trenda recalled how lively Mai Tai used to be. She owed everything from her blowjob skills to how to make quick money transporting to her Filipino mentor. Countless nights she had sat on Mai Tai's bed with her as she counted out money by the pound—and that's pound by weight, not currency. One of the first things she taught Trenda was how to protect herself. Besides teaching Trenda pressure points to attack that would debilitate a combatant, she also taught her how to handle a butterfly knife. She would make Trenda spend hours practicing how to flip it, fold it and the proper ways to slice and dice a mutha-fucka. She was also Mai Tai's only visitor during her hysterectomy procedure a decade ago. "I'm sorry…damn, I didn't know…"

Mai Tai dismissed her with a wave of her hand. "Ahhh, don't worry 'bout me; I done lived a *good* life. You know I always said, 'you burn hot, you burn fast.' And I was the hottest, fastest bitch around."

Trenda managed a slight smile. "Yeah, you was that fa sho. Wish I had half the skills you do, then maybe I wouldn't be caught up in this mix." She looked at her friend. "I'm sorry for buggin' you wit' my drama. I'll work it out…somehow, you-know-what-I'm-sayin'?"

After a moment of silence, Mai Tai sat back and looked across the table. "Quit all that sad talk. Bitch, I didn't say I wouldn't help you. I just said you was fucked."

Like the rising of the moon, a full smile rose on Trenda's face. "Bitch, why didn't you just say so!"

ഇാൻ

"I ain't workin' with that crazy broad, Nick. No way."

Nick swung and missed a fast ball. His healing wound hampered his swing. Earlier, he had instructed Beanie to meet him at the Sluggo batting cages in Towson. It was one of his favorite places to go on his off days. He glanced out of the protective netting at Beanie. "You really think you have an option?" A fastball shot out of the pitching machine. He swung and hit a ground ball. "Think about it, Bucko."

Beanie sat down at the table behind the protective netting and pulled out his cell phone. "Man, it ain't gonna work; she hates my ass."

Nick hit a solid line drive. "Sounds like you need to buy her some flowers with that money you made selling her pictures to the tabloids."

Beanie grinned as he checked his text messages. "What you know about that?"

Nick fouled tipped a ball against the netting. "You would be surprised at what I know, ass-face."

Beanie shook his head. "Why you always gotta be talkin' bad to folks? Damn, you *ever* had a good day?"

"Yes!" he screamed as he knocked the last pitch to the end of the cage. He then exited the cage, took off his helmet and wiped his forehead with the back of his hand. "Look, scum; don't get smart with me. Just get busy finding me a buyer."

Beanie put his phone down on the table. "Gonna be hard to do. Movin' weight ain't my specialty. Especially when I ain't even got a sample to show potential clients."

Nick took off his batting gloves and tucked them into his back pocket. "That's why you're her partner. I trust her a hell of a lot more with my merchandise than I do you. If they want a sample, you contact me. Your only job is to solicit buyers. With that mouth of yours, I'm surprised you didn't turn out to be a used car salesman."

"There *you* go. Always talkin' shit." Beanie stood and took his car keys out of his pocket. "I'm serious, Nick; I can't work with her. It would be all bad."

The menacing call Nick had received from a man with a thick Russian accent still chilled him. The anonymous voice promised Nick he would introduce himself to him if he didn't make good on his payment. And make it on time. He turned to Beanie. "Let me spell this out for you; go to your buds down on the west side and spread the word you have a brick of quality smack. Cast that info out there. As dry as the city has been the last few months, I'm sure you'll get a nibble."

Thirty-Nine

"I'm sorry, Mrs. Kain, but we're going to have to keep you under our care for another month or so," Dr. Moyer said. "Hopefully, depending on how you progress, the judge may see fit to let you go a little sooner."

"Are you *kidding*?" Beverly asked. Her handcuffs rattled against the gurney rail as she tried to raise her hands in protest. "I want to go *home*. My son needs me!"

Dr. Moyer shook his head sadly as he and two security guards walked beside her down the hallway. "That's the best I can offer at the moment. It's for your own good. I spoke to your mom earlier and she said she will take care of your son until you get home. No need to worry."

Disbelief filled Beverly's face. She was being moved to a mental care facility in Hagerstown, more suited to care for her. Disbelief gave way to rage. "You can't hold me! I *demand* you let me go!" She rocked back and forth on the gurney as they entered the elevator. The leather straps across her abdomen successfully restrained her. She glared at the doctor out of her puffy eyes. "I'm going to sue your ass, you…you *bastard*! I hate you! Hate you *all!*"

෨෬

At the same time Beverly was being hauled off to the nut house for an extended stay, Trenda watched Mai Tai test a sample of the heroin for purity. "Where you get that drug testin' stuff from?"

Mai Tai checked the color of the chemically treated smack in the glass test tube. "The Wizard of Oz."

"Funny."

She then grinned at Trenda. "This is the good shit."

"I figured that...but you think I can really find somebody to buy it before my deadline?"

Mai Tai rinsed the vial out and then tossed it into her kitchen trashcan. "You might; it's been hard to find good dope these days. The Baltimore cops have pretty much locked down the streets. I heard the mayor is on the warpath. All the bad press about her corrupt cops is messin' with her shot at gettin' reelected later this year."

Trenda reached down and scratched Joe-Joe between his ears. Being back hooked up with Mai Tai both thrilled and frightened her. The fact that she was standing next to one of the most well-known madams on the east coast, with a brick of heroin between them, and her being a fresh parolee made her panties wet. The thrill seeker in her was alive and well. "I just hope that trick, Nick, can keep the heat off me."

"I can't believe that fool is still out there tryin' to be a baller." Mai Tai removed her blue latex gloves and tossed them into the trash. "With his little-dick ass."

Trenda cocked her head. "What you talkin' 'bout? You fucked him or somethin'?"

Mai Tai's face soured. "You must be high! Hell naw, I ain't touched that wannabe bastard. The girls at my parlor in Ocean City told me. Said that dude loves to suck toes and get his lil' weenie sucked."

The image of Nick's lipless mouth on somebody's toes almost made her upchuck. "You mean to tell me that fool hits the massage parlors? He ever see you there?"

She had to lean against the table and rest before she could reply. "No way. I don't roll like that. I got people to handle most of my business for me, especially now that I'm half-dead."

The ease of which Mai Tai could speak about her impending demise spooked Trenda. She felt as if she were talking to a ghost. "You gotta quit talkin' like that. You still here."

"Bullshit." Mai Tai reached into the pocket of her robe and pulled out a lighter and partially smoked joint as fat as a pinkie finger. "Let's get one thing straight; I know ain't no cure for me and I'm cool with that. And if we gonna work together, you had better get used it and not treat me like I'm helpless. Got that, bitch?"

Trenda couldn't help but laugh as Mai Tai fired up the joint. Mai Tai was the hardest woman she had ever met. Even facing death she refused to cower. That defiant streak was part of the reason she was so drawn to her. "You a damn fool!" She backed away from the secondhand weed smoke. "I'm gonna have to go outside or somethin'. Can't take a chance of gettin' no contact high. That shit show up in my drug test and it's a wrap. Lucky for me I ain't gotta get tested 'til next Friday."

Mai Tai took two deep hits and then ground it out on the pewter ash tray next to the sink. "Can't have no fun around you, I see."

"Not if it's gonna get me locked up, you can't!"

Mai Tai smirked at her. "You ain't gotta worry; you got a guardian angel lookin' over you now."

"The hell you mean?"

"Your new owner ain't gonna let nothin' happen to his prized possession."

Trenda stopped fanning smoke out of her face. "You know I hate when you start talkin' in code; what you tryin' to say?"

Mai Tai took a seat at the table, in front of the dope. "Like I was sayin', Nick the Dick loves him some Asian girls. And he likes to brag. You know he got that little-man complex. And since my girls act all quiet, he gets real cocky. Especially when he gets a little fire water in him. Ever since them cops got murdered at the Lighthouse, he been braggin' to the ladies about how him and his boys are gonna take over the streets now that his competition was gone. He even mentioned you by name a few times, talkin' about how Darius wasted your talents cause he was too busy tryin' to get in your drawers. He swore if he ever got the chance, he would work you like a part-time job."

A stress headache sprouted in her temples. The fact that Nick thought of her as his indentured servant pissed her off on many different levels. The aspect of being beholden to another cop was not on her to-do list. Oh hell no. She paced the floor.

For troubles without number surround me; my sins have overtaken me, and I cannot see. They are more than the hairs of my head, and my heart fails within me.

—PSALM 40:12

As that Psalm reverberated in her head, she did her best to fight off the sense of impending doom. *I'm not goin' out like that...* She knew from experience that if Mai Tai said it was true, it was true. Still, she asked, "Why you ain't tell me this before?"

"Bitch, how was I supposed to tell you when you was locked up? It ain't like we been talkin' on a regular." A coughing fit attacked her and then subsided. "Besides that, I can't keep track of everything. I'm too busy dyin'."

Trenda studied her friend and calmed down a bit. She realized things could be a *lot* worse. She took a seat next to Mai Tai. "Okay... I'll deal with that business later." She tapped the kilo with her finger. "This is my priority. I ain't got but a week to move it."

"How much you tryin' to get for it?"

Trenda paused as her inner-hustler took over. *Nick wants fifty grand and I'm sure he's gonna try and screw me outta my pay. I had better try and get mine now.* "Sixty-five stacks."

"That's a little high, but considering how dry the streets are, you might get lucky." Mai Tai yawned. Joe-Joe walked over and rested his muzzle on her thigh. She scratched his head. "If I was at full strength, I *might* have been able to guarantee you I could move it in a week. I'm not sayin' I can't, just keeping' it real wit' you."

Trenda nibbled on her thumbnail. Her swift ride down Trouble Street picked up speed. Not only did she have Nick to contend with, thoughts of her father surfaced. She hadn't checked on him since she left his house almost a day ago. *And that bastard Nick knows where he lives.* She closed her eyes, ran a hand down her face, stuffed the dope back in her purse and stood up. "Aight... cool. Guess I better get movin'. Need to get myself ready to hit the turf and get my grind on."

Mai Tai got to her feet. "Quit lookin' so depressed." She walked up and patted Trenda on the back. "I got a gift for you."

Trenda broke from her thoughts and looked at her out the corner of her eye. "Yeah? How much is it gonna cost me?"

"Didn't I just tell yo ass it's a gift?"

"Shit, the way things been goin' for me lately, I gotta question everything, you-know-what-I'm-sayin'?"

"Even me? Damn..."

The look on her face told Trenda a small part of her was truly hurt by her last statement. She sighed. *You gotta trust somebody.* "My bad."

"You damn right it is!" She gave Trenda a half-smile. "Follow me." Inside the living room, Mai Tai went to the mantel. On top of it was rack containing a trio of samurai swords. Under the rack was a jade-handled butterfly knife. It had a vintage and deadly look. Mai Tai picked it up and flicked it open with lightning speed. "Look familiar?"

Trenda gazed at the razor-sharp stainless steel blade. It was the first butterfly knife she had ever seen. It was also Mai Tai's favorite; her Baby. She'd had it custom made in Singapore decades ago. "Yeah, I remember that blade. I remember you never let me play wit' it."

Mai Tai flicked it a few more times; going over some of the same techniques she had taught Trenda. After a few minutes of demonstrating her skills, she got winded and stopped. "You remember…how to use it?"

Trenda nodded as Mai Tai tossed her the knife. She had always loved the solid gold scorpion image that was embedded into the jade handle. "Can't believe you finally let me hold your precious blade." She flicked the nicely balanced knife a few times. "Damn, it feels real good, no wonder you didn't let nobody mess wit' it."

"That' right. Me and that thing been to hell and back. Took a few folks along for the ride, too."

"I just know you did." She held it out to Mai Tai. "Here you go."

She shook her head. "That's your gift; your *new* 'Baby.'"

A smile formed on Trenda's face. She never in her life thought she would own a knife as expensive and as deadly as that one. It reeked of mayhem.

"You gotta be bullshittin'!"

"You know me way better than that; bullshittin' ain't in my vocabulary. I ain't got the time or energy to use it no more." She went into her robe pocket and pulled out a black .38 caliber Ruger pistol. "Now I fling hollow points instead. Ain't got the energy for slashin' no more."

Trenda took a step back. She was very uncomfortable with the way Mai Tai handled the pistol. More than once during her reckless gun handling display, she ended up looking down the wrong end of the barrel. *That's the second gun barrel I done looked down in a week. I sure hope this ain't no trend.* "Okay, quick draw, I get it. Put that thing away."

Forty

"How's the shoulder?" Anton asked after taking a puff of his cigarette.

"Better," Nick said. He caught himself rubbing it subconsciously and stopped. "But not healed."

Anton and his goon exchange a glance and grinned. "Sorry to hear that, but I'm glad you were able to meet on such short notice." Anton walked over to the large two-way mirrored wall of his office wall and checked his hair. His car dealership featured some of the most exotic cars in the state. He adjusted the lapels of his designer suit and turned to Nick. "I trust our due date is on schedule?"

Nick fidgeted with the zipper of his leather, Harley-Davidson jacket. "Yeah, looks good...looks real good."

Anton sat on the edge of his desk. "Good, because I have some very uptight associates that wouldn't understand why the return on their investment didn't arrive as planned. Trust me; they are not as understanding as I am."

The goon picked up a large sandwich off of the desk and took a huge bite out of it. His eyes never left Nick. *What a freakin' barbarian*, Nick thought, disgusted as crumbs and condiment leavings fell out of the goon's mouth onto his baby-blue shirt. *Bastard needs a bib.* "Are we done? I gotta get back to my side of town."

Anton stood and adjusted his tie. "Yes my friend, you are free to go." The goon walked over and opened the office door for him. "Just keep in mind, you have one week left until our next meeting. And I trust you will have a nice gift for me."

"I'm sure I will." *God, I hate these fuckin' Ruskies*, he thought as he walked past the grinning goon. *Oh, how I would love to bash his hideous smile in with a sledgehammer.*

Outside the exclusive Dover, Delaware dealership, five of Nick's riding buddies/coworkers waited for him. A tall, chubby blond rider, standing next to a chromed-out Harley, looked at Nick and said, "Well? How did it go?"

"It sucked out loud as usual." Nick unhooked his helmet off of the handlebars of his bike. "Did you know those fuckers smell like cabbage?"

"Who?"

Nick shook his head. "What you mean, 'who'? You shit through feathers now?"

Chubby was totally perplexed. "Shit through feathers...what you talkin' about?"

Nick tilted his head and gazed at his dense friend. "You know; shit through feathers like a friggin' owl. Who? Owl? Get it?"

Oblivion registered in Chubby's eyes. *"Huh?"*

Nick smirked and pulled on his helmet. "Forget it, Brad. You *obviously* don't have enough gray matter to figure it out."

Brad flipped him both his middle fingers. "Sit and spin on these, you dick."

ॐ

"What a waste of humanity," Marv said as he watched the group of bikers ride off. Obsessed with the idea of bringing pride back to his profession, he decided to spend his off day studying

Nick. "Ain't enough honor in all six of those fools combined to fill a thimble." Marv was familiar with all of them. Four of the six were from different precincts. That troubled Marv. To his knowledge, not even Darius had spread his *alleged* unsavory dealings that far, that fast. He started the engine of his girlfriend's black Lexus coupe. Pretending to take it in for an oil change while she worked, he'd swapped cars with her to aid in his surveillance. Nick was all too familiar with his personal car—a pristine, pearl-white Jaguar.

Just before they got out of sight, Marv pulled out and followed them. He passed up a black and white Dover police car. *Wonder how many of them are on the take?* It pissed him off to even have to think of his fellow officers in that light. He gripped the wheel tight with anger. The fact that he was so limited in the aggressive actions necessary to accomplish his goal to pursue scum like Nick often discouraged him. That led to his current position. For the past four years, he had been looking into retiring from the city and becoming a private investigator. *Would be a hell of a lot more I could do about a piece of shit like Nick.*

As he tailed the bikers, Marv revisited what he knew about the owner of the car dealership. Anton and his dealership came up clean. Not even so much as a late garbage bill. After digging deeper—legally and illegally—he found out that several of Anton's goons had vast criminal records. Records that included crimes associated with the Russian mob back in Prague. *Ain't no way Anton is innocent...you are who you roll with, as far as I'm concerned.*

Between trying to keep up with Nick, Beverly posed a challenge. "I had no idea that woman was obsessed enough with revenge to risk blowing her witness protection cover," he said as he followed Nick and crew across the Maryland state line. *Her being committed for the next month is a big help. Hopefully by then she'll be stable enough to go back underground.* The thought of her tangling with Trenda worried him more than Darius's killers finding her did. His instincts told him they no longer posed a threat to her, but Trenda on the other hand...The stacks of information he had on Trenda showed she was no Mary Poppins. Although only having been convicted of crimes ranging from petty theft to assault and battery, a trail of blood and chaos followed Ms. Fuqua. His collection of snitches, miscreants and other underworld associates informed him of some of her rumored—yet improvable—murderous exploits. He winced as he drove over a rough set of railroad tracks too fast. *Nah, I think Beverly would do well to stay in her own lane when it comes to Ms. Fuqua...*

Forty-One

"Why so many cars parked out here?" Trenda said as she pulled up to her father's house. Three cars parked in the driveway and four more in front of the house. Worried something was wrong, she parked across the street and hurried to the door.

She rang the bell. Seconds later, she heard a stranger's voice. "Hello! You must be Trenda!"

The security gate was pushed open by a jolly white man who could have been a body-double for Santa Claus. "Yeah...uhhh... is my father here?"

His blue eyes were filled with warmth. "He sure is." He waved her inside. "He's in there taking center stage as usual."

She eased past the rotund gentleman. "Thanks."

Almost a dozen people milled about the dining room. Her father sat at the head of the dining room table. Everyone held a Bible. None of them appeared to be less than a hundred. Her father rose from his seat. His black and white clergy shirt was crisp and clean. "Hey, daughter of mine!"

"Hey, Daddy." All eyes found her. The eyes of a few of the men lingered on her too long. "I don't wanna disturb y'all; I'm gonna go up to my room."

He beckoned her to him with his hand. "No, no...I'd like to introduce you to some friends of the church."

After a round of handshakes, well-wishes and hugs, her forced smile was waning. She could tell many of them were itching to ask about her infamous story. That was until a deep voice behind her said, "Anybody want a bottled water?"

She turned and saw a handsome, young kinda-chubby black man holding five small bottles of water in his hands. *Hmmmm... thickolicious!* She held her hand out. "I'll take one."

His eyes widened. Delight filled his face as he quickly looked her up and down. "Sure!" He fumbled nervously and dropped two of the bottles. Embarrassed, he quickly bent over to pick them up. "I'm sorry, folks."

Trenda chuckled at the nervous fella. He looked to be around her age. She looked at his hands and saw no signs of a wedding ring. His hip haircut took away some of his innocent looks. *Boy, I tell ya, no matter how holy a man is, they all got a lust bone in 'em.* She bent down and helped him pick the bottles up. "I'll take this one, hon."

They rose at the same time. A large silver crucifix hung around the collar of his French-blue, clergy shirt. "Thanks for the help." He hugged the bottles to himself and attempted to offer her his hand. "I'm Gary."

She took his hand. "I'm Trenda."

They both turned to the sound of her father's voice. "Hey, Brother Colfax, that's my daughter I was telling you about." He smiled at Trenda. "Brother Colfax is going to take my place in the church soon."

She managed a smile. "That's good. It's about time you take a break."

"I've been grooming him for almost a year; I think he's just about ready."

Already feeling self-conscious because of her bed-head and not having changed clothes since yesterday, Trenda sought an exit.

"It was nice meetin' y'all but I have to go change." She looked back at Gary and held up her bottle. "Thanks for the water."

His smile was a yard wide. "My pleasure."

He kinda reminds me of ol' Box. She recognized the wanting look in his sanctified eyes. *James 1:14* came to mind:

But every man is tempted, when he is drawn away of his own lust, and enticed.

It might be fun to play with big boy, but I really ain't got time. The weight of her current problems took the fun out of the idea of flirting with the saintly chap. Also, the Bible Study session reminded of her not-so-innocent mother. She had hosted them faithfully every week, as long as Trenda could remember. That iced her mood even more.

Her father then said, "Hey, Trenda; we are about to start Bible Study. Would you like to join us?"

"Sorry, I can't right now. I have an important phone call to make before I leave. Thanks." She then headed for the stairs. "Was nice meetin' y'all."

⅚ℙℹ

"Damn!" Trenda said as she collapsed on her old bed. The whirlwind of recent events overwhelmed her. The springs of the twin bed she'd slept on as a youngster squeaked as she rolled onto her back. She stared at the empty white walls. The images of rap stars, R&B and movie star posters danced in her head briefly. Just as briefly as her parents would let them hang on her walls. "I gotta get rid of that brick."

Outside her window, the last of the afternoon sunlight peeked in and out of her tan curtains. She sat up, pulled off her sweater and plugged her cell phone into the wall socket. *I need a bath and a meal.* After stripping down to her underwear, she stuck her head out of the door and listened. It sounded as though everyone was engrossed in some heated Bible discussion. She walked across the hall to the linen closet and grabbed a large, rust-colored terrycloth towel and wrapped it around herself.

I didn't know they still made this stuff, Trenda thought as she inspected a bottle of her late-mother's Avon Skin So Soft bath oil. She longed for some candles. After pouring the bath oil into the piping-hot water, she eased herself into the tub. While she soaked, she thought. Disappointment set in once she realized she no longer had the phone numbers for her most reliable connections. And after a couple of years, it would be even harder to track them down. She slid down deeper into the water. She leaned her head back and closed her eyes. The dull ache in her va-jay-jay and anus began to subside. Prior to going to jail, living in her fast-paced environment was the norm. But after her stint in The Cock, away from the temptation, trouble and fast money in the streets, she questioned her skills. *And what if Nick reneges on the deal? Can I risk him goin' after my family if I don't get this money on time?*

After close to an hour of soaking and napping, she heard the muffled sound of her phone ringing in her room. *Must be Nick.* She sighed and got out the tub. As she dried off, she glanced at herself in the mirror, turned and looked at the jagged scar on her shoulder. That and the remnants of a small scar under her right eye served as reminders of how fast shit can go sideways. After tying her hair up in a towel and wrapping one around her tight body, she went to her room. Instead of checking the phone right away, she sat on her bed and lotioned up.

Ain't even had time to figure out what I'm gonna do with my life. That thought made her furrow her eyebrows. Her plan to just lay low until she dropped off of parole and bounce was shot to hell. She used the fingernail clip on her mother's key ring and clipped her toenails. The temptation to call Alexis, take StarShine's offer, get the money and run shamed her. She tossed the keys onto her nightstand. *That's some straight, selfish, coward thinkin'.*

From downstairs, she heard her father thanking everyone for coming as Bible Study came to an end. After opening her bag, she took out a pair of sexy teal boy shorts and bra and put them on. She unwrapped her hair and let it air dry. She grabbed a lock of her hair and pulled it down. It touched her chin. *Damn, this stuff is growin'.*

She exhaled loudly and picked up her phone. *Lemme see who called.* She saw a missed call from Mai Tai. The fact that she didn't leave a message was no surprise. Mai Tai always said never leave a trail when doing dirt. That included messages, notes or anything similar. She dialed Mai Tai's number, rubbed her belly button and waited for her to answer.

"What took you so long to call me back, bitch?"

Trenda simpered, walked over to her window and looked out on the spacious backyard. "Call me another bitch and I'm gonna cut you wit' your own knife."

"In that case, I hope you good at dodgin' bullets, bitch."

She looked at the spot behind the garage where she got her first kiss. From a boy. "Whatever...what you call me for?"

"If you *would* have answered your phone, you would have heard that I *might* have somebody interested in your package."

Trenda's eyes enlarged. "What? Who?"

"I'll tell you when you get here. You know I don't talk business on the phone."

Black skinny jeans, black boots and a black T-shirt. A large, neon-pink image of the Baby Phat, pussy cat logo dominated the front. The tail of the cat sat strategically between her tits. It was the last outfit that Dennis bought for her that she hadn't yet worn. She got dressed in record time. *Can't do too much with this stuff right now,* she thought as she tied her hair back in a bushy ponytail and slapped her New York Yankees cap down on her head. She paused to look out of the window. *Better take a jacket.* She went into her bag and pulled out her new black hoodie, pulled off the tags and put it on. After gathering up her phone, keys and purse, she hurried down the stairs.

"Where are you going in such a hurry?"

She practically skidded to a halt. "I gotta make a run. I'll be back in a while."

Her father peered into her eyes. "Oh…did you have dinner yet?"

"No…I'll get somethin' while I'm out."

He waved toward the kitchen. "There's a lot of food in there. The group always brings me too much dang food. I usually end up having to throw most of it out because it spoils in the icebox or I try and donate it to the shelter."

The aroma of fried chicken, greens, macaroni and cheese found her nostrils. She looked through the kitchen doorway and saw dish after dish of food lining the counter. Her stomach rumbled like an approaching freight train. "I'll get some when I get back." She checked the time on her phone. "I really gotta run. I have a meetin' of my own to get to."

He continued to scrutinize her. The look her gave her was unmistakable. It was the same look he had given her as a child when he could read a lie in her face. "Is it with that Jeff fellow?"

"Jeff who?"

He hobbled over and sat down in his recliner. "You know; that young man that left his number for you to call. He said he had a job offer for you."

It took her a second to catch on. "Oh...oh yeah. No, not him. I'm gonna catch up with him tomorrow."

He took off his glasses, rubbed his eyes and looked at her. "Trenda, whatever you are up to, keep Hebrews 4:13 in mind:

Nothing in all creation is hidden from God's sight. Everything is uncovered and laid bare before the eyes of him to whom we must give account."

Trenda scratched the back of her neck and looked away from him. Her stomach soured. The eerie feeling of being under the rule of her parents' heavy religious thumb, once again, bothered her. "Okay...I'll keep that in mind."

I bet he wasn't sweatin' Momma with that Bible shit when she was out ho'in', she thought as she started her car and drove off. Deep down inside, she had a feeling moving back home was a bad idea. "I'll deal wit' that later," she said as she pulled into Mai Tai's driveway an hour later. After getting buzzed in, she found Mai Tai waiting for her inside the garage. She got out of the car, walked over and leaned against the Hummer's chrome grill guard. *She looks better than she did earlier*, Trenda thought as she watched Mai Tai walk toward her. Her red and white, ankle-length, floral-designed, kimono dress hid her skeletal physique well. "What up, Madame X?"

Mai Tai swept back a lock of her long salt-and-pepper hair back. "I hope you ready to work, bitch."

Forty-Two

"Man, you *promise* you gonna be able to get my baby momma's shopliftin' charges dropped, Messy?" Beanie asked.

A bit past nine, in the mask of darkness, behind Griff's Junkyard, Messy Marv met with one of his most devious informants. He reached inside his leather jacket and scratched his ribcage, just below his shoulder-holstered 357 magnum. "Beanie, when have I ever not kept my word?"

Beanie scratched his thick, Philly-style beard. "This is different tho', homey; if she get convicted this time, with her record, she is gonna do at least five years. If that happens, what's gonna happen to my little girl?"

Marv sat down on the hood of the Lexus and played with the pair of 357 speed-loaders in his jacket pocket. The moonless night was exceptionally quiet in the downtrodden, industrial area. The intermittent barking of a junkyard dog half a block away echoed down the dark street. "For one thing, if she *was* to get some time, you might consider being a father to your kid and taking care of her *yourself.*"

Beanie sucked his teeth and paced in front of Marv. "Man, it ain't even about that...you don't know what I do with my kid... you don't know me like that."

Unmoved by his imitation outrage, Marv kept his eyes on him. "I *do* know you haven't paid child support since she was two. What's she now? Seven?"

Beanie stopped pacing, pulled a blunt from behind his ear and fired it up. "I paid some since then."

Marv stared at the hoodlum pacing in front of him and imagined him as a banker, teacher, baseball coach, computer tech or something other than a low-life, money-hungry snitch. *Makes me wonder if we are doomed as a race.* "I don't have time for a counseling session, Beanie; what is this valuable info you're supposed to have for me?"

Beanie took a long drag off of his smoke and tapped off the ashes. "Man, this info is worth a *lot*. That's on my momma; trust me."

Marv checked his watch. "Well? Isn't getting the mother of your child out of jail worth a lot?"

Beanie exhaled a large plum of marijuana smoke. "It's worth more than that; it's worth you gettin' me my driver's license back, too."

"You're pressing your luck, Beanie; I can't think of the last time you gave me something worth a crap." Marv folded his arms across his chest. "You have two minutes to impress me before I leave your ass standing here."

Beanie showed him a confident grin. "How 'bout I tell you one of your fellow officers is about to push some high-grade smack into the hood?"

Marv's expression didn't change. "That's not exactly breaking news. Have you watched the news lately? There's a boatload of crooked cop stories going around."

Beanie took another drag off of his cigarette. "Did I mention that this cop's new salesperson is Trenda Fuqua?"

Marv slowly stood up. "You better not be bullshittin' me."

"I'm serious as a stroke; you think I'm takin' a chance talkin' to you out here for some bullshit?"

Marv took a step closer to Beanie. "Tell me what you know."

"First, you gotta take care of my issues. I need to be able to drive without havin' to worry about your boys sweatin' me."

What an asshole. You would think taking care of his kid's mother would be the priority. "If I can verify what you have to say is true, I'll keep my part of the deal, and you know that. Who is she allegedly working with?"

Beanie maintained eye contact with Marv for a moment and then looked away. "You positive you gonna take care of me?"

"You're acting like this is the first time we've done business; you *know* how I work."

A long moment of silence passed. Beanie finally spoke. "Nick... Nick the Dick. He got a key of horse he's tryin' to move. And the way it sounds, he ain't got much time to move it. He got us out here lookin' for somebody to buy it real quick."

Marv tossed the information around his brain. He went back in time and began connecting dots. He went clear back to the night he ran into Nick when Slip got stabbed and later murdered in his hospital bed. The dead girl in the abandoned hardware store. Trenda being released. Nick getting cozy with the Russians. Tons of information swirled in his head. He refocused on Beanie. "I need times, places...do you have the dope?"

Beanie grinned and held a hand up to Marv. "Slow ya roll, Detective; slow ya roll. We are gonna have to renegotiate the terms of this deal."

ഇൻരു

As Marv and Beanie haggled, Trenda and Mai Tai were having a conversation of their own. The well-connected, loyal and resourceful Mai Tai was able to find a potential buyer. A Persian trucking company owner, and longtime massage parlor customer with a "happy ending" fetish named Hassan, mentioned something interesting to one of her girls he was dating a few weeks back. He bragged to her how easily some of his associates were able to fool the TSA and successfully smuggle illegal items into the United States from the Middle East. Items including narcotics. After leaving the garage, Mai Tai walked Trenda through the large rose garden in her backyard. They took a seat on the concrete bench next to her koi pond. As Mai Tai worked to catch her breath, Trenda said, "Dude smuggles stuff into the States; what makes you think he's gonna be interested in buying some dope? That don't sound right."

Mai Tai crossed her legs and scratched her bony ankle. "Let me finish. I had my girl rub him right and see what else she could find out. Turns out, his brother is a major heroin dealer in New Jersey."

Trenda leaned away as Mai Tai turned to cough. She then said, "Okay...so what's the connection? His brother wanna buy it?"

Joe-Joe walked over and sat at Mai Tai's feet. "He might...I had my girl set up a meeting with Hassan so we could talk business."

"When?"

"What time is it?"

Trenda pulled her phone out of her purse. "Almost ten. Why?"

"We're supposed to meet Hassan in a few hours."

Trenda lifted her eyebrows. "*Tonight?*"

"Yeah, bitch, *tonight*...no, actually this mornin'; Hassan has a truck terminal outside of Newark. We are supposed to meet him there so we can talk."

A sense of déjà vu snuck up on her. She hadn't been on a late-night mission in over three years. But she found the rush of the potential danger exhilarating. A little *too* exhilarating for her own good. *Can't believe this shit; just got out on parole and I'm about to take some more penitentiary chances...*"We?"

"Yeah, bitch, *we!* What? You thought I was gonna do ya work for you?" She stood up and Joe-Joe followed suit. "You oughta know by now that these kinda deals go down fast sometimes. And if his brother decides he wants to do somethin', I'd like to be ready to make it happen."

Trenda got to her feet. The thought of crossing state lines briefly worried her and then fled. She knew she was in too deep to worry about that. She looked Mai Tai in the face. "When we leavin'?"

"We need to leave now; it's gonna take about three hours to get there." She pointed at Trenda. "And I ain't drivin'."

Trenda followed Mai Tai and Joe-Joe down the flagstone walk-way, toward the house. "We gonna ride in the Corvette?"

Mai Tai paused next to the entrance to the garage. "Hell no! We gonna take *your* car. I don't wanna be ridin' dirty in mine. Yours will draw way less attention."

She's got a point, Trenda thought as she stepped inside the garage and looked at Mai Tai's fleet. "You gonna have to take care of the gas. I ain't got enough to make it there and back."

Mai Tai put her hands on her scrawny hips and shook her head. "Damn, what's next? You need me to get you some tampons, too?"

Trenda laughed. "Now you know you ain't right...the hell you expect? You know my ass is broke."

"I don't wanna hear it."

"Yeah, yeah, yeah." Trenda pulled out her car keys. "How long before you ready?"

"Ain't gonna take me long. Just gotta get my bag and a coat and we can roll."

A few hours later, just after one in the morning, Mai Tai checked the GPS on her phone. "Slow down. The terminal is just ahead on the left."

The section of town they were in was as quiet as a tomb. Freight companies and warehouses lined the streets for almost half a mile. Several sets of railroad tracks and vicious potholes tested the Buick's suspension. The only traffic they encountered was the occasional tractor-trailer heading for parts unknown. Trenda spotted a mid-sized trucking company a few yards ahead and pointed at it. "Is it that place right there?"

Mai Tai strained to read the darkened sign with the trucking companies name. "Do that sign say Quality Transport?"

Trenda slowed and flashed her high beams. "Yeah...but the gate is closed. Are we supposed to just wait here or what?"

"No...park in front and let me call Hassan."

Trenda parked across the street as Mai Tai made the call. A couple of minutes later, the old, automated, chain link gate rattled and began to open. Mai Tai ended the call and put her phone back in her purse. "Pull around to the back of that building behind the loading dock."

Orange and white trailers filled almost all forty of the loading dock stalls. The night crew was busy loading and unloading trailers. "Look at this fool!" Trenda yelled as she narrowly missed colliding with the yard hostler. He ignored her and hurriedly pulled a full trailer away from the dock. "Bastard!"

"Who taught you how to drive?" Mai Tai said as she coughed into her fist. "Gonna kill a bitch up in here."

"Funny."

Trenda pulled behind the mechanic shop. Light spilled from under the doorway. A black big-bodied BMW sat next to the rear entrance. "Park next to the Beemer and let me out."

"You want me to come wit' you?" Trenda said after she parked and shut off the engine.

Mai Tai reached into her red leather purse, pulled her pistol out, took off the safety and put it back inside. "No, just wait right here. If I ain't back in fifteen minutes, then you might wanna take off."

Trenda glared at her. "You expectin' trouble?"

Mai Tai unbuckled her seatbelt. "No, but I believe in bein' prepared. I ain't kiddin'; if I ain't back in exactly fifteen minutes, get outta here. Crash the damn gate if you have to."

Trenda knew her mentor well; questioning her was a waste of time. She pulled out her phone and noted the time. "Aight. At one-twenty-five, I'm out. With or without you."

Mai Tai opened her door. "You better be."

Trenda sat in silence and watched Mai Tai walk over and knock on the door. It opened almost immediately. The silhouette of a tall male spilled out with the bright light. *Hope this don't get crazy,* Trenda thought as Mai Tai went inside and the door closed behind her. She exhaled deeply and opened her purse. *Better get ready just in case.* She went into her purse and pulled out her new Baby. She flicked the butterfly knife a couple of times and then sat it on her lap.

While waiting, she stared at the cross hanging from the mirror and thought about her mother. She *still* found it hard to believe her straight-laced momma was once a prostitute! *Did the church really turn her life around?* She looked away from the cross and examined her own past. By her own count, she had committed almost every other crime in the book except prostitution. Including the most heinous of all; murder. Out of nowhere, a chill found her spine and crawled down it. *What if I get busted out here in Jersey? I doubt Nick got enough pull to keep me outta jail if I catch a felony out of state.*

The stress sucked all the air out of her. She suddenly felt suffocated. Just as she was about to let her window down, the door Mai Tai went into opened up. Out came her friend. She walked over to Trenda's window and tapped on it. "Open up."

Instead of letting the window down, Trenda grabbed her blade and opened her door. "Wassup? Everything cool?"

"Open the trunk and gimme the brick."

Trenda hopped out and put the blade in her back pocket. "He wanna buy it?"

Mai Tai waited impatiently. "No…he just wanna check it out. Make sure we ain't bullshittin'."

Trenda opened the trunk, lifted the spare and pulled out the brick. "How much longer? I need to get my ass back into Maryland."

Mai Tai took the dope out of her hands. "Ain't gonna be long. Why you stressin'? You actin' like this your first bar-be-que."

Unaccustomed nervousness set in. Trenda looked around the perimeter. "I'm just gettin' tired, you-know-what-I'm-sayin'?"

Mai Tai studied her for a moment and then patted her on the arm. "Okay…I'll be back in a few. Just chill."

Mai Tai went back inside. Instead of getting back in the car, Trenda paced back and forth next to her car. While analyzing her situation, she froze. A pair of Crown Victoria headlights pierced the darkness behind the garage. Her heart tried to spring out of her throat. She learned long ago in the game that learning to recognize cop cars was vital. Instinctively, she ducked behind the remains of a stripped down truck, before the headlights found her. *That looks like an undercover!*

The white car slowly drove past the mechanic shop and parked in a stall next to the main building. Trenda worked up her nerves and peeked around the front of the truck. To her relief, she saw the word Security and the orange QT logo on the Crown Vic's door. A security guard got, turned on his flashlight and began making his rounds. Seconds later, the door to the mechanic shop opened. Trenda heard Mai Tai's unmistakable cough along with a male voice. She then focused on their conversation. "You okay, my friend?"

"Yeah, I got it from here. Thanks, Hassan. I'll wait to hear from you."

"And you will, my friend. I can tell you are a straight shooter; I like that."

Cool, let's get the hell out of here. She crept from her hiding place, cracked her door open as quietly as she could and got back inside. Her nerves were shot. The thought of the long drive back dogged her.

Mai Tai opened the door, got in and handed the brick to Trenda. "Hey, put this thing back in the trunk so we can get out here."

Trenda saw a teaspoon-sized chunk was missing from the package. "Damn! You givin' my stuff away?"

"Bitch, calm down. You just a phone call away from sellin' it."

Trenda perked up. "You *serious*? *Already*?"

She gave Trenda a smug look. "You surprised? Obviously, you musta forgot who I am."

Forty-Three

"One more! One more! *Push it*, Marv!" Jim said as Marv struggled with his last bench press rep. Jim helped Marv place the three-hundred-pound weight on the pegs. "Good job!"

Twelve hours after his eye-opening meeting with Beanie, Marv and Jim met up at their favorite gym for a super-set workout. Over the years it had become a Saturday morning ritual for them. Marv sat up, picked up his towel off of the bench and wiped sweat off of his face. "Thanks." He stood and let Jim take his place on the weight bench. *Can't shake what Beanie told me...even though he's a liar, coward, thief and opportunistic hustler, something tells me he's being straight with me on this Nick and Trenda mess.*

"Hey, partner; you gonna spot me or what?" Jim asked as Marv stared off into space, lost in thought.

"Sorry 'bout that." He walked around the bench and stood ready to assist if needed. "Got my mind on what Beanie told me."

"Can't blame you; if what he told you is true, it could turn into a shit storm of massive proportions."

Marv wrapped his navy blue towel around his neck and looked down at Jim. "Yeah...gotta make damn sure before I make a move. Can't afford to go after Nick with faulty information. I don't wanna blow a chance to take him and his cronies down. I'm tired of cops like him making the rest of us look bad."

Jim managed to only get three reps in before Marv had to help him out. "Not only that, things could get really complicated if that piece of Russian garbage, Anton, is involved. Especially with his 'diplomatic immunity.'"

Marv barely heard him over the clank of weights and the high-energy house music being piped through the gym. He switched places with Jim for his last set. He looked up into Jim's eyes. "I wouldn't give a damn if he was Vladimir Putin himself. If I find out that Nick really is somehow connected to those Russian thugs, I'm gonna beat him 'til candy falls out."

Jim chuckled and shook his head. "I was afraid you were gonna say that."

"What do you mean?"

"Face it, Marv; you only have a couple years to go before you can retire with a fat pension. Is it really worth jeopardizing that for that collection of scum-puppies?"

Marv gave him a cold stare. Having been born and raised in Baltimore, he still had pride in his hometown. Even after watching his mother get beaten and robbed by a pair of Irish thugs as a five-year-old, he still loved his city. Even after his father and favorite uncle were shot to death in an after-hours club on the west side, he still loved his city. Even after the kindly Polish detective that was told to drop his investigation of his father's and uncle's murders by a racist administration, he still loved his city. Instead of running away from those memories after graduating from high school, he instead decided to become a protector of his city. And to his credit, he'd become one of the best. "You goddamned right it is."

&)CR

While Marv and Jim hit the showers at the gym, Trenda was awakened by a beam of afternoon sunlight. A space between her partially closed curtains allowed the light to land directly on her face. "What the hell?" She rolled over and pulled her pillow over her head. Stress disrupted her sleep. The heap of parole violations she had racked up since getting released was hard to ignore. She now had much more sympathy for the people she had met that went in and out of jail on a regular. *And I'm still rollin' around with a kilo of heroin in my trunk.*

She sighed, reached for her phone on the nightstand and checked the time. It was nearly one in the afternoon. It had only been about seven hours since she'd left Mai Tai's house and come home. The look her father gave her when he opened the door for her cut to the bone. The sadness in his face was hard to look at. It was as if he knew his wayward daughter was still lost in the wilderness. A dangerous, hellish wilderness.

She put the phone down and stared at the ceiling. *I sure hope Mai Tai's connection comes through. I wanna hurry up and get rid of that brick and get Nick off my back.* Mai Tai's condition sprang to mind. Having had several friends that had succumbed to HIV and other maladies, she wasn't freaked out by Mai Tai's illness. She was well educated on how the disease was spread. *I hope nothin' happens to that girl before this deal gets done. I'm runnin' out of time.*

೮ාಇ

The following five days were tense. Fending off Nick was a bitch. The closer she got to the deadline, the more often he called. Mai Tai was getting tired of her calls checking to see if she had heard from Hassan's brother. Then to cap it all off, her oldest brother, Ricky, called and instead of welcoming her back to the family, berated and belittled her. He torn her a new asshole for not only missing their mother's funeral, but for also contributing to her unhappiness. In return, she cussed him out in good fashion and vowed to disown him. *And to think I gotta protect him and his family from Nick's threats.*

While her father was away on church business, she took the opportunity to soak in the large master bathroom tub. Once done, she got out and dried off in front of the mirror. Looking for some cleanser to clean out the tub, she opened the cabinet under the sink and found a plastic tub full of her mother's combs and brushes. "What's this?" She pulled the tub out and sat it between the Jack-and-Jill-styled sinks. Inside, among the combs and brushes, was a flat iron. She pulled it out and inspected it. *Looks barely used.* She looked at her wild, curly Afro and plugged in the flat iron. *Yeah, let's do this.*

Two hours later, a totally different woman looked back at her in the mirror. "*Daaaaayum!* You fine, girl!" she said to her reflection. Her Afro had been transformed into a rusty red, flowing mane that fell between her shoulders. It was now even long enough to cover the jagged scar on top of her shoulder. The color contrast between her hair, skin tone and her eyes even shocked her. Once upon a time ago, she hated all the attention her looks garnered her. She smirked at herself as she held her hair up on top of her head and a couple of other mock styles. *I think I'm gonna enjoy it this go 'round.*

As she put away the flat iron, her phone rang. She walked her naked self to her room. "If that's Nick callin' again, I *swear* I'm gonna cuss him out." It was Nick. She ignored his call. Before she could put the phone down, it rang again. To her relief, Mai Tai's number was on the caller ID. "Wassup, girl?"

"I hope you sittin' down, bitch."

Trenda wiped her hair out of her face for the first time in years. "What you talkin' about?"

"I just got off the phone with Hassan; his brother wants to meet." Her phone beeped in her ear. She looked at the display and saw it was Nick and ignored him again. "Cool! He wanna spend?"

"Bitch, you know I don't talk business like this. Come see me and then we can talk."

Nick called again. She ignored him again. "What time you wanna meet?"

"The sooner the better. You know I ain't got no schedule and I'm subject to cut out at any minute."

She put her new Baby into her purse. "I'm comin'."

෴

"I can't *believe* this cunt!" Nick said as he slammed his fist on the dashboard of his truck. "She thinks she's slick; I can tell she's sending my calls to voicemail." He ran his hand through his hair with frustration. With only minutes before the start of his shift, he didn't have time to continue tracking Trenda down. Beanie was useless. He hadn't come up with a single prospective buyer. Three days remained before he was due to come up with Anton's money. He found it nearly impossible to relax. The fact that his mother called and thanked him for the lilies he had delivered to her Florida home freaked him out. Especially since he hadn't sent them. When Anton called the next day and asked Nick when was the last time he had sent flowers to his mother, his blood frosted over.

෴

In celebration of her new hairstyle, Trenda decided to dress up a bit. She mixed up her few outfits and ended up in her blue skinny jeans, olive blouse and her thigh-high, black boots. She let her hair flow. It graced her shoulders magnificently. A lock of it covered the left side of her face. As she walked to her car, her phone rang. She grimaced as she answered it. "What you doin' callin' me, asshole?"

"Is that how you talk to all your partners?" Beanie asked.

She paused before opening the car door. "Look, punk; I ain't got no words for you except this: I know you sold my pictures out to that magazine, even though I told you to erase them. I'm gonna make you pay for that. That's on my momma."

"Hold on, shorty! How you gonna blame me for that? I ain't the only person that took pictures of you, I'm sure."

"Bullshit! I can tell by the way I was pointin' my finger at you in the picture that it was yo' no-good ass."

"I'm not gonna argue with you, Shorty. And I'm sure not gonna let you threaten me for nothin'. Ain't gonna let no bitch punk me."

Her face went red with fury. "*Bitch*? Oh, hell naw. Yo' ass is good as dead…I'm comin' for you, Beanie. Believe it."

"Yeah, yeah, yeah, yada, yada, yada. I ain't worried about you and them Wolf tickets you sellin'. I just called to let you know Nick is lookin' for you an—"

Fuck this trick, Trenda thought as she ended the call.

Her father pulled into the driveway as she was pulling out. He rolled down his window and waved at her. "Are you going to be gone long? The crab feast at the church is tonight. Brother Colfax and I were hoping you would join us."

Oh no, there he goes tryin' to play matchmaker. She recalled him mentioning the crab feast *and* Brother Colfax to her a few days ago and sighed. "Sorry, Daddy. I got a meetin' to go to in a minute. It's gonna go on for a while. Not sure when I'm gonna be home."

Disappointment shaded his face. Oh...okay." He forced his frown into a smile. "You look really nice. Reminds of when your mother used to comb your hair like that."

She forced a fake smile of her own. "Thanks...I'll check on you later, okay?"

He adjusted his gray fedora and nodded. "Okay...be safe, Trenda. Please be safe."

He only called her by her name like that when he was worried. "Okay." She turned from him, backed into the street and headed to Annapolis.

ഇറ

Beanie puffed his jaws full of air and then exhaled after Trenda hung up on him. He knew he had gone too far. He was *very* familiar with Trenda's penchant for making good on her promises. Having personal knowledge of two unsolved murders associated with her, he wasn't crazy about being the third. His inner coward shook like gelatin in an earthquake. He stared out of the window of his car. *Gonna have to get up outta here. Fuck Nick, Trenda is way more dangerous.* A Machiavellian plan formed in his worried mind. He nodded his head. *I gotta get a hold of Messy Marv.*

ഇറ

"*Here*, Joe-Joe," Mai Tai said just as the dog was about to rush Trenda. The dog immediately stopped, turned and sat down. She looked more sickly than normal. She managed a weak smile. "Hey! Look at *you*! Who you tryin' to catch lookin' all hot?"

"I ain't tryin' to catch *nothin'* but a bag of cash." She closed her car door and dropped her keys into her purse. "Believe that."

"Coulda fooled me." She circled Trenda, admiring her ensemble. "You look *almost* as hot as I used to be back in the day."

Trenda had to laugh. "You off the hook."

"I know I am." Mai Tai opened the door leading into the back-yard and walked out. Trenda followed. "Time for business. Hassan's brother, Atash, made an offer."

"How much?"

"He said if the rest is as good as the sample, he's willin' to pay your price."

Relief tumbled off of Trenda. "Cool...when he wanna hook up?"

"He wants to meet someplace between here and Jersey. I said that I would call him back when I was ready to meet."

Trenda watched an Eastern Bluebird swoop down a few yards away and gather up some material for its nest. "You got a spot in mind where we can meet?"

"I was thinkin' my parlor in Dover would work. Ain't gotta worry about cops too much."

Damn...out of state again. "Okay...I'm in. Let's get it over wit'."

"All right, here we go." Mai Tai coughed up a nasty wad of phlegm, spat it out, went into the pocket of her baby-blue Adidas sweatsuit, pulled out her phone and dialed.

Trenda walked over to the koi pond as Mai Tai did her thing. She watched the colorful fish mill about. Several of them came to the surface, expecting to be fed. *Them fish look hungry as I am.*

"Okay, it's a go," Mai Tai said as she put the phone back in her jacket pocket. "He wasn't feelin' meeting in my parlor, but he did agree to meet somewhere neutral in Dover. We settled on meetin' at the Salisbury Inn. It's not too far from my parlor. He's on his way now there now. He said he's gonna get a room and call me back with the details. If you ready, we can leave right now."

Trenda recalled the low fuel light coming on as she pulled into Mai Tai's driveway. In her haste to get to Annapolis, she used the gas she had and planned on filling up on the way home. "Okay, but I need to stop and get some gas on the way." She pulled her wallet out her purse and checked her cash. "I got a little money; I was finally able to cash that check earlier this week."

"We ain't takin' your car this time; it smells like old folks."

"Excuse me?"

"I said, I ain't ridin' in your stanky beater today. We gonna take the 'Vette."

Trenda shook her head. "You lucky I like you."

Forty-Four

"This is a nice spot," Trenda said as she whipped the Corvette into the Salisbury Inn's parking garage just after sunset. By the looks of the crowded garage, business was booming. "I stayed here a while back."

Mai Tai coughed and grimaced. "Good…for you; but this… ain't no vacation." She unbuckled, opened her purse and pulled out a small, black, four-shot, .357 Derringer. "It's…all…business."

"Damn, chick! How many guns you got?"

Mai Tai checked the rounds. "Enough."

Trenda watched Mai Tai struggle to catch her breath. "You okay?"

"I'm good for a…dead bitch." She checked the brick in her purse. "Just remember…the plan. I'm gonna go…to the room and see what's up. I'll…call you to bring this up if…it's all good. He don't know… I brought you wit' me. And just like… when we met… Hassan; if you don't… hear…from me in fifteen minutes…cut out."

"I know the drill…I got this."

Mai Tai set her purse on the floor, took the gun, set the safety and then tucked it into her panties. She smirked at Trenda. "This the hardest thing been this close to my pussy in a long time."

Trenda wiped her hair out of her face. "You ain't got *no* sense."

Mai Tai got out and headed for the lobby. Trenda was saddened and impressed at how well her loose-fitting sweats completely hid the bulge of her gun. Her frail image stayed in her mind. *I just hope she can make it to the room...she looks weak as hell.*

Seven minutes later, Trenda got the call. "It's me...come up to room 4104 on the fourth floor."

"Showtime." She opened her purse in search of her blade. Her hand brushed against her rosary beads. Somehow they managed to get tangled in the knife. It gave her goosebumps. She felt as though she was being watched.

For his eyes are upon the ways of man, and he seeth all his goings.
—JOB 34:21

"I really don't need to be thinkin' about that right now; I need to focus." She untangled the knife, tucked it in her boot and grabbed Mai Tai's dope-filled purse and got out. Inside, she was swarmed by women and a smattering of men. Many of them black. *What the heck is this?*

A large banner answered her question; the National Nurses Association was having a conference in the main ballroom. Trenda weaved in and out of the women and made her way to the elevators. Everyone seemed to be going in the same direction. She checked Mai Tai's large burgundy leather purse and saw it was halfway unzipped. The cellophane wrapped brick winked at her. *Oh hell no!* She quickly zipped it up. *Almost got caught slippin' fa real.*

The elevator arrived and a herd of laughing, smiling women exited. A beautiful, chocolate hottie around Trenda's age paused and cocked her head. "Excuse me, do you work at Kent General, in Delaware?"

Trenda tucked the purse under her arm. "No...sorry."

"You sure? You look dead on like this lady I worked with while I was on a travel assignment." She shook her head. "You *definitely* have a double."

I ain't got time for small talk, broad, Trenda thought as the elevator emptied. "Thanks, but I'm from the west coast." She pushed the fourth-floor button. "Have fun."

"You, too!" She saw one of her friends and did a double-take. "Okay, girl, the presentation is about to start. I'll see you there."

To Trenda, it took the elevator a week to get to the fourth floor. To her surprise, she only encountered a couple of people. According to the directory on the wall across from the elevator, the room she was looking for was to the right. She rolled her head from side to side in an effort to relax. "Quit actin' like you ain't done this before." Twenty yards away, suite 4104 waited for her.

&)(&

Marv thought about the report he'd received from the CSI lab regarding Slip's murder scene as he made his way to Druid Hill Park. A portion of a fingerprint was found on the screwdriver found near where Slip was attacked. Marv slowed as he approached the Maryland Zoo inside the park. *Hard not to believe that's Trenda's fingerprint.* The computer analysis reported that there was a one in thirty-eight hundred chance that it belonged to Trenda. As he pulled into the vacant parking lot next to the main building, he spotted a male dressed in all black sitting on the stairs. *Now let me see why Mr. Beanie needed to see me so badly.* Marv parked his undercover car and got out. *He sounded as nervous as a cat in a dog pound.*

"What took you so long, man?" Beanie said as he took a hit off of a weed-filled blunt. "I been waitin' here almost two hours for you."

Marv pointed at his hand. He could barely make out Beanie's features in the darkness. "First of all, put that damned thing out before I arrest your ass; I'm on duty, asshole."

"Aight, man, aight." He dropped the blunt and mashed it with his foot. "You satisfied?"

"No, but if you keep pissing me off, I'll get a lot of satisfaction from locking your ass up."

"Okay, be cool. I don't need no more drama tonight."

"So what's this big emergency? It better be good; I'm way too busy these days to be dropping what I'm doing for bullshit."

Beanie shook his head. "Man, you gotta help me; that crazy broad threatened to kill me."

"What broad?"

"Trenda...she threatened my life!"

Marv grimaced. "Are you telling me I drove way the hell out here because somebody scared you? You better have a better reason than that or I'm gonna take you in for real."

"Man, that broad is nuts! She ain't never not followed through on a threat...I should know..." He caught himself before giving up too much information to the lawman in front of him. There was no guarantee Marv wouldn't lock him up if he said the wrong thing. He had to think of something to appease him. "She also has the kilo of heroin Nick gave her."

୧୦୧୪

Before knocking on the hotel room door, Trenda leaned over and checked the position of Baby inside her boot. Instincts and experience taught her to be ready for any and everything. She knocked. A moment later, one of the biggest men she had ever seen opened the door a crack. "Can I help you?" the gigantic, well-dressed, Middle Eastern man asked.

He was easily four hundred pounds if he was an ounce. She had to look up, past his long, black beard into his dark eyes. They were in stark contrast to his white turban. "I'm wit' Mai Tai." She pointed at her purse. "I got somethin' for her."

He turned his head and said something in his native tongue. Another male voice replied. He looked at her and pulled the door open. "Welcome."

Inside the fairly average suite, Mai Tai and a handsome Arab-looking man sat on opposite ends of a root beer-colored sofa. Mai Tai looked bad. She stood, walked over and met Trenda in the middle of the room. "You cool?"

Trenda looked over her shoulder at the slim handsome fellow. "Yeah... wassup wit' these dudes?"

As she spoke, the stranger walked over and joined them. His nice-smelling cologne matched his tasteful, gold, linen suit. Instead of the Ali Baba-like beard like the giant wore, his was neatly trimmed. He looked more like an American hipster than a foreigner. He smiled at the ladies. "Well, Mai Tai, who is this lovely lady?"

"This is my daughter, Mya." She winked at Trenda. "Mya, this is Atash."

Atash chuckled. "I see beauty runs in your family."

Trenda raised an eyebrow. *Wow, she actually remembered that alias!* She then turned and offered her hand to Atash. "Pleased to meet you."

Lust radiated from him like rays of sunlight. He took Trenda's hand and kissed it. "No, Goddess; the pleasure is *all* mine, I assure you." He shamelessly massaged her body with his eyes. "Your presence alone has made the trip here worthwhile. And your eyes...they as green and beautiful as the lawn of my home in Miami; I'd love to show it to you one day."

"Thanks, but..." She eased her hand out of his. "Can we just get down to business?"

He ignored her question and circled her. "I like what I see, Mya...are you available for dinner tonight?"

Mai Tai coughed into her fist. "Hey, Atash. This ain't Match. com; how 'bout we get this over wit'?"

The giant walked over and stood behind Mai Tai. Atash finally took his attention from Trenda and turned to Mai Tai. "Relax, my friend. If what you have is as good at the sample you provided, we have a deal."

The big dude is way too jumpy, Trenda thought. She patted the purse containing the goods. "I got it right here; where's your money?"

Mai Tai walked up next to Trenda and had a coughing fit. Atash and the giant grimaced and took a few steps back. The giant gave Mai Tai a dirty look. "Cover your mouth, woman!"

Mai Tai bristled. "Quit being a pussy, big boy. What I got you can't catch from a cough."

His eyes widened as he placed his hand over his mouth and nose. "Atash! Did you hear that? This old cunt is contaminated!"

Trenda saw Mai Tai reach for her crotch. *Oh shit!* She managed to grab Mai Tai's wrist just before she was able to get to her concealed weapon. "Chill out, ma...be cool."

Atash placed a hand on the giant's chest. "You too, Faysal... calm down," He looked at Trenda. "I'm sure our friends mean us no harm."

Every nerve in Trenda's body tingled. And not in a good way. She took a deep, calming breath. "The sooner we handle this, the sooner we can all go home." She unzipped the purse, pulled out the brick, showed it to Atash and then put it back. "You ready?"

His eyes locked on the brick. "Yes...I have the payment back there in the bedroom." He began walking and waved for her to follow. "Come with me, Goddess."

Mai Tai spoke to Trenda while still giving Faysal the evil eye. "You go do your thing; I'll keep fatso here company."

Faysal's wide face soured. "Atash, please hurry. The sooner we get away from this wench, the better."

As he held the bedroom door open for Trenda, he winked at Faysal. "This will be over soon, my friend."

Forty-Five

After nearly a week of observation in the Winston County Mental Health Center, Beverly sat back at her desk and smiled. She had finally finished the three handwritten letters she had written to Trenda's father and brothers. *This should do the trick*, she thought as she placed a stamp on the letter addressed to Trenda's father's church. The amount of foul language in the letters was impressive. So was the research she had done to find information on Trenda's family. Most of it she had gotten from news stories and interviews about her late husband's demise. Not a single member of Trenda's family was spared her venom. The things she said about Trenda's niece were most disturbing.

She placed the letters in a neat stack and then walked over and peered out of her barred window, into the dark night. "I can't wait to send these off." Although the room was reminiscent of a hotel suite, the burly guards sprinkled throughout the compound reminded her that she was in an upper-class mental asylum.

Forty-Six

"I just can't get over how exotic you are," Atash said as he closed the bedroom door behind them. "Such beauty deserves to be protected...cherished."

This arrogant bastard is workin' my last nerve. She sat on the bed and let her hand dangle near the boot that contained Baby. "For the last time, I'm not here for pleasure; I came to make this transaction and bounce. So how 'bout you show me the money?"

He smiled. "Feisty... I like that." He then went to the closet, pulled out a black briefcase, walked over and tossed it on the bed. "Count it if you wish."

"I think I will." She took the purse off of her shoulder, sat it on the floor and opened the briefcase. It was layered with stacks of twenty, fifty and hundred dollar bills. *This what I'm talkin' 'bout.* After a quick count, she found it was five thousand dollars short. She turned to confront him and froze. "What the *fuck* you think you doin'?"

To her utter dismay, he held his penis in one hand, and the missing five grand in the other. "Your asking price was a little too high for me, but if you really want it, you can earn it by taking care of little Atash."

She sprung to her feet. "You must be out ya monkey-ass mind!" She glared at him. "That might work back is Egypt or wherever you from, but that shit don't apply out here, fool!"

Quicker than she could react, he rushed over and caught her

on the side of the head with a backhand. The lion's head-shaped gold ring on his hand almost fractured her skull. She fell to the bed, stunned. He hovered over her and glowered. "Listen here, little whore; *no* woman talks to Atash like that, *no* woman!"

As she fought to regain her senses, her vision blurred. She faintly heard Mai Tai yelling to see if she was okay. *That bastard slapped me!* Her focus came back just in time to see him crack the bedroom door open. He attempted to assure Mai Tai everything was fine. Alas, he'd made a grave mistake; he turned his back on a very angry and hostile woman, filled with fatal intentions. By the time he heard the click of Baby being unleashed, the tip of the blade pierced his linen shirt and entered his right kidney. "Slap me again, muthafucka!" He whipped around, full of pain and shock. In a flash, Trenda laid his throat open with the efficiency of a ninja. "Slap me again!"

Faysal reached for the Desert Eagle pistol holstered under his jacket. "Crazy bitch!"

Before he got it out the holster, three .357 hollow point slugs shattered his spine. He toppled over like a gigantic domino. Adrenaline flowed through Trenda like a like a tidal wave. She looked over at Mai Tai. The smoking gun hung at her side. "Let's get the hell outta here!"

A disturbing calmness emanated from Mai Tai. She pointed at the bed. "Grab the money."

She gave Mai Tai a quizzical look as she wiped blood off of Baby onto Atash's shirt. "*What?* We gotta *go!*"

As Trenda folded up the butterfly knife and put it back in her boot, Mai Tai nonchalantly walked over, closed the briefcase and handed it to Trenda. "Take this and go." When Trenda hesitated, she yelled, "*Hurry up, bitch!*"

Trenda's paralysis broke. She took the case and gave Mai Tai one last pleading look. "You ain't comin'?"

She simply shook her head. "I'm gonna clean this up, you have to go, baby...let me go, Trenda."

Before her emotions took hold, Trenda spun around and left. Blessedly, the hall was empty. She slowed her urgent stride to a normal pace and headed for the elevators.

℘℃

"How many times do we have to go over this? All you have is hearsay. That and five bucks will get me a gallon of gas." Marv checked his watch. "I'm outta here. Good luck."

Desperation filled Beanie's face. The thought of encountering Trenda after their last conversation was almost enough to make him piss himself. His phone rang, shattering the silence of their dark meeting place. His eyes bulged when he saw the number on the Caller ID. He showed it to Marv. "*It's her!*"

"Answer it, dummy."

℘℃

As Trenda conversed with Beanie, Mai Tai was busy cleaning up the crime scene. With most of the hotel being booked for the nurses' convention, and them attending a function down in the grand ballroom, no one heard all the commotion in Atash's suite. Using what little energy she had left, she laid her pistol on the sofa and methodically wiped down every surface Trenda could have touched. Including the cellophane wrapping on the kilo. She then went into the kitchenette, opened a drawer and pulled out a steak knife. *This oughta do.* She went into the bedroom and kneeled down next to Atash's still body. After pulling up his blood-soaked shirt, she located the butterfly knife's entry wound, plunged the steak knife inside up to the handle and pulled it out.

With extreme effort, she then rolled him over onto his back and re-slit his throat. Satisfied with her work, she dropped the knife, staggered to her feet, went and got her Derringer and placed the barrel in her mouth. *What the hell; I had a good run.* She then swallowed the last bullet.

ഇരുന്ന

"Christ! It's about time she called me back," Nick said after checking his personal cell phone. While taking a burglary suspect into custody a short time ago, he found that he had missed a call from Trenda. "And the cunt didn't bother to leave me a message."

ഇരുന്ന

"Say that again, I'm in a bad spot, I can't hear you all that good," Beanie said as both he and Marv listened to Trenda via Beanie's speakerphone. "Where you say you wanna meet to drop off the money for Nick?"

"Look, listen up! For the third time, have him meet me in the tunnel on Race Track Road, at the Bowie Race Track at ten-thirty. Got it?"

Marv nodded at Beanie as he jotted down the location and a few other notes. Beanie then said, "Aight...I'll pass it on to Nick," He paused, then said, "You good wit' me comin', too?"

"Beanie, if I was you, I would be tryin' to put as much real estate between me and you as possible."

Before he could reply, Trenda ended the call. He looked at Marv. "I *told* you she's out to get me. What you gonna do 'bout that?"

Marv finished his notes and checked the time. "I don't know

about you, but it's time for me to get out of here. I have a date in Bowie here shortly and I need to get prepared for it." He watched Beanie squirm with fear. "I suggest you find a rock to crawl under until this storm blows through."

Forty-Seven

Figures *that trick, Nick, wouldn't answer his phone,* Trenda thought as she pulled into Mai Tai's garage. Considering the night she'd had, the Corvette was *too* noticeable to ride in. Once the garage door closed, she hopped out, grabbed the bag out of the trunk and paused. *Better get my cut right now.* She realized that at some point her luck would run out. She opened the case, removed fifteen grand, and put it in her trunk in the same spot she had carried the heroin in. *Sure hope Mai Tai made it out safe...I'm worried 'bout that girl.*

A part of her *knew* she had seen the last of her mentor and friend, but she wallowed in denial. She had little time to worry. Delivering the dirty money to Nick was top priority. The headaches she'd suffered worrying about the safety of her family were too much. The double murder she had just been a part of also weighed on her. Before getting back into the Buick, she realized that she still had Mai Tai's keys. *I'll hold onto them, just in case she needs me to let her in.*

ഌൠ

"Yes, your Honor, I'm positive. All I need is for you to sign off on this wire and I can *promise* you enough evidence for a conviction...you have my word on it."

Judge Holloway pondered Marv's desperate request. The Colonel Sanders look-a-like finally caved in and signed the order. "You better bring me back some results, Detective. I don't normally respond to well to people showing up on my doorstep at this hour." He handed the order to Marv. "But with your track record, I'm sure you know what you're doing. Besides that, you know old-timers like me are usually in bed before ten."

Thank God for small favors, Nick thought as he hopped in his car and sped off. He had less than an hour make the forty-mile ride to the Bowie Race Track. The prospect of busting that vermin, Nick, almost gave him an erection. He arrived at the track with fifteen minutes to spare. He found a spot fifty yards from the meet point and parked. From his vantage point, he could see anyone that approached the tunnel.

While he waited for Trenda, he went into his trunk and pulled out a small black duffle bag. Inside was a box containing what looked like a transistor radio and a hands-free headset. "I hope this thing is all the lab boys say it is." He pressed a button on the handset and a green light flashed three times, then went blue. He placed it on his ear and then turned on the radio-looking device. "Check one, two...check."

The LED lights on the front of the receiver blinked green, indicating a strong signal. He then pressed the PLAY button on the receiver and heard "Check one, two...check," loud and clear.

࠾ᑐᏇ

"I don't know what that fool is drivin', but I sure hope I ain't missed him," Trenda said as she pulled up minutes before her scheduled rendezvous with Nick. She checked the time on her dashboard clock. "I'll give him ten minutes, then I'll call him."

While she waited, she decided to get out and remove the brief-case full of cash from the trunk.

ଓଋ

After watching the Buick park on the opposite side of the tunnel, Marv put the recording equipment back in the bag, grabbed his flashlight and got out of the car. *Gotta play this just right.* He walked over to the tunnel entrance and walked toward her.

ଓଋ

In the night's silence, she heard footsteps echoing off of the tunnel walls. She strained her eyes to make out whose silhouette was approaching. *That don't look like Nick...Nick ain't ever been that tall.* "That you, Nick?"

Fifty feet away, the shadowy figure turned on a powerful flash-light and aimed it in her eyes. "No, I'm Detective Brice of the Baltimore PD. Can I have a word with you, Ms. Fuqua?"

Her heart dropped to her ankles. The image of Big Mo' laughing in her face as she returned to The Cock both frightened and repulsed her. She shook her head and then stomped her foot. *"Fuck!"*

ଓଋ

An hour remained before the end of Nick's shift. Having spoken to neither Trenda nor Beanie all night had thoroughly pissed him off. The two calls he'd sent to voicemail from Anton didn't help matters. He turned his beacons on a red Toyota Camry with no brake lights that he had been trailing. The prospect of losing out on his $25 millilon deal with the Russians sickened him. The beat down awaiting his failure to deliver the thirty grand he owed gnawed at his anti-panic switch. In the midst of writing the fix-it ticket, his personal cell phone rang.

Forty-Eight

"'m leaving right now. Don't you move, you hear me?" Nick said as he fast walked out of the station to his truck. "I'll be there in twenty minutes."

After Marv had her to lead him to the secluded spot where Nick had first handed her off the stolen heroin, he parked around the corner out of sight. He sat in Trenda's car, looked her in the eye and nodded. They were both listening to Trenda's conversation via the receiver Marv was holding.

She spoke into the earpiece. "Aight, I'll be here in the same spot where you passed me off the kilo."

"I got it, I got it. You think I don't know my own drop-off points? I'm the one that took you there, remember, genius?"

After Nick ended the call, Trenda looked at Marv. "That enough evidence? Can I go now?" She pointed her thumb at the briefcase on the backseat. "You got the money."

He shook his head as he saved the conversation on the receiving device. "I'm going to need you to hand it off to him in order to make these charges stick."

She turned and stared out of the window at a train chugging down the tracks in the distance. "What if I don't? All you got on me is a satchel of money that I coulda found on the street."

He sat the receiver on the dashboard and turned to her. "Well, did I mention we found a screwdriver in the alley where a man was assaulted? The blood on the screwdriver just so happened to match his. And guess what?"

She had a white-hot desire to be onboard that train, going anywhere as long as it was out of Maryland. Defeat was beating on the door of her confidence with a battering ram. She kept her eyes on the speeding train. "What?"

"We also found a partial fingerprint that pretty much matches yours." After no response from her, he continued. "Look, Trenda, I'm going to be straight with you. I'm *much* more interested in stopping this clown, Nick, than I am in arresting you. Of course, if I have to, I will, but if you cooperate, that may not be necessary."

Discretion shall preserve thee, understanding shall keep thee
—PROVERBS 2:11

After revisiting that bit of the Bible, Trenda drew in a deep breath and let it go. Even though her face remained emotionless, the urge to fight was leaving her. She felt herself getting physically ill from stress. As the train disappeared from sight, she said, "What do you want me to do?"

ഇ◌ଓ

"That's right, Anton; I'll have your dough shortly," Nick said as he sped through the streets of West Baltimore. "I'm on the way to get it as we speak."

"I'm glad to hear that, Nick. I was beginning to think I was going to have to cancel our contract and go with another distributor."

Nick shot through a red light, a quarter of a mile from his destination. "You'll soon learn *I'm* the man out here, now that my competition got dissolved a couple of years ago. My network is gonna make that asshole, Darius's, look like the Girl Scouts."

"Don't get too cocky, officer; you haven't delivered me my money yet. Until then, you're still a marked man. Don't you forget that."

What I wouldn't give to put a burning slug between his rude, Russian eyes, he thought after Anton hung up on him. According to his watch, he would arrive right on time. A few minutes later, he spotted Trenda's car a couple of blocks ahead, parked in front of an abandoned brownstone. He slowed to a crawl and observed the area. *Looks as empty as a whore's promise.* He pulled up behind the Buick and parked. A confident grin grew on his face as he got out. *Time to step my game up, as the Negros say.*

∞)∞

"That's it, you piece of shit. Smile for the camera," Marv said as the large telephoto lens of his night vision-equipped camera took multiple shots of Nick. After kicking in the back door of the brownstone, and warding off a family of rats, he'd found a second-floor bedroom window suitable for surveillance. He plugged a set of earphones into the receiver and turned up the volume as Nick approached the Buick.

Before he got to the driver's side door, Trenda got out and closed the door. Five feet away from Trenda, he paused, stunned by how gorgeous she was. "No wonder Darius couldn't keep his hands off you. You're one hot gal."

Trenda wiped her hair back in an effort to make sure the earpiece had no trouble picking up their conversation. She gave him a sexy smile. "Is that right, officer?"

Pleased with her perceived warmth, he took a couple of more steps toward her. "Yes it is, sexy one. And once my network takes over where Darius failed, there might be a spot available for someone as resourceful as yourself." He boldly placed a hand on her waist and rubbed her hip. "You have no idea how long I've wanted to bang you."

"Really? Well, Officer Nick." She stroked the top of his buzz-cut hairdo. "Tell me what else you'd like me to do for you?"

He took her hand and kissed her wrist. "How about you start by giving me my money? That always gets my pecker up."

"Sure thing, love." She rubbed the side of his pale face. "I have to tell you, the buyer sure was impressed with the quality of that smack. He said he ain't came across no heroin that pure in a long time."

He grinned and rubbed her right tit. "And he won't. You can tell him that there's plenty more where that came from, but the only way he's gonna get it is through me."

She turned slightly to her left, allowing him to rub the other breast. "You must have some serious connections."

His grin slowly faded. He took his hand off of her tits, took a step back and looked around. His cop instincts had finally over-ruled his lust for the beauty in front of him. "Enough of this bullshit." He pulled a pistol from behind his back and pointed it at her. "Get me my money...*now*."

She continued to grin. "Sure thing, Suga." She eased past him, letting her hand brush against the small bulge in his crotch. "It's in the backseat."

Before she could open the door, he grabbed her wrist. "Step back. I'll get it. If you try anything, I'll put a bullet in your pretty ass."

She tossed her hair over her shoulder. "No problem, baby. Help ya self."

He studied her face, then opened the door and looked around inside the car. *Something about this bitch ain't right, but I don't have time to figure it out right now.* He grabbed the briefcase and closed the rear door. "I trust it's all here."

"Go ahead and count it. I figured you could do that when you give me my cut."

His loud chuckle echoed down the street. "Your cut?" He laughed as he placed the case on the trunk and opened it. His face lit up as he picked up a bundled stack of hundreds. He put the pistol on the trunk, wiggled a single bill out of the stack, and handed it to her. "There you go, lady. Thanks for your services."

Trenda looked at the bill pinched between her fingers. "This it? All I get for selling your dope for you is a hundred bucks?"

He picked up the pistol, tossed the stack back inside the case and closed it. "That's a start; you can work your way up the pay scale if you continue to produce results like this." He waved the pistol at her. "And trust me, I'm going to be looking for you for more than your courier services." He pointed the gun at her crotch. "I'm going to christen that sweet, chocolate pussy as well."

ഇൻൻ

"Got cha!" Marv said as he took several more shots of Nick putting the briefcase inside his truck and speeding off. He pulled a two-way radio out of his duffle bag and called his partner. "Jim, it's a go! I repeat, it's a go! The suspect is dirty and headed your way!"

Forty-Nine

Three days later, the news was abuzz. Two stories dominated the local headlines. One was the discovery of three dead bodies in what a police report described as a drug deal in Delaware gone wrong. A wave of sadness swept over her. *Poor Mai Tai...I can never repay her for what she did for me.* The second was the report of more Baltimore police corruption. This time, it was good news. One of the biggest perpetrators was busted in a sting operation orchestrated by a pair of BPD detectives. An informant, that refused to be identified, told one source he had information on who had helped the detectives in the sting. He said for the right price he would provide the information.

"I bet that's that bastard Beanie," Trenda thought out loud as she sipped a cup of coffee at her father's kitchen table, while reading his newspaper. She hadn't been out of the house since her ordeal with Nick and Marv. "I knew I shoulda silenced his ass a long time ago."

"Oh my Lord," her father said after checking the mailbox. "This is terrible!"

Trenda got up out of her seat. "What's wrong, Daddy?"

He walked into the kitchen with a letter in his hand and a shocked look on his face. Both of her brothers, unbeknownst to them, had received an equally venomous version of the same letter. He held it up. "This...this is blasphemy!"

Trenda walked over and took the letter out of his hand. Her jaw dropped as she read the first, handwritten paragraph:

Dear Father Fuqua, you old fuck, thanks for contributing to the birth of the bitch that had my husband killed. I swear on your life, your whore-daughter is going to pay for all the anguish she has caused my family. I don't give a shit if I have to spend every dime I have, I'm going to have the pleasure of watching that miserable cunt bleed to death. I want her to fucking suffer as my son will, having to grow up—

She could read no more. She looked at her father and shook her head. "Daddy, I don't know—"

He raised a shaky finger and glared at her. "Get out! Get out of my house right now! You, you...*heathen!*"

A blizzard of emotions and thoughts stormed in her head. The look in her father's extremely angry face told her rebuttal would be futile. She ran upstairs, grabbed her bag, stuffed it with as many of her possessions as she could grab, and ran out of the house. A string of her father's curses followed her out of the door.

"Fuck this shit, I'm out!" she yelled as she sped to the freeway and got on. She alternated between extreme anger and overwhelming sadness as she drove. She didn't stop until she arrived in the city of Allegheny, on the far edge of Maryland.

Fifty

After a month of isolation in an extended stay hotel, on the outskirts of Maryland, living off of the fifteen grand she'd skimmed of the deal with Nick, Trenda almost choked on the slice of cold pizza she was eating. On the TV screen was a reporter doing a story from her father's house. In a somber voice, the blond young newsman reported on the passing of beloved Baltimore priest, Herman Fuqua, father of the notorious Trenda Fuqua.

෧෬

Three days later, on a warm spring afternoon, Trenda stood in the back of the crowd of people watching her father's white casket get lowered into the ground, next to her mother's plot. Among them, in the front row, were detectives Marv Brice and his partner, Jim. Dressed in all black, including dark shades, a large black hat and full veil, it was practically impossible to tell who she was. As Brother Colfax and her two brothers each shared in the tearful eulogy, a familiar face stood out in the crowd. A woman in a short black dress, black hat and dark glasses stood next to the white hearse filming the event. *Why is that broad smilin'? Don't she know this is a funeral?*

Trenda watched as the mystery lady filmed her oldest brother breaking down to his knees in tears as his wife and Brother Colfax tried to console him. When she took off her shades in order to get a better view of the sorrow, Trenda's heart stopped.

It was Beverly.

Her first impulse was to run through the crowd, grab her by the throat and plunge Baby into her smiling face. She slowed her breathing and let a bit of logic sneak past her anger. *Be cool, be cool; too many folks here to get crazy.* Apparently satisfied with her footage, she put the digital camera in her purse, put her shades back on and turned to leave.

She could feel her life at a crossroad. Going after Beverly with not only a crowd there, but cops as well, was beyond foolish. Her life whizzed past her eyes as she made up her mind. She eased back from the crowd and trailed Beverly from afar. She followed clandestinely as Beverly leisurely walked to her rental car and got inside.

Shit! I gotta get to my car!

Trenda was parked ten cars back on the asphalt, fifty yards from the funeral crowd. She hurried as fast as she could without drawing attention to herself. As she started the Buick, Beverly was leaving the cemetery grounds. Trenda tore the hat and veil off and tossed it onto the backseat. "Can't believe that hoe had the nerve to show up at my daddy's funeral and had the nerve to be filmin' my family!"

Several blocks behind Beverly, Trenda fought to keep up with her sworn enemy. A while later, and after almost losing her a couple of times, she was relieved to see her pull into the parking lot of the Comfort Inn, near the BWI airport. Trenda parked several stalls away from Beverly's car and watched her walk into the hotel lobby. The giddiness in her stride further angered Trenda. *Laugh now, cry later, bitch.*

As soon as Beverly was out of sight, Trenda grabbed her black purse, got out of her car and hurried to the lobby entrance. As she approached the lobby desk, her heart dropped. Beverly disappeared inside the elevator doors. *Damn, how am I gonna find out what floor she's on?*

"Can I help you, ma'am?"

Startled, Trenda spun around and saw a middle-aged black woman at the counter smiling at her. "Huh?"

"Are you okay?"

Trenda adjusted her dark shades. "Oh…yeah. I got separated from my cousin; she just came in here and I forgot what room she was in."

"Oh, was she dressed in black and about your height?"

Trenda nodded. "Yeah, we just got back from my uncle's funeral…"

The receptionist gave her a sympathetic look. "I'm so sorry to hear of your loss; my thoughts and prayers go out to you and your family." She glanced at her computer screen. "I remember checking her in yesterday. She's in room 212; second floor."

Trenda gave an Academy Award-winning sorrowful look. "Thank you…thank you so much."

On the way up the elevator, Trenda opened her purse and looked down at the jade-handled killing machine inside. The jade reminded her of her rosary beads she had left back in her own hotel room. After being thrown out of her father's house, she'd tossed them into the kitchenette garbage can, vowing to never trust in God again. *I ain't countin' on nobody but me from now on.*

She milled around the hallway until the housekeeper empting the trash cans pushed his cart into the elevator and disappeared. She then walked over to Beverly's door and knocked.

ഇരു

"Yes, I'd also like a Diet Pepsi with that. Thank you," Beverly said as she hung up with the pizza delivery company down the road. She fell back on the bed and smiled at the ceiling. *Her brothers blubbering like little girls was funny as hell!* Beverly thought with glee. *I'll be sure to save a copy of the recording for their whore of a sister to watch...perhaps I'll play it for her right before I kill her.*

Ten minutes later, there was a knock at her door. She hopped off of the bed. "Wow! They *do* deliver fast!"

⁂

Trenda removed Baby and held it in her closed fist. To her surprise, Beverly opened the door and said, "You sure are—" An animalistic rage coated her face. *"You! How?"*

Before she could slam the door closed, Trenda bum-rushed her, knocking her on her ass. She closed the door with her foot and flicked Baby open. "Yeah, it's me, bitch."

Beverly, on her back, tried to kick, hit and scratch Trenda. "Get away from me, you fucking murderer!"

Trenda managed to dodge her attack and stomp Beverly on the belly. She pointed the deadly blade at her as she struggled to catch her breath. "Kick me again and I'll cut ya damned tongue out."

The manic fury that Beverly displayed gave way to child-like cowering. Tears streamed out of her eyes. She closed them and whimpered, "Please...please don't...please don't kill me...my son..."

Trenda ground her teeth with anger. "Fuck you, bitch." She placed her knee on Beverly's chest, put the tip of Baby on her jugular and prepared to slice it open. Out the corner of her eye, she saw a familiar face. A much younger, but still familiar, face. As Beverly softly wept, Trenda looked at a framed photograph of

Darius Jr. sitting on top of the nightstand. The innocence in that face doused some of her lava-hot wrath. The tip of the blade drew a drop of blood as Trenda gazed at the joyful look on the baby's face. His pointy birthday hat was almost the same shade of green as her eyes.

"My baby...please...please..."

Beverly's whimpering found its way past Trenda's rage-induced psychosis. She looked down at the cowering woman. The tip of the blade was centimeters from her jugular vein. *Shit.* She pulled the knife back, gripped Beverly by the chin and made her look her in her eyes. "Listen to me good; this is the last time we're gonna have this conversation. I ain't had *shit* to do with your husband gettin' killed. If you saw that tape of me and him, you can see he wasn't no damn angel." She nodded toward the picture of her son. "I'm sorry ya kid ain't gonna meet his daddy, but..." Beverly clenched her eyes and cried harder. "You got the rest of ya life to tell him what he need to know about his daddy...you gonna have to show him how to be a *real* man..." She grimaced at the unstable woman.

"Look at me, goddamn it!" she yelled as Beverly tried to turn away from her, crying her eyes out. Trenda gripped her chin again and looked in her wet eyes. "I'm gonna let you go. If I *ever* hear from you, or hear about you botherin' *any* of my family again, our next meetin' is gonna end *way* different than this. And don't even *think* about callin' the cops; you do that and I promise you, I'll reach out and touch you no matter where you are. You got that?"

Beverly sniveled pathetically, then whispered, "Yes...yes...yes... I...I." A fresh flow of tears started.

Trenda stood up and watched Beverly ball up into the fetal position, sobbing like an infant. She wiped the drops of blood off of the tip onto her dress, closed it up, put it back in her purse, and left.

ഇര

As she drove away from Beverly's hotel, Trenda realized her life was at a dead end. The money she had left over wasn't going to last forever. She also understood that surviving the rest of her parole without getting drawn into the street life was a pipe dream. Deep in her heart she knew who she was; there was no need in sugar-coating it. The possibility of giving her life to God, like she was raised to do, wasn't gonna happen. She adjusted her shades and picked up her cell phone. "Fuck it; if I'm goin' to hell, I might as well enjoy the ride." She pulled over, searched her purse for the card Alexis had given her, found the number for StarShine Entertainment, and dialed.

"Hey, Alexis, this is Trenda Fuqua. I hope you still got that check; I'm ready to talk."

ABOUT THE AUTHOR

Curtis L. Alcutt's initial effort, *Dyme Hit List*, focuses on Rio, a single African-American man who grapples with finding his soulmate after a lifetime of being a womanizer. His neighbor, Carmen, has all the qualities Rio wants....but can he commit to her?

Bullets & Ballads, his follow-up novel, is an erotic, psychological, drama set in the music industry. The main character, a musical genius named Apollo, is twisted into a steamy love triangle featuring Nyrobi, a gorgeous, wealthy and sexually liberated older woman and a loving, sexy and talented songstress named Tricia.

He is the author of *Sins of a Siren*. He also has an erotic short story entitled, "Not Tonight," published in Zane's *New York Times* bestselling erotic anthology, *Caramel Flava*. Curtis also co-authored the self-help book, *Your Road Map to a Book*, published by his literary foundation, WriteWay2Freedom. His heated short story, "Drastic Measures," is featured in the erotic anthology, *After Dark Delights*.

Curtis L. Alcutt's literary style is "no-holds barred" erotica combined with everyday experiences the reader is guaranteed to relate to. "I believe my story ideas come from being a shy, quiet child, always observant instead of talking," says Alcutt. "Growing up, I passed by the windows of bookstores and remember never seeing any novels with black people on the covers. I wondered what it would be like to see African-Americans instead. My love of writing song lyrics further fueled my desire to become a writer. My novel concepts were stored away for quite some time. After reading a few African-American novels I decided now is the time to write."

Curtis L. Alcutt was born and bred in Oakland, California. He walked many career paths before deciding to give writing a try. "I've been a roofer, garbage man, courier, truck driver, computer network administrator and even co-owner of an auto body shop. Back in the early nineties, I had a record deal as the rapper, 'Big C.' For many different reasons the deal fell through, but I never let it discourage my pursuit of self-expression."

Visit the author's website, www.curtisalcutt.com, and find him on Facebook.